THE TYRANNY OF IC.......

E. Liz Bramich was born in Birmingham and educated at a local Grammar School. She took a B.Sc. in Zoology from the University of Leeds. A teaching career followed in Warwickshire and Lancashire. Married with two children, she now lives in Inverness.

E. Liz Bramich is the author of *Anyone for Carrot Cake?*

*all the best
E. Liz Bramich*

THE TYRANNY OF ICHTHUS

E. Liz Bramich

For my family

'Woe unto them that call evil good and good evil.'

Isaiah V v20

This is a work of fiction. Names, characters, businesses, places, events, locales and incidents are either the products of the author's imagination or used in a fictitious manner. Any resemblance to actual persons, alive or deceased, or actual events is purely coincidental.

The views and opinions expressed in the novel are those of the characters only and do not reflect or represent the views and opinions held by the author.

Copyright © E. Liz Bramich 2018

CHAPTER ONE

Thursday, 14 May, 1992.

'Over my dead body'...

Maudie looked at her husband, Tom Portland, her mouth agape and her eyes wide open in utter disbelief.

'Yes, those were his precise words. I know it sounds unbelievable but, there you are...that's what he said.' Tom was reporting to his wife, Maudie, the row he had had with Ted Slater, the Headteacher.

It was past six o'clock when Tom walked in through the front door. Jack and Freddie, their two sons, already fed, were upstairs in their bedrooms. She had just poured two, large glasses of wine but she delayed getting their meal because Tom had looked so distraught. The fury he had experienced earlier in the day now re-surfaced with such ferocity that he appeared to be close to tears.

'What right has Icky to talk to you like that?'

She used the nick-name they had devised for the Head. She jumped in a flash on to her high horse, as if preparing for battle against Ted Slater.

'Well, that's the way it is in the promotion stakes... if you don`t have the support of the Head, you'll never get on.' He let out a long sigh of despair. 'Icky says he didn't get his Headship 'til he was nearly fifty so why should I be any different?'

'Let's try to understand why he's got it in for you. What have you done to him that has appalled him so much that he should talk to you like that?'

'The man's nuts... I can't do right for doing wrong. Any normal boss would appreciate all the times when I've had to stand in for him at a moment's notice. He dismisses my qualities, yet he makes use of them all the time when it suits him, which is more often than not. For some reason, he doesn't want me to get promoted...to any Headship, let alone Southwich.'

'I think that Icky must be going doolally or he`s just plain jealous,' said Maudie.

Tom drained his glass, re-filled it and drained it again. He sat slumped in his chair, silently seething. Maudie had already plated up their dinner...his favourite mid-week meal...beef and mushroom casserole...but most of it was left untouched on his plate. Although hungry for promotion, he had lost his appetite for food having been so incensed at Ted Slater`s arrogance and high-handedness. He recollected the previous twelve hours.

The day had started well enough – a good omen, Tom had thought, as it happened, somewhat prematurely. A brilliantly, warm, sunny, morning in mid-May had changed abruptly as the

Portland family ate their breakfast together at the kitchen table. Both he and his wife had always insisted that they sat down as a family to eat and to talk together. The first sign of the deteriorating weather was an increase in the wind speed. There were gusts which shook the trees so violently that twigs and cones were torn from the branches of the great Douglas fir in the neighbouring garden with such violence that Tom wondered whether he would witness any structural damage on his journey to school, a journey of twenty miles or so along tree-lined country roads. He had not wanted to be late on this day of all days.

'Maudie, come and see what`s happened,'

Tom had shouted to his wife as he opened the front door. Whilst they watched, their containers of *Kingsblood* tulips, beautiful at six o`clock that morning had been buffeted so much by the sudden gale that there was a scattering of bright red petals all over the driveway, like droplets of blood from a battered and bleeding body.

Tom had known that this moment would arrive sooner or later. He had had many show-downs with his boss in the past, but this was likely to be a massive row of the first order. He had, as was the custom in the institution in which he worked, made an appointment to meet with his boss – Ted Slater. Appointments were essential as this particular 'boss' spent more time outside the four walls of Southwich High School attending as many committee meetings as he could contrive, leaving his loyal, over-worked Deputy to hold the fort in his absence. He had done it too often. His excuse had always been that his presence on a variety of committees was, in fact, good for the school because it meant that he was 'in the know' at the start of any new initiatives. Tom had been grateful on so many occasions for the experience in leadership which his boss's deliberate external involvement had granted him. It had never been the Head`s intention to help his Deputy, it was simply a matter of feeding his own vanity. But the practice had been going on for too long. Slater had always praised Tom's organisational skills. His teaching skills were way above those of his subordinates, and he had apparently always been popular with staff and pupils alike. The parents were grateful to him for the time he had been prepared to spend with their children who were in need of his help for one reason or another.

Tom had unsuccessfully applied for several promotions whilst in his current post which was now in its thirteenth year. Until his Deputy Headship, he had been successful in job applications. In fact, he had never failed to get whatever job he had wanted ...but not anymore. What could possibly have gone wrong? His record had always been beyond reproach. Tom was beginning to lose some of his self-confidence and he had not liked the feeling. His ultimate conclusion was that Ted Slater was envious of his competence and popularity and that in some way Tom`s attributes demoted Slater from that celestial pedestal on which he liked to perch in order to receive admiration from the lesser mortals who surrounded him and who were at his beck and call.

At nine-thirty exactly, Tom was in the secretary`s office, waiting to be invited into the inner sanctum. Mrs Bird was a brisk, efficient but kindly woman who would quite readily tell the Headteacher what she thought about any issue concerning the school, its staff and its pupils. She exhibited much common sense and only a fool would have not listened to her. Ted Slater was no fool... but he frequently did not heed her advice.

'Sorry, Tom...he's on the phone as usual.'

Tom could do nothing but wait patiently as he gazed out of the window. The wind was still as gusty as ever and the Dutch Elm disease-resistant tree which the School Council had decided to purchase some years before was shaking violently. At this rate, he thought, it would perish by being uprooted. He walked to the door and then back to the window. His cheeks were in constant flux as he clenched his teeth in annoyance at being made to wait yet again. He had never got used to it...but he should have done so because it had been the norm for thirteen years.

Jennifer Bird, aware that Tom was agitated, initiated pleasantries with him.

'How's the family, Tom?'

'Doing well, thanks...Maudie is enjoying her job at the library, especially when she gets to go on the mobile service. The boys are happy at school too. Jack will be going to University in October...he has a place at Warwick, to read Law. Freddie is coasting at the moment but there's time for us to sort him out before things become critical... and what about your Bobbie? What's he up to these days?'

Robert Bird, 'Bobbie' to his family, was not the typical product of Southwich. He was the only son of Jennifer and Harold Bird and he was their pride and joy. Mrs Bird was in her element now as she started to expound on his latest exploits. He had taken a BA in Anthropology and Archaeology from Manchester University. Upon graduation, he had decided to investigate, for himself, far flung places in the little-explored regions of the world. Bobbie was in his early thirties and he was what could only be described as an adventurer. He travelled to wherever his fancy took him. He had an abiding interest in the planet and all that that entailed. His travels had taken him all over the globe. He was also a published author known as 'Robin Bird' writing mainly in scholastic journals.

'He`s up the Brazilian Amazon at the moment but before that, his most recent trip was to Peru. He brought me some souvenir shrunken heads…horrid things! She shivered at the thought of those obnoxious artefacts. The house is rapidly becoming swamped by his collections of unusual and exotic curiosities. I give them away to anyone who shows some interest. Dr Slater has a 'head' in his cabinet…you`ll see it if you look'.

The telephone in Mrs Bird`s office rang three times. She ignored it.

'OK Tom…Dr Slater will see you now. Good luck!'

The Headteacher had devised a system of signals to alert his secretary to his immediate needs. One ring on her phone suggested, 'I`ll have my coffee now'; two rings instructed her, 'Get this idiot out of my office!' and three rings implied, 'OK, send the blighter in.'

Ted Slater had his back to the door through which Tom had entered. He was smoothing, daintily, with his left hand, his thick, wavy, silvery thatch of which he was excessively proud. He spent a fortune on visits to his hairdresser who maintained it at a constant length by a weekly trim, shampoo and blow-dry. He rested his right hand on his hip. He was jacket-less, and his blue, cotton shirt sleeves were casually rolled up, exposing a pale, smooth-skinned lower arm. The fourth finger of his left hand carried a heavy gold signet ring with an inset diamond. As he moved his hand over his silver locks, the gold and diamond, in his ring, glinted and sparkled as they reflected the bright, morning sunshine. On his wrist, he sported a gold-bracelet bearing an expensive watch …his fortieth birthday present to himself.

'It`s a grand day today, Tom.'

He spoke with a hybrid accent, refined or dialectic according to his perception of the target audience. He turned and sat down, looking at the page of his diary which was open on his desk. Not a glance did he cast in Tom`s direction.

'Just a sec, I need to make a quick call.'

 Having rung his wife, he sat back in his chair, stretching his legs to their full length under the desk, once again patting his expensively coiffured hair, gazing into the middle distance so that he appeared to be looking at some object to the right of Tom's head, apparently totally ignoring his 'right-hand man'. He started drumming on his desk-top with the fingers of his left hand. Tom could plainly see the time displayed on the dial…it was a quarter past ten. Tom could see easily through the Head's wily tactics…his attempts to upset and frustrate him because he had the power to do so. The Head suspected that Tom's request for this meeting would concern his intended early retirement from Southwich High School at the end of the following academic year and the consequent Headship vacancy. Just at that moment, the phone rang.

'I`ll just take this call...it could be important.'

Tom was fuming inwardly, but he stayed calm. There was no advantage to him in advertising to Ted Slater that he was annoyed; that would be playing right into his hands.

Tom took the opportunity to look at the various items scattered around Slater`s office...on walls, shelves and on the desk. Hanging on the wall, above his desk, was an enlarged print of Jacob Epstein's bronze sculpture, *St. Michael's Victory over the Devil.* Adjacent to the window, was a simple wooden cross symbolising that he was a Christian and, ipso facto, a good, honest fellow. Tom had been taken in by that for a while but the passage of time had persuaded him otherwise. He searched for the shrunken head. The shelves housed several photographs with Ted Slater occupying a central, prominent position... with the School`s First XI cricket team and the football squad... shaking hands with the Leader of the County Council...hob-nobbing, at a Rotary Club dinner, with Jonas Spry - a local footballer who had achieved status in the Premier Football League. Spry had been the guest after-dinner speaker at one of the many 'freebies' to which Slater had been invited. In a display cabinet, there were objects of special interest to Ted Slater...curios and artefacts which Slater had collected during his travels as a young man and gifts from friends and acquaintances who were familiar with his interest in the unusual and the exotic. There, it was, in full view - the shrunken head - what a grotesque ornament! Tom visualised the shrunken head of Ted Slater, and it made him chuckle, momentarily.

He looked at the desk. An antique, burr walnut, portable writing desk took pride of place, together with a 'James Deakin' silver-plated inkstand...now devoid of ink. A silver hip-flask had been carelessly left on the desk, an oversight about which Slater would be annoyed. A container of sharpened pencils was situated to the left of the centre of the desk. Slater was a left-hander who frequently used a pencil for his jottings. He now selected one and absent-mindedly started to pick his teeth with it. Tom shuddered. Slung carelessly over the back of the chair was his jacket. Tom could see, in the lapel, the metallic, fish-shaped *Ichthus* badge which had given rise to his nickname – Icky. It suggested to Tom a sinister, secret society. On a bookshelf, was an unlikely combination of titles including *The Pilgrim's Progress*, *Snakes of the World*, *The Myths and Legends of Ancient Greece*, *Paradise Lost* and *The Cultivation of Exotic Plants*. A large, black, leather-bound, Authorised Version of the *King James' Bible* was prominent.

'Sanctimonious sod', thought Tom.

Also lined up, in strict order of height, was a substantial collection of Chemistry text books. Slater, who majored in Chemistry for his B.Ed. degree, occasionally would select one of these as a teaching aid when he acted in the capacity of a relief teacher...a gesture which he thought would persuade his staff that he was a conscientious fellow...but they were not so naïve that they had been taken in by such overt acts of artifice.

The Head initiated the conversation,

'Yer know, Tom, yer`ll never get appointed to my job because, yer know what? I`ll thwart ye at every turn. Yer`ll get this promotion over my dead body! Just yer watch and see whether I`m reet.'

Still, there had been no invitation for Tom to take a seat. This lack of courtesy was not unusual. It was one of the Head`s methods to keep his staff and other visitors in a perpetual state of inferiority because Ted Slater had, at all costs, to be at the top of the pile in whatever task he was involved. On this occasion, his tactics were to no avail because Tom had not been discomposed. In his present state of mind, he preferred to stand in front of his malevolent adversary.

The Head now looked at Tom straight between the eyes, Slater's own steely-blue, slightly blood-shot eyes, peering out from a thin-lipped face whose florid complexion and bulbous purple-hued nose were in stark contrast to his silvery mane. His whole visage exemplified his habit of downing several tots of whisky every evening and frequent quaffs from his hip-flask during fraught days. If his alter-ego had been the scheming Francis Urquhart, Tom would not have been surprised.

'I'm not sure that I`d wish that on you, Headmaster, but make no mistake, I'll do my damnedest to succeed. The number of times you've frustrated me over the last nine years when I have attempted to move on…well…I've lost count. But, at last, before long, I'll get my chance to apply for your job…the job I really want…and you'll not be able to blight it. It will be out of your hands. The governors will decide. They'll consult the Local Authority officers who know me well enough, as do the parents and our kids. I doubt you have enough sway with all these factions to 'thwart' me...your words. You'll at last be seen for what you are – a vain, vindictive hypocrite interested only in presenting to the world what a morally conscientious educationalist you are and a leader who pretends to act altruistically out of Christian duty. You're nothing but a sanctimonious, duplicitous bastard.'

This altercation had ended as had dozens before it with Tom Portland, the forty-five year old Deputy Head, waiting defiantly for the next emotive salvo, from the capacious armoury of the embattled Head. As usual, eyes blazing, arms flailing, voice cracking, the incensed Ted Slater uttered a pulse-revving shriek and took on a bodily posture which gave him the appearance of Satan confronting the mounting army of the Almighty. His face, contorted and purple with rage, with sinews and swollen, throbbing veins protruding from his neck, was just as evil as his infernal alma mater's but there was little of Satan's awareness of inevitable defeat. The Head was the Almighty! How dare the upstart Deputy presume to criticise one like he who led by divine providence? Had he not been assured by hours of intimate communication with the great headmaster of the skies that Heavenly guidance would be granted perpetually? Was he not universally revered? Had he not been elevated by the Local Authority as one of the county's leading Heads?

Exhausted and livid, Tom turned his back, in disgust, at Ted Slater's typical dramatic though pious and self-satisfied response. Tom had spent half the morning on this meeting which had resulted in another unsatisfactory conclusion. There was still the daily routine of running the school to be accomplished. Tom knew perfectly well that Ted Slater, by then, would have donned his coat and have been off the premises before someone else on the staff could demand his attention.

Jennifer Bird, from her perch in the adjacent office, could hear every word uttered by Ted Slater and his Deputy. Resorting to the holding of an empty glass tumbler against the wall or the putting of her ear to the keyhole was unnecessary in that school building, shoddily constructed in the 1960s? The partition walls, vibrating whenever a door slammed to, seeming to be paper thin, being cheaply fabricated from plasterboard sheets nailed to a timber frame, offered little privacy. Confidential discussions were best avoided in those administrative offices at Southwich High School.

Drinking her coffee whilst poring over that morning's delivery of invoices, she was unaware of Tom's head as it appeared at the partly open door. He had been walking down the corridor having stormed out of the Head's room when he had been enticed by the aroma emanating from her coffee machine. He could not resist the temptation to revisit the Bursar to reaffirm the existence of a normal world, inhabited by recognisably amiable people, outside Slater`s office.

'Hey, your coffee smells wonderful. I could just do with a cup myself after that little fracas.'

'You two been at it again?' she quizzed, knowing very well exactly what had passed between the Head and his Deputy.

She took from a drawer a china mug on which was an image of a sparrowhawk and proceeded to fill it from her percolator. He accepted it gratefully and began to sip the steaming liquid. He watched her with admiration. Tom viewed her as an angel-mother-figure surreptitiously guarding the unwary from the entrance to Hades, ready to catch and nurture any demoralised soul who had the misfortune to fall unsuspecting into the clutches of the devilish figure who gloweringly occupied the dark chasm beyond the interconnecting door.

'For the first time in twelve years, that old slave-driver has expressed a personal view honestly.' complained Tom. 'I wanted to talk to him about my application for his job on his retirement and he exploded like a cache of fireworks accidentally ignited by a stray spark. He used the phrase 'over my dead body' in his protestations about my intended application, threatening to 'thwart' my every move. He became incensed further when I remained calm and said I hoped it wouldn't come to that. What'll you bet he'll deny it all?'

Mrs Bird declined the wager. She was mesmerised by the Head's diabolic power. She knew how disingenuous, hypocritical and sanctimonious an old goat he was and yet he possessed a charismatic charm which still had a hypnotic effect on her. She felt a deep regard for Tom but there was that lingering awe for the Head's authority. He was now, in his later years, such an avid churchgoer, so passionate about his religion that she wondered whether he truly deserved the criticisms made by his members of staff. Were they misjudging him unfairly? She was in a quandary as to her real feelings about the man. She spoke,

'I wish you two silly buggers would stop falling out. He can't be as bad as you make out. Why do you wind each other up so? It'll be six of one and half a dozen of the other, I'll be bound. Anyway he's just left', she informed Tom. 'I've just seen him totter out to his car, weaving all over the pathway. He's obviously been at the booze again.'

Her office overlooked the car parking area which lay beyond a neat, well-maintained lawn in the centre of which had been planted the disease resistant Elm tree. She was in a perfect position to observe all the comings and goings of personnel entering and leaving the main entrance and Ted Slater's frequent visits to his car had not gone unnoticed by her. Knowing his predilection for a tot of whisky, she assumed that his toing and froing was to indulge in his secret drinking habit.

Tom finished his drink, gave his thanks to Mrs Bird and headed off down the corridor to his own office, all the while thinking about what she had just told him about the Head and her opinion on their altercation. So this was Tom's dilemma... Whenever the Head and he rowed, at least half the mud stuck to him. He cogitated bitterly on his misfortune. The only way to avoid rows with Ted Slater was to adopt the worshipful, obsequious manner which had been utilised successfully by members of his staff such as that oleaginous creature Peter Smalley.

The cause of Ted`s dependence on drink preyed on Tom's mind.. Ted seemed to want for nothing. He had a secure family life. The local politicians, the county education officers and his church acquaintances appeared to regard him most highly. Tom was at a loss to understand his boss. Having such information about Ted Slater made Tom determined to watch him more closely, to look out for unsteadiness in his movements and to exercise his sense of smell in Ted's vicinity so that he could make up his own mind about the state of Ted`s addiction. Ted Slater remained absent for the rest of the day leaving Tom to pick up the pieces and do his own job as well.

After the largely uneaten meal, Tom and Maudie settled down to discuss their future. Maudie initiated the discussion,

'You've been his dogsbody now for nearly thirteen years…Icky won't let you go…he's got you trapped…you're too useful to him.'

Tom could only nod in agreement.

'So, what's going to be our plan? Are you going to carry on like this or not?'

Tom, deep in thought, cogitating on his various options, offered an opinion,

'I could try for a sideways move… Icky might support that. On the other hand, if I'm so useful to him, why would he? Is it worth a try? I could try for a move out of the county so that we could make a fresh start somewhere new… but what about your job and the boys?'

'I don't mind moving away to somewhere new. We're still young and fit enough to make a fresh start. Jack will soon be away at Warwick and it's doubtful that he'll ever live permanently at home in the future. Freddie's at just the right age to move to a new school. Anyway, my lover, don't fret about it. Worry never solved anything. We'll beat that bastard yet!' Maudie became quite agitated at the thought of an ongoing battle with Ted Slater.

They watched *Question Time*. Usually enjoying the verbal jousting between the panellists, they sometimes joined in the debate but on this occasion Tom`s attention was only half on the programme. He could not settle finally, bed invited them and they accepted the invitation gratefully. Tom was asleep before they'd said their 'goodnights'. But Maudie's brain continued to work overtime until, at last, she drifted off into a fitful sleep, interrupted periodically by visions of the demonic Ted Slater seated on a throne engulfed by dancing flames , surrounded by poles to which were chained all of his lapdogs.

Jennifer Bird carried out, meticulously, her secretarial and bursarial duties and left her desk clear at five o'clock. So efficient was she that despite recalling all the events of the day during this period, her business-like attention to detail had been unaffected. There was no doubt that she was a valuable asset to Ted Slater. She knew that he was irascible and petulant requiring perpetual praise and encouragement to bolster his self-confidence and that he also appeared to be somewhat cavalier with regard to the school's petty cash, ostensibly personally purchasing for the staff's consumption, all manner of drinks and tasty morsels from time to time, all the while clawing his expenditure back from her petty cash. He needed his staff to be aware of his generosity...putting his hand in his pocket for the good of his staff...but she alone knew the truth. So far she had been prepared to 'turn a blind eye' to his doubtful scruples. What was the secret of these dastardly men who could bewitch apparently well-grounded, normally sensible women so that they would come running at the slightest twitch of their little fingers? She was like a pure and innocent virgin being drawn towards the rakish libertine, knowing that her virtue was likely to be sacrificed in the liaison but she could not help herself. It was true to say that Jennifer Bird was and had been for many years enchanted by her boss. She was aware of all his foibles and failings and yet she was bound to him by invisible chains from which she had not the ability or the desire to attempt to escape. She had loved the man for many years but had not liked him. She had been deliberate in her compromise of her situation. She must be viewed by all to be a stalwart supporter of Ted Slater and overtly idolise him because to do otherwise would not be favourable to her objectives. During his thirteen years as Head, she knew that none of the independent thinkers prospered, the sycophants, only, had succeeded.

Her mind still full of images of Ted Slater's offences over her time at his side, she drove *Delilah*, her dark red Nissan Cherry Coupe at a speed commensurate with its jaunty appearance to her picture-book eighteenth century cottage dwelling, named appropriately 'Robin's Nest', constructed of grey brick under a thatched roof whose front door was at that time of year festooned with scented, dusty-blue, wisteria, around whose twisted stems climbed the beautiful morning glory, all the while considering the state of health, both physical and mental, of Ted Slater.

CHAPTER TWO

Friday, 15 May, 1992.

Tom glanced at the alarm clock for the third time. The bedroom was already ablaze with the brilliant shafts of sunshine penetrating the chinks between the layers of window blinds and curtains. It had seemed a long night. It was five o'clock. A gritty sensation in his eyes confirmed his continuing weariness. He looked across at his peacefully sleeping wife and not wishing to disturb her slumbers, silently, he slid out of bed and crept out of the room. He had had a bad night. He had gone to sleep easily enough but then the nightmares began and seemed to continue throughout the night.

In his dream, he had driven into a small, pleasant market town, busy with people and traffic because it was market day. Managing to park his silver-grey Ford in the rapidly filling car park, he headed for the nearest coffee bar. He saw that Jennifer Bird was behind the counter pouring his coffee from a percolator. Behind her, mounted on the wall, was a huge river serpent – a Green Anaconda, over thirty feet in length with a diameter of over twelve inches, which Bobbie had brought back from his travels in the Amazon rain forests. The walls were covered with pictures of birds from the Brazilian rain forest –the exotic, colourful parrots, hornbills and toucans and the sinister, dark raptors – eagles, vultures and hawks. Over the counter was an enormous cabinet housing a stuffed Amazonian Alligator gar, its long jaw armed with a double row of sharp, flesh tearing teeth. The torpedo-shaped body, with brown back and yellow belly was three metres long and it dominated the café. On the counter, a huge aquarium containing sand and various pieces of Sumatra wood housed a number of Peruvian angelfish and False rummy-nose tetra both from the Rio Nanay. On the walls, from hooks, hanging by their hair were dozens of shrunken heads from the Jivaroan tribes of Peru, all of them having the distorted, facial appearance of Ted Slater. Leaving behind his coffee in the cup, unconsumed, Tom had fled from the café, heading back to the car park which was full of silver-grey Fords. Try as he might, running from car to car, he could not find his car in order to make his escape. At that point, he woke up, sweat pouring from his body, his feet caught in the tangle of damp sheets which had enfolded him.

      He staggered down stairs to the kitchen where, in order to revive himself, he made a pot of tea which he carried outside into the garden. He sat on the bench which was receiving the full heat from the morning sun and looked across at a table on which were several containers overflowing with brightly coloured violas and pansies-the blue and yellow 'Morpheus', the purple and orange 'Sorbet Orange Jump Up' and the 'Velour Purple and White.' In the beaming sunshine, they turned their cheerful, beaming faces to him and caused a smile to appear on his careworn face. The mere sight of them lifted his mood and spurred his return to the kitchen in order to make a start on the preparation of the family breakfast. He felt ready to go forward into another day's battle. He, actually started to sing, whilst in the shower, so enlivened was he by the vision of his pansies and the splendour of the morning.

Thomas Michael Portland, at forty five years of age and a height of five feet ten inches still maintained a strong physique even though his waistline had thickened somewhat over the passing years. As a youth and as a student, his main sporting interest had been in the weight training area of the gymnasium and he had continued until the recent past when he was advised by his doctor that he should get his exercise by some other means. Not handsome as described in the conventional romantic novel, he had a magnetic personality which caused attraction in many but repulsion in some. His dark hair, now slightly thinning and with grey hairs appearing on a daily basis, was cut in a short, easily-managed style. He visited the barber once a month not once a week as did Ted Slater. Rogue hairs from his dark, bushy eyebrows curled over his heavy, black spectacle frames making for a slightly dishevelled appearance. He was clean shaven, although at the end of the day, the growth of his facial hair might have been construed as fashionable stubble. His complexion was clear with a healthy glow aided by the sun which was kind to him for its rays did not burn him but created an even golden tan which was the envy of many. His hands were hairy, masculine, substantially sized with an agreeable shape with well-kept nails. Maudie would admit that she had been initially attracted by this physical feature - a safe, trustworthy pair of hands. Parents could trust him in his dealings with their offspring. Men could trust him with their wives. Female colleagues felt secure to be alone with him. He was a faithful husband in his marriage to Maudie. He wore a plain nine carat gold wedding ring to show to all-comers that he was a married man. He was sickened by the illicit liaisons that he witnessed every day amongst his own colleagues. Some considered him to be old-fashioned in his outlook. His eyes, blue-green, forever alert - observing - watching and inspecting his fellows and his surroundings easily enabled his assessment of his environment where he was able to take appropriate action as required. Colleagues had learned to ensure that their conduct was absolutely faultless in his presence and if he was unimpressed with anyone, a quizzical glance in their direction usually engineered the appropriate response.

He was a man who took pains to look smart without ostentation. However, sartorial elegance was not his top priority, unlike some of his colleagues, for example Ted Slater, the Head, who was the most expensively attired person he knew. Today, Tom chose from his wardrobe, a dark blue suit, selected by his wife on one of her regular visits to the gents' outfitters at sale time. He had at least thirty suits, all of which had been obtained by Maudie at a considerable reduction, enabling Tom to wear a different suit every day for a month. Tom had little time or interest in keeping up with the trends in male fashion. He was content to let his wife choose his clothes for him. He belonged to that group of individuals who saved for a never arriving 'rainy day', keeping faith with the economic principles practised by his humble, hardworking, respectable parents and grandparents before him. 'Waste not: want not' was one of the clarion calls of the non-conformist, puritan ethic which echoed relentlessly down the years from childhood experience. An expensive cream shirt, similarly purchased by Maudie, and a tie in maroon, tied in a Windsor knot completed his attire. He attached some initialled, gold cufflinks - an anniversary gift from Maudie, to his shirt cuffs, completing his ensemble with black socks and some comfortable, highly-polished, black shoes. His dress could be described as sartorially conservative with a small *c*. and this description suited the personality of the man himself. Some thought him to be arrogant and self-satisfied, but those were colleagues whose conduct, both personal and professional fell short of his high standards. He was a simple man in that there was no artifice in him. He was a straight talker, honest to a fault, and although some did not like him, they knew where they stood with him. Unfortunately for Tom, his very laudable, outspoken nature did not go down well with some colleagues in the hierarchy at City Hall. It would have better served his interests professionally to have been more political with a small *p*.

He was a committed family man. He was satisfied that home-life, at least, was highly satisfactory. His wife, Maudie Portland, was an exemplary pattern of the working mother. She held down a full-time job in the local library and gave him unremitting support. He was full of admiration for her ability to juggle all of her tasks without letting any of them slip from her grasp. He was immensely proud of his two sons and their academic and sporting achievements. His character was beyond reproach and he was dismissive of those with lower standards than his own. This did not endear him to those of his colleagues with a debased moral code whether amoral or immoral or both. He was ethical to the *n*th degree and this was widely acknowledged by his supporters and detractors alike. Scrupulously honest and truthful in all his affairs, he was the exact antithesis of the mendacious Ted Slater. But Tom was always striving to be better. He would not allow himself to become self-satisfied. He would always believe, in whatever action he took, that there could be a better way of its execution.

Tom had long since severed all connections with religion of any kind. He did not fear the wrath of the Almighty simply because he denied 'his' very existence. His parents had remained conscientious in their worship and attendance at their chosen church but Tom, during his formative years, so thoroughly immersed was he, that he had become drowned in religion. Finally, as a twenty-year old student, he had abandoned it having witnessed too many examples of so-called self-professed 'Christians' acting in most unchristian-like manners, whilst he, a non-believer , was the most 'Christian ' of men. He was suspicious of the badge of office – that fish- *Ichthus*, which he saw more and more, to his dismay, sported by, in his opinion, the most irreligious individuals who regarded it as a way of ingratiating themselves with those of higher rank who might prove useful in the race for promotion. Such a person, in his circle of acquaintance was Peter Smalley.

Peter Smalley had joined the staff at Southwich three years earlier in Tom's tenth year of Deputy Headship. Tom had been on the interviewing panel. Smalley was tall, thin, with a sallow complexion and black, slicked back hair which revealed a pronounced widow's peak. He walked with a slight stoop. Tom could visualise him rising slowly from a coffin in the dead of night. He had not been overly impressed with this man who was being interviewed for one of the most senior academic posts in the school. Smalley had come with an exemplary reference from his former post in North Yorkshire. Tom was always suspicious of such glowing testimonials; sometimes they were too good to be true. Tom had noted that Smalley, like Ted Slater, wore in his lapel a small shiny badge…a stylised fish…the dreaded Ichthus. He was duly appointed to the post of Head of Science.

In due course, details of his private life emerged and were circulated on the jungle telegraph. He was twice divorced with three small children by two different mothers. Tom could not understand how a man, so entrenched in religion, could have revoked his marriage vows not once but twice. Now, unattached, he was co-habiting with another member of the Southwich Staff - Trudie Long, herself a serial cohabiter. Tom also found out, quite by chance, that Smalley's former Head was a devout atheist.

Peter Smalley did not row with the Head as Tom did on almost a daily basis. Had Tom to behave as Smalley -- the adoption of a worshipful, obsequious manner - in order to avoid the daily conflict? Peter Smalley was regarded highly by Slater despite a classroom performance and a general commitment to Southwich High School which any objective spectator could recognise as leaving much to be desired. Never a day went by when the Head was in school that Smalley failed to call on him, on some pretext or other. In his dealings with Slater, he was sycophantic and servile which contrasted markedly with the arrogance and sang-froid with which he approached all other colleagues and pupils.

Smalley had taken a dislike to Tom Portland from the time of his appointment as Head of Science in school. His personal history, that of a divorcee cohabiting with Trudie, a modern linguist already on the staff who had, before his arrival, already lived with and discarded the Head of P.E. – the handsome, fine figure of a man, Keith Dawson, and the tall, dour, craggy Scottish

History teacher, Donny Ross, had not endeared him to the Deputy Head. Smalley felt himself under suspicion from the supposed, high moral tone of Tom who had not tried to disguise his cynical view that divorce and cohabitation, far from being a handicap against professional advancement was a palpable recommendation in school as much as in political life.

It had seemed to Tom that the modern attitude to the sexual proclivities of human beings predominated in the mind sets of the butchers, bakers and candlestick makers who influenced the appointment of teaching staff responsible for the transmission of values to the children in the school. To Tom, it seemed that Governors' moral responsibility to provide all pupils with worthy role-models had become less of an obligation than permitting all teachers freedom to conduct private lives as they chose. Those personnel possessing the 'old' values of marriage 'until death do us part' and the reverence of family values were at a positive disadvantage. The Director of Education had warned Tom to avoid pontificating on this matter and it would have been foolish to have disregarded this advice coming as it did from the very person most likely to enable professional mobility. Tom and Maudie had considered that the moral climate, in which family values were scorned, was much to be regretted. Indeed, in their opinions, it was one of the school's primary functions to convey these values.

Tom's outlook on life and his relationships with his colleagues occupied his thoughts, throughout his drive to school – a journey of thirty minutes or so. His antagonistic relationship with Slater upset him but how could the self-respecting man of high moral fibre that he was maintain a relationship of mutual trust with a Headteacher who responded positively only to adulation? As he entered the school gates, his mind turned to strategies he might employ in the likely conflicts with some of his other adversaries, notably Peter Smalley and Phoebe Spong, his fellow Deputy Head.

He walked along the pedestrian pathway from the car park to the main entrance of the characterless , single-storied, flat-roofed extension, whose outer surface was cladded with some faded panels to obscure the shoddy construction beneath and which housed a host of characters most of whom he loved and a few whom he loathed.

An hour later, having deposited in a compartment of his brain all contemplations of skulduggery on the part of his adversaries, Tom made his way towards the Assembly Hall to stand on policing duty as the Upper School's hordes trudged unwillingly into Assembly.

The Upper School gathered on a Friday morning for Assembly which was mainly for the dissemination of notices and announcements. It was conducted by the Headteacher or more usually by one of his Deputies. Friday mornings seemed to be a favourite day for out-of-school committee meetings. The Head, a practising Christian, pursued a routine of hymn singing and lengthy prayers, largely ignoring the smirks and smiles and whispered comments of his unwilling audience. However, aware of how the educational tide was turning, he had encouraged the Music teacher, Vernon Longstaffe, to find uplifting songs in lieu of hymns for the pupils to sing.

'Morning, Sir', chirped a series of open-faced, sunnily disposed fifteen and sixteen-year olds as they marched reluctantly into the School Hall for the Senior Assembly.

'Straighten your tie...tuck your shirt in...where`s your tie?...are you wearing lipstick?...wait outside my office after assembly…..STOP pushing!'

Such were the regular remonstrations with his beloved flock. They accepted his hectoring tone affectionately. After all, he was only doing his job! The pupils of Southwich High School knew and respected Tom as a fair, kindly and understanding person who they knew instinctively would tolerate no nonsense but who nevertheless saw each one of them as an individual. The jungle telegraph of pupil communication concerning staff natures was remarkable. It did not take long for the rawest Year Seven pupil to discover who was who and how one had best behave towards specific teachers.

Tom was well known in Southwich. Having been Deputy Head in the school for thirteen years, his reputation had preceded him. The parents knew him well. Frankly, they liked him. He gave parents a feeling of their importance. He made them feel welcome in school. The most nervous working-class, single-parent who approached the school in trepidation had been made invariably to feel a person of worth. This was one of Tom's strengths. Perhaps it was a function of his working class inheritance. He was almost universally acknowledged as a man who responded convincingly and warmly, one who genuinely respected those with whom he dealt. The parent who liked a teacher rarely turned out a child who had failed to absorb that liking. Knowing the respect in which his Deputy was held in the community made Slater's scepticism about Tom all the more painful.

      Tom walked purposefully to the front of the assembled Upper School. A single movement of the hand was enough to bring three hundred and sixty or so excitable teenagers to attention. The Head of Music, Mr. Vernon Longstaffe, wittily nicknamed 'Prod' by generations of Southwich pupils struck up a restful rendition of *Somewhere over the Rainbow.* The peace was disturbed by a growing crescendo of rustling as pupils turned in their seats in order to gain a sneaky first sight of the Headteacher. His late arrival had already caused Longstaffe to have to repeat the theme from a recent musical production three times. This was an almost unvarying circumstance at the beginning of Assemblies. The pupils were inured to Dr Slater's dishevelled appearance. They were all amused by his insistence upon carrying his mortar board and wearing his academic dress which was usually only half on his shoulders as he hurried along, the long black sleeves of his gown streaming behind him like those of a bat out of Hell. They were intrigued by the shiny 'fish' badge which glimmered ostentatiously in his lapel.

      Dr Edward (Ted) Slater was six feet tall, with a thin but wiry frame. He had been a good footballer in his youth, but the ravages of time and indulgence were beginning to manifest themselves. He was inordinately vain, especially about his expensively coiffured head of wavy, silver hair. He was delighted by his nickname of the 'Silver Fox'. So proud was he of his silver hair that he ignored the reddening of the whites of his eyes, the multiplicity of broken veins in his cheeks and the purplish tinge to his nose which grew ever more intense with each passing day. Now an increasing lack of exercise with the resulting increase in his portliness and an anxious, awareness of the onset of old age and pensionable status added to which, was the constant battle with his Deputy, had caused his daily tot of whisky to become an hourly one. Many had been the occasions when Slater had appeared at evening events evidently the worse for alcoholic satiation. The school was largely unaware of this. For now, he presented a figure which reminded the educated reader of 'Mr Bumble the Beadle' from *Oliver Twist*. The same assurance of moral ascendancy, of arrogant superiority and determination to make everyone tremblingly aware of his influence over their futures was painfully apparent.

    The Headteacher surveyed the waiting masses critically. He frowned aggressively at Paul Sawyer, the independently minded Head of Technology who was slipping in late at the back of the Assembly Hall. He smiled deliberately at his current favourite, Peter Smalley, the Head of Science who smiled obsequiously in return. He looked around vainly for his other Deputy, Mrs Phoebe Spong who, as usual, was nowhere to be seen. No doubt, he considered, she would be sidling covertly into the back entrance, late and full of excuses about impossible traffic conditions. Just as certainly, she would be presenting herself in his office at the end of assembly, disingenuously claiming to have some issue of importance to discuss with him whilst actually endeavouring to elicit his sympathy for the obvious bruising around her eyes and forehead received at the hands or feet of an inebriated husband who was another of the county's favoured

Heads. He noticed with considerable irritation that Alan Bairstow, his favoured Head of Mathematics was once again seated next to the young, female Science teacher who was looking up with fond admiration into Bairstow's eyes.

The Senior School rose as one to their feet like a well-rehearsed choir as Longstaffe ceased his repeated rendition and Tom requested their respect for the approaching Head. Slater was about to walk down the central aisle when a hullabaloo broke out in the Dining Room behind the closed doors. Evidently, Phoebe Spong had arrived; a pupil late for Assembly had been collared and berated for her tardiness.

Phoebe Spong was universally execrated by the pupils. She was a malevolent hypocrite whose only interest was to use them either as sacrificial pawns in order to improve her career chances or as sources of prurient titillation in intimate counselling sessions. When a sexual problem was evident, she became immediately animated. Such occasions were rare, however, because the pupils failed to include her in their requests for counselling. They approached teachers whom they could trust and she was not on their list. The everyday business of teaching and control were sources of dreadful boredom to her. She approached all pupils in the same belligerent manner. There had been only a couple of assaults against staff in Southwich's history; each had been committed against Mrs Spong. Teetering on the edge of his assembly's delivery, it seemed to Ted Slater that a third assault was about to occur.

'GET OFF my fucking back!' the highly pitched voice of the teenage girl, like the fire alarm, reverberated, so disturbing the pregnant silence of the waiting assembly.

Broad grins appeared on the faces of the rosy-cheeked youngsters who confidently believed that this Assembly was going to be memorable. The silence was almost tangible; all breathing appeared to cease as the next outburst was anticipated. They were left unsatisfied. They began to chatter among themselves ...all making similar observations.

'Sponge-face is at it again'

This example of Phoebe Spong's many nick-names was the one most favoured amongst the pupils. Her complexion was puffy, squashy and bore pock marks from an old childhood infection. It had a yellowish tinge reminiscent of an old yellow sponge kept in the garage for car cleaning purposes. The source of her sallow colouring was discovered to be self-tanning lotion which she used liberally around her eyes to conceal the bruises delivered to her by her brute of a husband. She was of medium height but attempted to appear taller by her straight-backed, marching mode of walking with her chin pugnaciously thrust forward. Totally black haired with not a grey hair in sight but cut severely in a short style with a straight fringe, which she sported above garishly painted, fleshy, protruding lips a vague moustache, often the bane of the dark-haired individual. Her so-called 'laughter lines', should have been renamed 'misery-lines' for there was a permanent scowl on her face. Laughing was not to be found in her repertoire. To add to her despotic aura she wore a 'uniform' of dark, sombre, military –styled suits, all of the highest quality, reminiscent of those worn by an authoritarian regime.

Forty-five years old, married to another Headteacher, she had two children, both at University, and apparently 'living the kind of student life which does not lead to a 'good' degree' some of her colleagues had been heard to say.

'God help those two...having a mother like that. It's no wonder they are as they are. You can see it coming...they will embarrass her at every opportunity. Serve her right for being such a harridan. She must have treated her own children as she treats our pupils,' another colleague had added.

Her relationship with her husband was appallingly strained since neither of them was prepared to 'play second fiddle'. In consequence Phoebe had conducted a series of extra-marital relationships which had culminated in a long-standing affair with a local solicitor. In an attempt to normalise her view of herself, she constantly sought out the company of those who shared her social experience of marital infidelity. Such company was readily available amongst the teaching and associated personnel of the educational fraternity. It had been a source of genuine alarm to her colleague, Tom, that domestic disharmony such as Phoebe exemplified should be exhibited with such abandon as she, he maintained, ought to display a worthy rôle-model to easily influenced youth. It seemed to Tom that his profession was singularly ill-equipped to convey without massive hypocrisy the values of family, loyalty and responsibility. Had not the Authority's adviser in Moral Guidance and Pupil Welfare left for employment in a neighbouring authority and almost immediately cohabited with the Religious Studies Adviser? The educational world which Tom inhabited had elevated Lust to the level of voluptuous naughtiness, a thing to be smiled at benignly like a father might his son's first amorous exploit.

Tom gestured with his eyes and an effortless motion of his hands in order to regain the respectful silence and attention of the Upper School as the Headteacher made his way to the platform. There was something essentially impracticable about the way Ted Slater insisted upon wearing his academic gown for Assemblies. The pupils, unfamiliar with academic dress, regarded his habit as an eccentricity and referred to him as 'Batman' in consequence. It was, in fact, a symbol of his self-conscious ascendancy; he stood out strenuously against the generality of staff wearing academic dress on public occasions like Speech Day since some non-graduate staff were ineligible but his every working thought was directed towards the maintenance of his own superiority; democratic equality amongst his staff he identified as the quasi-reason which justified his own precedence.

As Ted Slater strode masterfully down the central aisle, he gazed critically at pupils who appeared not to be standing in perfect reverence. He frowned malevolently at an individual whose attention was directed towards his neighbour. Just as he arrived at his table on the platform, placing his Assembly notes on the table-mounted lectern, the solemn atmosphere he craved was broken by the heavy sounds of a cloudburst.

'Damn this soddin' weather!' Ted Slater fumed.

The day had started brightly enough. Slater had been impressed on his arrival at school by the late spring sunshine illuminating the flower borders adjacent to the car park. Rose bushes were beginning to show their first signs of springtime renewal with the promise of a fine display a few weeks thence. The daffodils were past their best but they had been replaced by a grand display of Tulips - *Queen of the Night and Princess Irene* .The combination of the dark purple, almost black with the bright orange petals created a dramatic regal display outside his office window which Slater found most gratifying.

But now all had changed. Dark skies with their ominous outpourings added a note of depression which matched his mood. The rain came thundering down in 'stair rods', rattling against the floor-to-ceiling windows of the Assembly Hall. One joker on the staff, Carwyn Jones remarked,

'This`ll save the county a few bob on a window cleaner. God doesn't charge for this service,' he laughed.

The pupils gasped out loud in undisguised pleasure at another distraction to their boredom. They fidgeted, turned to grin at their peers and expressed their delight to their neighbours. Ted Slater put his hand to his forehead.

'Oh God! For Christ's sake, give me strength to bring this bloody rabble back to order,' he cried out silently to his Maker.

Ted Slater, totally discomposed by the thunderous and turbulent weather outside his control, almost began to weep. He had to summon all of his energy to get himself back on an even keel in order to deliver his messages to the Assembly. His misanthropic mood did not help his situation and he struggled to regain that feigned bonhomie he normally presented to the Upper School Assembly. The colour rose in his already florid complexion. The attention of the disturbed congregation was further strained as he attempted to sort out the jumble of papers which constituted his Assembly notes. After what appeared minutes of fumbling, Slater nervously announced the hymn. It was with a kind of exaggerated relief that the gathering launched into a rendition of *The Streets of London.* Longstaffe began his accompaniment of the singing with his usual gusto and though singing was frowned upon by the majority of the pupils, to sing was less troublesome than to experience the wrath of the Headteacher should they fail to achieve the level of sound which he identified with conformist enthusiasm.

Tom sang with apparent relish. He enjoyed a limited tonal range. The hymn selected by Longstaffe, deliberately intended to enable half-broken teenage voices to avoid frog-like croaking, suited his modest capabilities equally. It was a constant source of annoyance to Slater who indulged a self-conceit of his own prowess in everything including singing that his Deputy whom he conceived could not 'sing for toffee' should imagine himself to possess that ability. This symptomized Tom's major problem with Ted Slater. The Headteacher was incorrigibly competitive. He could brook no rival. He required desperately for his sanity a feeling of superiority. Anyone who conducted their affairs of whatever nature, alongside his, was the object of intense jealousy immediately comparison between the two could be made. Tom had been tremendously embarrassed by the Headteacher's petulant displays of envy over matters which no-one with normal mental stability would notice. Tom's purchase of a new car would seem as a deliberate attempt to upstage him. His offer to drive home the Chairman of Governors had been seen as a piece of patent toadying. Tom's popularity with parents drove him into a frenzy of mortification. The purchase of a fine house, far superior to that of any other member of staff, including Slater filled him with fierce resentment. His inevitable response was vengeance. The one professional aim in life which Tom nursed above all else was to be responsible ultimately for his own school. In attempting to achieve this goal, Tom could be sure of his arousing Slater's retaliating, remorseless responses. Tom would pay for his presumption.

    Longstaffe hammered the keys of the piano whilst appearing to make every pupil feel his eyes on them. For him, here was a very moral duty. The disturbance of the previous few minutes was to be overcome by his Pied Piper of Hamlyn-like influence. He was a man of genuine ethical conviction, the son of a non-conformist minister, a touch boyishly naïve and irremediably idealistic yet he aroused unquestioned loyalty amongst the pupils of Southwich High School where he had practised his art for over twenty five years. Inspired by the moral forcefulness of his eyes, the pupils were launched, almost against their better wishes, into a passable performance of the hymn. There were still odd nods and exchanged glances of amused cynicism and eager anticipation of the next faux pas from their bumbling Headteacher but by and large the school sang. This had been one of the remarkable features of the school. Whilst others had given up fatuous attempts to maintain a semblance of choral conformity, Longstaffe had, by virtue of personal command, maintained a tradition of musical enterprise in the school which surprised all objective commentators.

Slater knew that the sounds of altercation shattering the solemnity of the morning worship had to be scotched. Though it pained him to acknowledge it, there was no alternative but to send his luckless Deputy from alongside him. No-one in school was as likely as he to introduce a calming note into the embattled confrontation between Phoebe Spong and the incensed pupil. Tom made an undemonstrative exit through the rear door of the platform whilst the pupils sang on.

Whilst they sang, Slater's mind was racing in overdrive. However would he deal, without escalation of confrontation, with Phoebe's universal inability to handle potentially difficult pupils? The encroaching noises of embattlement had ended from the precise moment of Tom' intervention but though a temporary respite had been achieved, he knew that his Deputy's intervention would leave him with a triple problem of ensuring suitable treatment of the offending pupil, counselling Phoebe to side-step such unseemly confrontations and making sure that Tom did not come out of the affair smelling of roses. Phoebe, he was positive, would prove to be the usual ally in ensuring the latter. She could be depended upon to make complaint that Portland had caused her to lose face before the insolent pupil. This, then, was Slater's perpetual dilemma. He knew of Portland's utility in defusing explosive circumstances but his own ascendancy had to be maintained at all costs. Not for a moment was the upstart Deputy to be permitted an ounce of credit.

The singing abated and Slater sallied forth upon his usual address... The thoughts were clear in his mind but articulating them in a comprehensive manner to adolescents of widely ranging abilities was beyond his capability. He possessed a butterfly mind which struggled to keep pace with its racing thoughts. Ideas which he thought he had expressed remained unstated so that the stated notions made little sense. Most pupils and staff had given up attempting to make sense of the unconnected ramblings which constituted his usual sermon. Yet he entertained considerable conceit about his public speaking prowess. It was true that he had gained plentiful experience through Church and Sporting connections. Nevertheless, he struggled to achieve an oral style which communicated ideas clearly.

His ability to read out loud was so inferior to that of Tom that it greatly affected his performance. Mercifully, his dispatching of Tom from Assembly meant that Tom could not display that usual look of disdain which the Headteacher imagined to be an unvarying response when he himself performed publicly.

Slater announced his theme of 'selfless service'. By way of introduction, he read from St. Luke, Chapter ten. It concerned the Good Samaritan. He stumbled laboriously over the verses, lacking the authority and conviction of tone which would make the reading register upon the sleepy minds of his passive audience.

'Which of these three, do you think, was a good neighbour to the man who fell into the hands of robbers?'

He read in a voice without deviation from the monotone which had exemplified the reading of the whole passage. He proceeded into a mishmash of self-congratulatory reminiscences about his visit the previous evening to the local hospital in order to sit alongside a sick church member… his moment of personal dilemma whilst playing centre-forward and captain in the University first eleven and a piece of half-remembered trivia from his days in the National Service. Whatever the theme of his Assembly, these same three illustrations were always drawn upon. Those members of staff who were brave enough to entertain critical thoughts of the Headteacher raised mental eyebrows at the descent into the invariable exemplars. Such were the responses of Paul Sawyer, the Head of Technology, and of Irma de la Haye, the Head of English and the school's major Union representative. Teachers like Smalley- the 'Uriah Heap' of the Science department and Alan Bairstow, the suave, artfully careerist and self-appointed 'Casanova' of the Maths department simply remained mentally nonchalant in case silent articulation of criticism would invite seer-like recognition of their disloyalty by the feared Headteacher.

Without warning or explanation, Slater shifted to a diatribe against thoughtlessness and selfishness in pupils and adults alike.

'I want you all to be like the Good Samaritan – to help others even if it costs you dearly.'

With a suddenness which awakened his audience from their slumbers, he announced his final prayer whose audibility was stifled by the hectoring sound of the bell signalling the beginning of period one.

Grasping his notes, Bible and mortarboard, Slater stepped forward in order to leave the platform. Pupils and staff shuffled into the obligatory standing position only to be surprised by the instruction to sit down once more. An afterthought had occurred to him which haltingly, he acknowledged. He had remembered suddenly that he must announce the tragic death of one of the pupils who had been absent for some months.

'It is with great regret that I have to inform you of the tragic death of Philip Johnson from Year Ten who you all know to have been suffering from leukaemia.'

There was at first a stunned silence followed immediately by half-hidden titters of embarrassed laughter coming from a limited area of the Assembly Hall. Slater's face reddened to an explosive state of near-apoplexy. Stifling a natural urge to bellow his displeasure, he became aware of a small red-faced year ten pupil in the middle of the disturbed group. All around him, pupils gesticulated knowingly, shouting out gleefully,

'He doesn't look very dead to me!'

Philip Johnson was very much alive and looking distinctly uncomfortable with all this talk about his death. Recognising the intense gravity of the situation, Longstaffe raised himself from his piano stool and manfully intervened.

'Excuse me Mr. Slater, the name of the deceased boy is John Philpott.'

'My apologies to everyone - especially to you... Philip Johnson. Now settle down. Please stand.'

In abject confusion, Slater stumbled down the steps from the platform, making his way in torment towards the back of the hall. The pupils stood dutifully in a jittery sway, trying hard to avert their embarrassed faces from that of the retreating Headteacher. As he reached the doors and the pupils collapsed exhausted to their seats, the silence was disturbed by an explosion - a crack of thunder immediately over the school. The windows immediately became awash with torrential rainfall, strident in its intensity. The darkened skies were then illuminated momentarily by ostentatious, forked lightning which made the dim lights of the hall appear to flicker pathetically. A buzz of nervous chatter arose amongst the pupils. From his extensive repertoire, Longstaffe started to play with great vigour, *Vivaldi's Storm* to which stirring tones, the pupils began to make their exit.

Irma de la Haye turned instinctively to the neighbouring Paul Sawyer,

'Well... doesn't that just take the biscuit? What a silly bugger he is! It makes you wonder what barmy trick he`ll perform next. He must be on something... booze at the very least.'

Sawyer was lost for words. He nodded his agreement, his face contorted in disbelief. Perhaps overcome by the ferocity of the storm and horror at the enormity of Slater`s mighty gaffe, Irma continued,

'This is the best example of 'the pathetic fallacy', I`ve ever witnessed. What a plonker he is!'

Just as swiftly, Alan Bairstow dismissed any emergence of his own dissatisfaction and took his position in order to direct out of the hall the by-now highly indignant and therefore voluble pupils.

Peter Smalley, whatever critical response which might have been lurking in his mind was consciously squashed. Totally unaware of any hypocrisy which it might imply, he studiously entertained the thought,

'Sod it, Christian brotherhood demands that I catch the opportunity to congratulate Dr. Slater on the Biblical appropriateness of his Assembly and to add that the unfortunate error which occurred at its conclusion was no more than anyone with his crushing weight of responsibilities might suffer. Furthermore, he has shown tremendous presence in correcting the petty lapse of memory.'

With these thoughts rehearsed in his mind, like a snake he slid through the throng of excited pupils and headed for the Headteacher's office, instinctively fiddling with his lapel in order to ensure the prominence of his Ichthus badge.

Ted Slater, back in the safety of his office gazed out of his window. Sadly, the sudden squall, with its damaging downward spears of hard rain took its toll on his tulip display causing their irreparable trauma well before their allotted life span had been reached. He opened the top drawer of his filing cabinet and reached inside. At the back of the drawer he felt for the familiar comfort of his hipflask. At this moment, he needed a drink more than he had ever needed one before. He had swallowed only a couple of mouthfuls when the inevitable knock on his door occurred. Where was his doorkeeper, when he needed her?

CHAPTER THREE

Friday, 15 May, 1992.

The Tyranny of Ichthus was a phrase which Tom Portland had initiated cynically within the openly irreligious section of the Southwich staff. It was a matter not difficult to detect that since Slater's appointment to the Headship, a growing number of staff given to ingratiating themselves with him, had ,like himself, taken to wearing on the lapel of the jacket the metallic ,sometimes Sterling Silver, sometimes White Gold, fish badge symbolic of Christian belief. The fawning women, as did a few of the men, wore the fish, inlaid with mother of pearl, as a pendant. Tom had been fascinated by how little effect the said decoration had exerted upon the social behaviour of its wearers. The effects upon him of an upbringing in a quietly modest Christian family had been to sensitise him to ethical issues though he had been left with an inalienable agnosticism. He was deeply suspicious of any open advertisement of ecclesiastical belonging. In some ways he regretted his loss of faith; he had hoped that like his parents he would find it a comfortable home rather than the prison which it appeared to provide for a good many of his professional acquaintance.

      Peter Smalley's footprints were virtually imprinted on the floor of the Administration corridor which led to the Headteacher's office. It was a daily, if not more frequently, habit of his to seek out the Headteacher on some pretext. After that incredibly, excruciating, toe-curling Assembly, he could hardly contain his desire to meet his mentor at the earliest opportunity. His tip-toed approach was silent, his soft-soled shoes making no sound as he oiled his way along the grey-painted concrete floor of the Administrative corridor. As he drew near the Secretary's office, he glanced around, eyes wide, in order to ensure that prying eyes were unaware of his visit. He need not have worried as all members of staff were still in or around the Assembly Hall, supervising the pupils, but it was a well-rehearsed habit when he was approaching the Head's office. He slid silently past her door so that she could not intercept and possibly foil his intended mission. He brushed some imaginary speck from his cuff and felt his lapel for his stainless steel 'fish.' His quiet, almost inaudible tap on the door was answered by an artificially stentorian,

'Come in.'

Were it possible for a six foot male to have oozed like an oil slick around the door, Smalley would have managed it.

Slater greeted Smalley like a 'Godfather' might one of his henchmen. There was a degree of condescending patronage, his universal urge to retain ascendancy and yet sufficient familiarity to ensure a feeling in the subordinate of his worth to the enterprise.

'Ah, Peter, what can we do for you today? I'm glad you popped in. I feel in need of a little moral support after that cock-up out there.'

Slater's acknowledgement of error was not unusual. He was simply selective in the personnel with whom it was shared. Such a confession was essentially disingenuous; he admitted failure in order to elicit contradiction. Thus reassured, the most appalling faux pas could be relegated, in his mind, to the level of minor lapses, the inevitable consequences of an over-worked brain.

'Dr Slater, you ought not to take these things so much to heart. I thought that you recovered magnificently from a slip of the tongue which would have reduced the ordinary mortal to a...a...a...'

Smalley stumbled over his final words. He wanted desperately to choose a phrase which would adequately convey the sense of confusion and embarrassment which another might experience after such a critical error but whichever phrase came to mind carried with it the danger of appearing to describe the Headteacher pejoratively. And so he was unable to select the appropriate term. Not that it mattered. Slater was not interested in any platitudes being spewed from the sycophant's lips, all he wanted to observe was the appropriate body language and Smalley did not disoblige. Immediately, the Headteacher appeared refreshed and mightily relieved.

'Oh, thank you, Peter. I find the support of colleagues like yourself a great support at times like these when support is so supportive.'

Smalley, an intelligent man, was amazed at the gibberish expressed by Slater but it was not in his interests to be critical.

Instead, he searched his brain for something to say that would endear him still further to the Headteacher.

Buzzing around in Slater's mind were sensations of bewilderment at the prospect of having to resolve Phoebe Spong's self-imposed misfortunes, the need to make use of the skills of Portland without becoming indebted to him, his obligations to half a dozen short- and long-term professional and social commitments together with a nagging anxiety about the altercation with his wife earlier that morning. It was little wonder that self-expression upon the matter in hand failed him so regularly that he fell back upon a well-worn facial expression of tired resignation.

'Well, Sir, I would like you to know that I thought your Assembly was super. In these irreligious times, it was so refreshing to hear a message like yours this morning, infused with God's precious wisdom. God bless you Sir. It's a pleasure to work for one so patently chosen by Our Lord for...'

Again he failed to finish his sentence. The last thing he wanted was for the Headteacher to recognise his insincerity which overlong statements might reveal. So he contented himself in permitting Slater, who once again unaware of the unfinished sentence, the opportunity to interrupt gratefully. There was an aura of religiosity about Smalley's compliment and it was as though precision of expression was immaterial. Signposts of meanings were enough. *God, wisdom, Our Lord,* were quite sufficient an approximation of intention. This, together with Smalley's admiring demeanour was all that was required.

'Thanks, again, Peter, repeated Slater. 'When you become a Head, and I'm jolly sure you will, you will find that support is…is…is…'

'The Lord's work?'

Smalley interjected interrogatively, cautiously witnessing Slater's difficulty in concluding his reply.

'Yes indeed, Peter. God bless you .Now, about this bloody Science lesson of mine…What in the name of sweet Jesus am I to do this afternoon? You know that yesterday I had a little mishap with the sodium. How is Jones by the way? I believe that the hospital released him early last evening. He really shouldn't have peered over the front bench, you know.'

'Oh. He's fine, foolish boy. It certainly was no fault of yours, Sir. They've all been told thousands of times that when demonstrations are taking place, they must keep in their seats with their safety spectacles over their eyes, not perched on top of their heads.'

'Yes, indeed, Peter. I have been teaching Chemistry for thirty years now and I've never had such an accident before.'

The accident in question had occurred when Slater had been demonstrating the reaction of sodium with water. He enjoyed delivering lessons of this sort since they were dramatic and dangerous and through them he could exemplify the exciting, colourful, passionate person he so much craved to be. The unfortunate Nicholas Jones had gazed in fascination too closely at the frantic, haphazard zooming hither and thither of the tiny ball of dull, silvery metal over the surface of the water. Slater, of course, had been totally unaware of the boy's exposure so engrossed was he in the zeal of didactic ecstasy. As the excited sodium suddenly exploded, Jones received a myriad of tiny fragments of the element full in his unprotected face. Peter Smalley cleverly nodded his acknowledgement. He maintained a dead-pan expression. Not for a moment did he permit his facial expression to display that he recognised, as usual, his superior was being economical with the truth. Conspicuously spattered on the floor of the Chemistry laboratory in which the Headteacher occasionally deigned to teach a lesson was evidence of frequent chemical spillages and experimental mishaps. The previous demonstration, only three weeks before, involved the setting up of a mercury barometer. Slater had to clear the lab as a slight error on his part had caused a massive spillage of mercury. This fascinating, fluid metal bounced in a myriad of tiny silvery spheres in all directions forming mobile, shining, silvery pools on the bench and on the floor, disappearing into every crack and crevice in its path, where, in secret, it waited to emit its toxicity to the unsuspecting pupil. The hard-working, underpaid laboratory assistant was summoned yet again to clear up after the clumsy manipulations of the Headteacher, and in doing so, used up a large quantity of the departmental stock of Flowers of Sulphur in the attempt to reduce the hazard. The laboratory was put out of use for two days.

   The Headteacher selected the most thrilling topics for his intermittent forays into the Chemistry laboratory. He regarded himself as a latter-day 'Merlin', as he attempted to arouse admiration for his magical and dramatic capabilities. In reality, he was a poor teacher. He was regarded by pupils and principled staff to be like Mr Sugden in *Kes* – a figure of ridicule, a cheat and unfit to be a teacher. The marking of books and the keeping of consistent records, which he demanded of his staff, to him, had always been a matter of secondary importance. He viewed the pupils as a means of facilitating his own self-dramatization and his staff as enablers in his quest for supremacy.

Smalley suggested that since he was teaching a parallel set that afternoon, perhaps the Headmaster would like him to combine groups in order that he might get on with more pressing management duties.

'God bless you, Peter. Normally, I'd refuse your thoughtful offer, but, today, I've so much on my plate that I'll accept. Thanks.'

In fact, this outcome was the rule rather than the exception. Virtually every lesson for which he allowed Tom Portland to timetable him, he failed to attend so that the Head of Department was obliged to combine groups. The Headteacher's appearance on the timetable was in order to convince staff that he was a committed teaching Head, thus to be conceived as a conscientious fellow. Naturally, he depended upon the loyalty of the subject head to preserve his cover. With Smalley, his secret was secure. The reward was bound to be early promotion, Smalley convinced himself. Smalley, in fact, was quite pleased to take on the Head's classes for another reason. It pre-empted the explosive chemical experiments of which Slater was so fond, and which caused Smalley extra paperwork in the form of accident reports and the mollification of the Laboratory assistant whose job it was to clear up Slater's mess. Smalley heaved a great silent sigh. He wished that the Head had chosen to teach in the RE Department, since that subject was nearest to his heart. He could not fathom why Slater, incompetent Chemist as he was did not teach the Scriptures since it was in that area of study that he acquired his Doctorate.

Smalley glided out of the Head's sight, like a slug might on its slimy trail. Slater collapsed into his chair, head in hands, as images of failed experiments in the lab and the recent hullabaloo in his Assembly overcame him.

The door had barely closed on Smalley when the phone rang. Smalley went down on one knee as if genuflecting at the altar, in order to adjust an imaginary loose shoe lace. His ear was close to the door.

'Of course, you may come now, my dear. I'm free for the rest of the morning. We must sort out this business as soon as possible.'

Smalley was in no doubt that this was Phoebe Spong on the phone. It was often the case that she and he were in competition for audiences with the Head. He now made a speedy exit from the area. Phoebe would be at the Head's door in no time and Smalley wished his appearances in that vicinity to be covert. In his anxiety to remove himself from the scene, he slid almost silently down the corridor, his crepe soles squeaking now and again on the concrete floor.

CHAPTER FOUR

Friday, 15 May, 1992.

Tom Portland, having been dispatched from the Assembly Hall, reached the Entrance Hall in less than a minute. His face bore a grim expression. Leaving one adversary to face another was part of his day's work, but it was becoming a tiresome affair even for the peace-maker that he was. In the few seconds before his arrival at the site of battle, he adopted a calmer disposition because he knew that to be otherwise would be less productive.

His female counterpart, Phoebe Spong, was scolding, loudly, the luckless teenager for her foul language and insolence, denying the girl's accusation of 'being on her back', assuring the girl that her treatment for the offence was no different from that meted out to any other pupil. She saw it as part of her job to control the excessive use of cosmetics worn by pupils during the school day. The obvious wearing of make-up was forbidden for all pupils. The girl appeared to be quietening in her protestations, surrendering to the truth of the matter. At this point of triumph, Phoebe Spong, instead of withdrawing, was about to go in for the kill, her war-painted face contorted with anger and distaste for the youngster.

Lesly Atherton, the offending pupil, was characteristic of many of Southwich's pupils. At fifteen years of age, she possessed the social sophistication of a mature woman. She lived with her mother and the current, live-in boyfriend on the council estate, situated adjacent to the school grounds. There were four younger siblings who had to be fed, watered and delivered to their respective nursery and primary schools whilst the mother and the boyfriend continued to sleep off the excesses of the previous night's consumption of drink and drugs. Lesly's lifestyle as chief carer for her siblings, at least in the mornings, led to her notorious unpunctuality and an undesirable, unkempt appearance. She found herself in a desperate situation from which there was no immediate escape. The lack of maternal advice on personal grooming, the enforced domestic chores and the necessary child-care imposed on her, caused her, in her frustration at her lot, to anger easily, and to get involved with spats with her peers and teachers alike. A child, herself, suffering from an excessive social deprivation, being wet, cold and hungry, was unlikely to take Phoebe Spong's criticisms without a severe reaction to the hated female Deputy.

Tom approached cautiously. For Lesly, like all other pupils, he entertained a warm sympathy. She could be a nuisance. A little self-justifying and truculent but as a member of his own English group, she enjoyed extraordinary talent both in the maturity of her command of fluent, practical English and in a sensitively intelligent response to Literature texts. Orally, she was a powerful presence in the group, well able to express opinions plainly and she was a natural group leader.

Tom's problem was to calm the situation, to appear to support his colleague and at the same time to give Phoebe and Lesly the opportunity to emerge without serious loss of face. He knew that with Phoebe, he was bound to lose whatever the outcome. She resented intensely the quality of his relationship with pupils. The secret was that he respected them. He conceived of all pupils as basically sound; he preferred them to adults, forgiving their foibles as manifestations of adult contamination. He could see little to distinguish children from adults apart from the length of their teeth and a degree of sophistication. He wished never to pretend friendship with pupils; he simply believed in the natural bridge-building potential between the teenager's and the adult's perceptions. Phoebe Spong was unable to forge such links since she needed pupils as she needed most adults, as material upon which she might practise in order to manufacture career advancement. Tom's popularity she interpreted as a consequence of ingratiation. His ability to control children by a manifestly muted presence she was unable and unwilling to fathom. At that moment, she was embarrassed by his approach. Being well aware that he must have heard the commotion from the Assembly platform, she was determined to rescue from the situation what she could. This, she could understand only in terms of the pupil's admission to total responsibility.

As Phoebe witnessed Tom's arrival, she engaged fourth gear of moral outrage and high-pitched, high-handed dogmatic tone.

'This girl, Mr Portland, has had the impertinence to swear at me in the hearing of the entire Upper School Assembly. This cannot be tolerated. I have challenged her on her lateness, her poor appearance and her make-up and all I've had in return is downright insolence. She is a foul-mouthed slut and a disgrace to the school!'

Hearing the word *slut*, Lesly became incensed. Like one who has had to fight for her breakfast, she flew towards Phoebe Spong with fists ready to do damage. But Tom was quicker than she. Like lightening, he intervened between the two of them, catching Lesly's hand just preventing it from making contact with the already bruised forehead of his colleague. He was a physically alert and strong man after a lifetime's sporting commitment. Firmly but gently, Lesly was manoeuvred away. His voice was not raised; soothingly, his physical movement was accompanied by no more than a tut-tutting of the tongue. Having placed a comfortable distance between them, in a placatory manner he released Lesly, suggesting that she might usefully remove herself to his office. Cursing, she flounced from the scene in that direction.

'A fat lot of good you were,' recriminated Phoebe. 'Typical of you, that I'm assaulted by a screaming cow of a girl and you immediately take her side and come your usual smarmy manner, giving her the opportunity to leave me looking a fool.'

'Facts...you were not assaulted; I did not take her side; you made yourself look a fool.' Tom was able to speak to her in a forthright manner, as soon as the girl was out of earshot.

'I'm going to insist that Slater exclude her immediately and, furthermore, I'll invoke the official grievance procedure against you on the grounds of your failure to support a colleague in a row with a pupil. In addition, I'm disgusted by the way you, as a man, put your hands on the girls. I saw the way you handled her. You're always touching the girls. The women on the staff will join me in having you impeached for perpetual sexual harassment. So put that in your pipe and smoke it.'

Before Tom could further defend his actions, Phoebe, head back with chin forward, barged past him and strutted off in the direction of the staffroom where she hoped to find sympathetic feminine ears receptive to her passionate objections to the treatment of her by her opposite number. Tom, astounded by this outburst, for a moment or two, was rooted to the spot, unable to separate into their sequence the events of the previous few minutes. His thoughtfulness was interrupted by the reassuring voice of Jennifer Bird, whose face appeared at the louvered office window overlooking the entrance hall.

'Don't worry, Tom; I saw what happened and I heard everything. You were magnificent. Don't let that evil woman get you down. I saw the way you handled the girl. No worries there. Phoebe Spong has been after you for months on some trumped up sexual harassment charge. It's all the rage amongst the feminist lobby. She thinks she's got you in a corner, but don't fret, I'm on your side. I'll look after your interests.'

Tom had indeed been aware that the teaching union favoured by Phoebe Spong, Sian Waite, Monica Dickinson, Alan Bairstow, Peter Smalley and Trudie Long – The Secondary School Teachers' Association, had recently put out draft documents on sexual harassment. He had anticipated that this feminist-dominated group would be anxious to avail themselves of the opportunity offered by these new complaints, warranted or otherwise, against male staff, in order to establish superiority in the widespread, eternal battle of the sexes which existed within the school.

    Tom immediately quelled his nascent anger and basked in a long sigh of relief that Jennifer Bird had had the presence of mind to observe the whole episode. He was well aware of Phoebe's former allegations about his inappropriate dealings with the girls. Since she so patently failed to cope with teenage girls, she nursed a tremendous resentment against anyone who had that ability and especially against Tom simply because he was a man. He was supposed to manage the academic and administrative aspects of school life. It was she who was responsible for Pastoral guidance, and she, as a result of her ineffectiveness, was aggrieved at his continual successes with both pupils and their parents in relation to their appeals for help in academic or personal matters. She was too blind to acknowledge his value as she saw it as a threat to her existence. She considered him to be a perpetual thorn in her side and she was determined to put him down by whatever means, devious or otherwise that she could muster.

    'Hell hath no fury like a woman scorned', he had observed privately, and he knew that it was only a matter of time before the axe fell. But he did not harbour serious anxiety on that account since he knew his own mind to be without blemish. Pupils of whichever gender were sacrosanct; pupils were safe with him. He would have excluded from the establishment any colleague he suspected of inappropriate dealings with either boys or girls. And his cleanliness of mind was universally recognised by his objective,

unbiased colleagues. *'Safety enough'*, he had thought in his innocence.

'Thanks Jennifer. That's a relief! However am I going to cope with that woman?'

'Come in here, Tom, I've made some coffee for the girls in the office. Come and join us and calm yourself down before you go and deal with Lesly Atherton.'

As he entered the office, Jennifer and her two colleagues smiled reassuringly at him. Tom wallowed in the comforting atmosphere which was always proffered by the Secretary and her staff.

'I think Phoebe Spong needs sorting out', suggested Lucy Bright, the younger of the two office ancillaries.

'And I'm going to tell Dr Slater precisely what I think of her', added Jennifer Bird. 'Seriously, Tom, you will have to watch yourself with her, though. She clearly is after ruining you. She's a liar of the first order. Whatever you do, never let yourself get caught alone with her. Have all your dealings with someone there.'

It hurt Tom to the quick that he was obliged to assent to the wisdom of this advice. Passionately, he needed confirmation that his dealings with women were unimpeachable. He asked each of the three office staff to corroborate the point. Warmly and with evident emotion, the three in their turn reassured him that so far as they were concerned, 'he was an OK guy'; they thought the world of him; they knew beyond a shadow of a doubt that his manner towards women and girls was beyond reproach.

Tom consumed his coffee and left to attend to Lesly Atherton as the pupils were beginning to emerge, somewhat haphazardly, likes shoals of silver fish, from the Assembly Hall.

CHAPTER FIVE

Friday, 15 May, 1992.

As Tom neared his office he heard audible weeping sounds. During his walk from the entrance hall, after experiencing irritation at the excitability of the pupils as they emerged from their Assembly, he had considered the wisdom of interviewing Lesly Atherton without chaperone. His reluctant advice to colleagues was to interview pupils always in the presence of a third person. The need to give this advice was a continual source of angst to him. Pupils, he considered, could never alone be the instigators of malicious allegation against staff but society had so poisoned the minds of youth that he knew it to be a necessary precaution. That he should have to avail himself of this unsavoury safety device irked him immensely.

'If I'm clean', he had reasoned, *'then my purity of motive will be protection enough.'*

The girl's emotional condition, he contended was such that the presence of another adult would merely agitate her the more. He decided to see her alone.

Tom entered his office quietly but in a spirit of evident concern. The girl was slumped in one of the easy chairs, knees grasped by her arms, crying freely with her thumb in her mouth.

She adjusted her position as he entered the room.

'Oh, I'm so sorry, Sir', she blubbered. 'You shouldn't have had to sort it out. That Spongeface is really horrible. All I did was to come in late and she was down on me like a ton of bricks. I hate her and so do all the girls.'

Tom wiped a tear of empathy from his own eyes. He sat contemplatively in his own chair at his desk, leaving the length of the room between them. He looked thoughtfully at the photographs of his wife, Maudie, and their two sons, Jack and Freddie, staring down sympathetically at his predicament. His gaze passed to the print of Renoir's *A Little Boy Writing* which he had chosen for his room since it seemed, alongside his family portraits, to sum up what he was about in the teaching profession. He searched Maudie's face for inspiration. None was forthcoming. He did not know what to do for the best. Clearly, the girl had offended; she must apologise at least. But privately, he knew it would have taken the patience of a saint for a pupil of Lesly's background to have spoken respectfully to Phoebe Spong that morning.

Tom's calm contemplation before embarking on a response to Lesly seemed to act as a balm to the girl. His mere presence eased her agitation. Something of the man's restfulness seemed to be contagious. It was she who broke the silence in a much more restrained fashion.

'What d' you want me to do, Sir?'

That was Tom's cue. He much preferred pupils to come up with resolutions of their own in disciplinary situations. Punishment, it seemed to Tom, was a fatuous pretence unless genuinely sought by the recalcitrant. Punishment, he saw as a kind of religious penance. Unless redemption was sought consciously by the perpetrator, the wrongdoing remained unregretted. Punishment when unacceptable to the pupil was mere retribution – a sort of teacher's vengeance and likely to be regarded by the unrepentant pupil as vindictive. Discipline was a matter of developing sound relationships and punishment need only occur when a party to the relationship had spoiled it.

'Perhaps more pertinent, Lesly, is the question, 'What do *you want* to do'?

'I suppose I ought to apologise to her'?

'Yes, Lesly, I think you ought.'

'D' you think Dr Slater will expel me, Sir?'

'No, Lesly, I don't. I will speak to Dr Slater on your behalf. I will tell him that you are prepared to apologise in writing and in person for rudeness to Mrs Spong, for losing your temper and for making as though to hit her. I know that you did not hit her, although you obviously have me to thank for that.'

'Yes Sir. I do have you to thank. I'm very grateful. I will do as you ask. Thank you, Sir.'

'OK, Lesly. Now, I have a price for my part in the resolution. I want you to promise that this is the last time that you will behave in this way.'

'Yes, Sir, I promise.'

'Would you like me to put you in touch with one of the ladies on the staff who might be able to help you further?'

'No thank you, Sir, I would prefer to speak to you.'

Tom found himself once more in a dilemma. If pupils sought counsel, surely they should be entitled to choose their own counsellor. Clearly, here was a girl who needed help in facing difficult relationships and to dodge the responsibility of helping her simply because she was female seemed moral cowardice of the first order. He decided to temporise.

'Perhaps I should talk to your mother? Perhaps she and I together could help you improve your relationships in school?'

'If you like, Sir. But I don't think you'll find her much help. We don't get on. She's always with her fella – out boozing or else sleeping it off. I have to look after the other kids and do the cleaning as well.'

'Well, Lesly, we'll see what can be managed. In the meantime, perhaps you would go to your first lesson and be available should you be called by Dr Slater or myself.'

'OK, Sir. Thank you, Sir.'

When the girl had left his office, Tom sat, scratching his head, trying to make some sense of his morning so far. It was still only a quarter to ten and he felt as drained as if he had done a day's hard labour.

He considered the possible episode which inevitably would occur when he went to discuss with Slater the morning's incident.

Because of Jennifer Bird's support, he did not worry unduly about the malicious allegation but he forecast that Phoebe had already started on her mission to poison the receptive minds of colleagues who had been targets of Tom's criticism in the past. She would have no trouble persuading Slater that Tom had mismanaged the altercation between herself and Lesly Atherton.

    He decided to ring the Head in order to seek permission to discuss the dispute. Slater answered the phone immediately.

    'Oh, it's you, Tom', he answered in an irascible tone. 'Judging by what I've heard already from Phoebe, you'd better get up here straightaway.'

    'What about my lesson? I'm teaching the second lesson at a quarter past ten so I'll have to….' He did not get the chance to finish his sentence.

    'Get it covered, man,' he growled down the phone.' We can't tidy this one up in a few minutes. You *really* do put me in some tricky situations, you know.'

Tom could almost sense the vibration as the phone was slammed down. He had a mental image of Slater weaving around his office like some great Silver Pike waiting to devour the next unsuspecting interloper into his domain.

    With metallic-rimmed, owl-like, reading spectacles perched on his silver thatch, Slater was pacing up and down his office like a neurotic, imprisoned creature, not knowing what, in his jumbled brain, to address next- the angry messages from his wife or the Spong- Atherton-Portland fiasco. Tom's knock on his door caused him to come to a decision very quickly.

Lacking his normal patience, Tom hung up, but not before Slater had made his move first. He then had the disagreeable task of obliging an unfortunate colleague to cover his Year Ten class, which contained a few mischief makers. He called in at the classroom of Monica Dickinson, the Head of Personal and Social education to give her the bad news. He regretted having to offload his work on to another member of staff but he was in a cleft stick and there was no alternative. He reported to her the reason for his action. Her response was cold. Phoebe Spong had already alerted her to the episode.

'Typical,' she observed irritably, 'you management wallahs cock up yer relationships and then we 'ave t' lose us precious free periods whilst you patch 'em up! Don't forget to credit me wi' th' cover, I've already lost one free this week!'

Tom accepted all this misanthropy stoically enough, not that he had a great deal of alternative, standing as the two of them were before a group of Year Eleven pupils who, in silence, were listening for all they were worth. Whilst he was closing the door, he heard Monica reminding the pupils disturbed by his interruption of the theme of her PSE lesson-*How might we generate warm, successful relationships in society?*

Monica was unique in the staffroom, in that she always spoke with a broad northern accent, frequently lapsing into dialect when over-excited. She was fortunate that Slater, who himself reverted to his northern pronunciations on occasions, was open –minded enough to ignore the accent and see the cleverness of the person beneath. The Head was well aware, within the County, of the desire to engineer inclusive staffing policies. She was an independent thinker with a good brain; she was also an intense feminist and a hater of men.

As Tom reached the end of the Administrative corridor, Phoebe stormed past him, in her usual haughty manner, straight backed, head high and chin thrust out pugnaciously, having the bearing of one about to achieve a considerable victory.

CHAPTER SIX

Friday, 15 May, 1992.

Tom, his anger having subsided somewhat, courteously knocked on Slater's door. The stormy weather which had caused such disruption to the Upper School Assembly continued without abating. Thunderclaps persisted in their rolling around the heavens with forked lightning threatening but staying at a distance. Darkness had descended and the school corridor was dimly lit giving a depressing atmosphere of doom, gloom and foreboding. He did not wait to be invited inside. He opened the door and strode in, ready for whatever Slater was going to hurl at him. The freshness caused by the sudden storm had turned the air chilly and he shivered as though entering an ice box and not the gates of Hell. Percolating from Longstaffe's Music room were Strains of Wagner's *Ride of the Valkyries,* one of Slater's favourite pieces of music. Tom appreciated the aptness of the light, the music and the weather all culminating in the perfect storm. He stared at the patterned carpet which he had seen many times previously but now he could see images he had never noticed before. In front of him lay an intricate network of webs with gigantic spiders ready to paralyse him with toxins from their poisonous fangs if he took the wrong route through the maze of hostility presented to him from the two factions in the staffroom- the jealous, spiteful Phoebe Spong and her fellows and the hypocritical, sycophantic devotees of Ichthus and most of all from the great white shark called Ted Slater who loomed up from behind his desk.

Slater, his face a vision of unredeemed malevolence, his blood-red, eyes narrowed, his owl glasses perched on the end of his bulbous, purplish beak-like nose, stared over them at Tom, with no smile of recognition but simply made an affected, duplicitous, enquiry,

'Now, Tom, give me an honest account of what happened when you left my Assembly.'

Tom took a seat facing the Head's desk. No such invitation had been offered, but he felt the need to sit down while he composed his answer. He was not deliberately being stubborn in his reluctance to reply, he was simply gathering all the information together so that he could articulate with precision and with strict adherence to the facts of the case.

'Am I to understand that Mrs Spong has already informed you of the details?' Tom asked.

'She has, though I don't see what that has to do with what I've asked of you', was the irritable reply from Slater, his head, aggressively thrust forward in Tom's direction.

Tom proceeded to describe in fine detail the event, which he had witnessed, of the altercation between Phoebe Spong and Lesly Atherton, the slanging match and the attempted but thwarted assault on the teacher by the pupil which followed and the subsequent counselling of the girl by himself and the threats hurled at him by Spong in her fury at his intervention.

'Phoebe's version of the story is rather different,' Slater batted back.

'No doubt. It usually is.'

'She alleges that the girl struck her above the eyebrow and that she has a bruise to prove it. She further alleges that you manhandled the girl in a most unseemly manner. Furthermore, she alleges that your support favoured the pupil and not the teacher.'

'Mrs Spong's bruise existed before this incident. She has been trying to camouflage it for days with fake tan. She is orchestrating, among those staff, receptive to her cause, an antagonism towards male colleagues whom they dislike for one reason or another. An easy accusation is that of sexual harassment. I am surprised that you are being taken in by her disingenuousness. It's about time you stamped on these ridiculous allegations of my mishandling of girls and female staff. This mischievous ploy by certain, disillusioned women of alleging inappropriate behaviour by their male colleagues is becoming seriously damaging to us all.' Tom, looking at his boss intently in the eye, told him straight.

'Tom, you are a *touchy-feely* sort of guy, aren't you. You can't deny it. You have to keep your distance and you have to stop upsetting the women.' The Head gave, by the changing, softening tone of his voice, the impression that he was sympathetic to Tom's predicament. 'Now what do you know about this bruise and the assault on her?'

'I can't explain the bruise, except that it was already in existence. There was no assault. I intercepted the attack.'

'Phoebe is demanding that the girl be expelled. What's your view?'

Tom explained how the domestic situation was having a deleterious effect on the girl in many other ways as well as in her aggressive behaviour.

'She needs our help and understanding, not vengeful retaliation. You would expect the person in charge of Pastoral Welfare to be well aware of that,' Tom said, his words reminding Slater of Spong's role of Pastoral Head. 'Lesly will apologise, to her, in person and in writing. She has promised not to repeat such unacceptable behaviour in future. I am prepared to give her the benefit of the doubt. I will see that she carries out her apologies and then, in my opinion, the matter should be closed. I suggest that you take up my offer on her behalf to apologise to Mrs Spong'

It was becoming evident to Slater that his Deputy was displaying the kind of sang-froid which invariably irritated him. It was probably just the kind of self-conscious moral correctness which caused the desire to bring him down a peg or two in women like Phoebe Spong. Why was it that Tom created this kind of response in a small section of female colleagues and himself? Slater could not comprehend. It drove him into an agitated frenzy when he witnessed Tom's apparent freedom and ease of relationship with parents, the women in the office, the male staff and women like Irma de la Haye. The mutual regard shared by

Tom and the de la Haye woman angered him. By virtue of her role as representative of the major Union and her intellect, was she not a massive thorn in his flesh and ought not his Deputy side with him out of sheer professional duty?

Phoebe was a nasty, vindictive woman a fact with which Slater privately concurred, but he preferred to favour her rather than Tom whose 'whiter than white' personality annoyed him intensely. How was it possible that an outright atheist like Tom could demonstrate such Christian values? Slater was becoming so weary of all the rows and bitchiness amongst his staff that he was strongly considering retiring early. He could have off-loaded Tom, so easily, several times, to other Headships for which Tom had made application. This would have made life much easier in many ways but he preferred to be an obstacle to Tom's aspirations even if it caused him to suffer. In any case, who else could run the school as efficiently as Tom, enabling himself to take so much time off the premises? If he had let Tom go, he would have had to spend most of his days managing his school, a task which, increasingly, he found a bore. Tom *had* to stay and be kept in his place. He just had to ensure that the saintly Tom did not succeed him. He decided that he could usefully take some time out of school in order to canvass his local church elders with a view to his entry into the church and possible ordination. The workaholic Portland could act as Head in Slater's absence. Hopefully that tactic would suspend Tom's constant demands and interrogations about his references and why he was failing to get the promotion he so fervently desired. Slater considered that the fawning Smalley might be a suitable successor to his post. Smalley was a toady - First Class, but he did not give Slater any trouble, and so for that he would be rewarded.

Slater put his contemplations about his future in the church on hold whilst he returned to the tiresome matter in hand. It was becoming likely, also, that Tom was indeed in the clear. The complaints from Phoebe were manifestly malicious. He knew of her jealousy and vindictiveness towards Tom. He knew also how intemperate and venomous she could be towards pupils. The bruise on her forehead he assumed to have its source outside school. She had several times in the past confided to him her domestic situation with her easily angered husband. Slater could quite understand how the frustrations of the husband could be vented by an attack on this woman, but *that* was none of his concern. Much as he was appalled by Phoebe's deceit, he was prepared to overlook it. To him, she was a useful weapon in his artillery, a useful ally in his continuing war with his other Deputy and an invaluable defence in the frustrating of Tom's primary goal of achieving the Headship of Southwich High School. Portland was not to be allowed, at any cost, to walk straight into the Headship which Slater hoped to vacate. He realised to his chagrin that he would not be able to use this incident to tarnish Tom. He was not a reckless fool. He needed to tread a careful path to achieve the destruction of his Deputy. He knew that he had to wait patiently for another opportunity which would occur in due course. Of that there was no doubt.

He began to consider the possible obstacles he could place in Tom's pathway to Headship. The obvious one was his own refusal to back him. People like Smalley and Spong were useful obstructive forces, but these were countered by Tom' supporters. There had to be a way of removing them from the scenario. Slater's principal obstacle - the Chair of Governors, Violet Bluett, had been overcome on the previous evening. This particular lady had thought very highly of Tom, confiding this information to Slater and so he knew that if she were in a position to make the final decision about his successor then she would certainly appoint Tom. And so Slater had to dislocate her from her position of authority on the Board of Governors. This proved to be a simple task. He simply overloaded her with so many commitments that Governorship of the school became incompatible with her duties as a local Labour Councillor. Getting his preferred nominee to the vacant post had also been easy. Ms Jacqui Erne had come to the rescue immediately the resignation had been confirmed. Slater was in a cheerful mood as he anticipated the look on Tom's face when he delivered the news when the time was right. In the meantime, Tom would have to be permitted to escape the hook.

'I'll get back to you with my decision as soon as I've spoken to Phoebe again. Now about our row earlier today, I'm sorry I got so worked up. I'm under a lot of pressure at the moment.'

Slater hid a sly smile. This apparent sudden hint of friendliness would certainly confuse Tom, who hoping and believing that he might have had a change of heart about him, would be thrown off the scent about his plans. Slater desperately wanted people to think highly of him and his Deputy was no exception. He was anxious that Tom should believe the deception that his superior supported his career ambitions. Indeed, there was a vague desire to see Tom appointed to a Headship if only to demonstrate that he engineered his own staff's career mobility. This, however, did not extend to the post of Head of Southwich High School, where there was a danger that any comparisons between Tom and himself might favour Tom rather than himself. Each time he had sat down in order to write a reference for one of Tom's many Headship applications, he could not bring himself to speak in terms sufficiently complimentary to render Tom's success likely. On one occasion, after having a row with Tom, he had deliberately given a poor assessment of his ability to have a harmonious relationship with senior colleagues. Tom, having suspected for some time that his stumbling block had to be the reference made by Slater, managed to intercept it, an action of which he was not proud, but he had to discover the truth about Slater. Tom, normally slow to anger, was furious. Like a volcano, he erupted with such violence, that the inevitable destruction followed. Slater became all the more determined that 'the bugger should be kept in his place'. Tom had not profited in any way. However, the incident of the interception had blown over. Slater had considered having Tom impeached over it but he decided that 'discretion was the better form of valour' lest his criticisms of his Deputy's suitability for Headship should be subjected to Union and Local Authority investigation. For Tom's part, tarnished by his action, he decided to drop the matter, since any victory would have been Pyrrhic. He could not beat the Establishment of which Slater was very much a part. It was a source of never-ending amazement to Tom that Slater, despite his managerial incompetence, possessed a face which fitted within the County's Advisory Set. He concluded that it might have had something to do with that emblem that they all wore in their lapels.

'He's after my sympathy now,' thought Tom, as he internalised Slater's claim of stress. *'I'll humour him a little. What harm can it do? And I want a satisfactory outcome to this embarrassment.'*

Furthermore, Tom experienced little pride over his contretemps with his superior. His nature was essentially affable and peaceable; that they should be able to return to the mutual respect of their earlier relationship, when he had preferred to relate to his boss as would be expected from his role, was an outcome which he much preferred,

'I too am sorry about our row, Ted.'

Tom lapsed occasionally into the familiarity of first name terms. Ted Slater had recommended it upon his appointment but the appropriateness of its use became unseemly as their relationship deteriorated. 'But you must understand that I have worked my balls off for you for thirteen years and your reluctance to support my Headship ambitions is hard to take.'

'You have it wrong again, Tom. Of course I support you. You have the makings of a bloody good Head. It's just that when you become your old...old...'

Once again, Slater was unable to seize the word for which he was searching. Tom made the same mistake of finding his words for him.

'Aggressive, belligerent, combative, dogmatic...perhaps one of these words was the one you wanted?'

'For Christ's sake, Tom, there you go again. You really do piss me off when you start to lord it over me with your fancy words. You're like a bloody walking dictionary. Why can't you realise that your use of language makes people feel you're…you're…you're…'

'Patronising them?'

'Fuck it, man; you don't know when to stop, do you?'

Slater failed to complete his point. He placed his highly coloured, almost dangerously reddened face into his hands. Tears welled in his eyed. Beads of perspiration glistened on his increasingly, lined forehead. He prayed silently for the strength to see him through this difficult conversation. Tom looked quizzically at him. It was challenging to avoid a sympathetic response and yet nagging away at him was the realisation that this demonstration was a well-used ploy by the Head in order to massage his interlocutor into reacting pliably. Tom was sorely tempted to provoke him more. He had long wished to remind the Head of Christ's admonishment in Matthew Chapter five about the use of oaths, *'Swear not at all…But let your communication be Yea, yea;?Nay, nay; for whatsoever is more than these cometh from evil.'* Slater's tendency to curse volubly struck Tom as characteristic of his religious hypocrisy. He did it, of course out of a lifetime's conscious determination to make himself acceptable in male company. The fact that swearing, mildly or otherwise, proved that his professed Christianity was false, never occurred to him. Clearly, this was not the moment for such a below-the-belt swipe so Tom dismissed the thought.

'Who am I, anyway, to start preaching to him?' Tom cogitated.

His familiarity with Biblical exemplars arose from deep within his familial past and had little relevance to his own ethical position. The Bible conveyed material not greatly more pertinent than Grimm's Fairy Tales as afar as Tom was concerned .He could see little evidence through the history of the previous five thousand years that the Bible's devotees had improved the lot of their fellow man or indeed, their own virtue.

'Look, Ted, don't let's wrangle. This really does ill-become the potential we share for positive contribution to this school's welfare. We must work together so let's do it maturely.'

'You're right, of course. But that's the trouble for me, Tom. You're always bloody right! And you do have a habit of…'

Slater stopped himself. Whether it was because words failed him again or because he could see the old wrangle recommencing, Tom was unaware.

'What is causing you strain at the moment?' Tom enquired solicitously.

'This bloody job, of course. Do you know, during the half term holiday, I was trying to fix some wall lights in the sitting-room? I just couldn't get it right. I broke down in tears at my own incompetence. My wife laid into me saying that it was that bloody school and that bloody Deputy of mine which were the causes of my depression. That's when I became determined to go ahead with my early retirement application. She and I seem to be drifting apart. Only yesterday, she complained that I had shown no interest in her in bed for three months. And it's true, you know; I seem to have so little energy. I'm permanently exhausted. I drink myself to sleep every night. This morning, she's already been on the phone haranguing me over something I forgot to do before I left home to come to this place.'

He raised his eyes towards Tom, passionately attempting to elicit the kind of response he had received from Smalley. As ever, Tom experienced the usual sympathy but he could not bring himself to utter the pedestrian response which his superior craved.

'Your early retirement is just what you need, Ted. I can't deny observation of your strain. I am sorry for it. Why don't you take a few days off?'

Slater felt a resurgence of the irritation. That was the last thing he wanted.

'You'd like that, wouldn't you Tom - another opportunity to play Headmaster and to show that you have enough balls for the pair of us?' Slater spat out.

If he had displayed a forked tongue, Tom would not have been surprised. Tom, appalled at the venomous response to his concern, remained calm under duress. He countered,

'Nothing was further from my mind, Ted. You may find it difficult to accept but I do feel a genuine sympathy for you. Clearly you are under strain. Why don't you credit me with the human decency as a colleague ought to do?'

'Oh, I'm sorry Tom. You're right again. Let me tell what I am planning to do in retirement. I have applied to embark on a part-time theological course in order to prepare for the Ministry.'

'Yes, I know, Ted. Since you have not chosen to share this with me, I had declined to mention it but you have informed others of your intentions. As you know well, you can't stop gossip from being exchanged. No-one is totally confidential.'

Slater was well aware of this fact. Indeed, one of his ways of circulating information was to share an issue in confidence deliberately in order to engineer its promotion through the jungle telegraph. Such had been the case in this instance. Jill Field, the IT teacher, was the one in question. Tell Jill anything and the whole staff would know faster than if a staff meeting were called to disseminate the information. He was, however anxious to discover Tom's response to his decision.

'What do you think of my plan?'

Tom made no reply; he was back in the minefield. Slater required emotional support from all his acquaintance and he needed their approval. Tom could see that to lose the moral ascendancy which Headship represented could be satisfactorily replaced only by a role in the Church but he was also aware that the *calling,* as Slater would have it, did not exist. The desire to enter the Church arose, he felt sure, from Ted's self-dramatization and conceit. But these thoughts were going to remain private. Slater continued,

'My parents are both dead so they can give no opinion. My kids, however, are disgruntled. My daughter is frankly appalled; my son is less than excited. Neither of them, as you know, have the slightest interest in the Church. My wife and I have failed to take them along with us in the faith. Much as we love them both, we have been embarrassed by the way each has thrown our values back into our faces.'

Tom knew well to what the Head was referring. Both offspring had taken partners after graduation without observing the conventionalities of a Church marriage.

'You mustn't blame yourselves on that account, Ted. They are children of their generation.'

'And our generation too - I am surprised you didn't add, as you usually do, Tom. My wife is, of course, a little sceptical but she will warm to the idea, I'm sure, especially when she realises that perhaps I'll have more time to devote to her.'

'Right, Ted, I'm convinced that you are making the right move. You will be able to do a lot of good', under his breath adding, *'preaching to the converted.'*

Tom was anxious to get back to his lesson. He knew that if he had not engineered the end of the conversation, Ted would have carried it on until break. Tom was a committed teacher, leaving classes only with reluctance. In a classroom situation, he was at ease. The tension of managerial relationships was avoided. There was work to mark and homework to set. He never forgot that the reason he entered his chosen profession was a desire to influence the minds of children and with it the direction of their lives. Failure to teach when responsibility demanded it was a gross dereliction of duty and one that Tom did not seek. The pride he took in his teaching was a constant source of irritation to both the Head and Phoebe Spong each of whom assumed that his insistence on this duty as first priority was inevitably an affectation.

'Very well, Tom. Thanks for your time. I'll sort it out with Phoebe. In fact, I'll do it now before break. I've decided to follow your advice about Lesly Atherton. Get her to apologise as you recommend and we'll leave it at that.'

Tom was about to leave when he was recalled.

'By the way, Tom, Jennifer Bird told me all about the *kerfuffle* in the entrance hall. Her story does you much credit. Whatever a handful of females on the staff think about you, you certainly attract an awful lot of support from those secretaries. I wonder why that is?'

Much relieved, Tom was again about to take his leave, nursing a little irritation that Slater had chosen to keep to himself until so late in their conversation the intelligence just shared. '

'*Part of his usual ascendancy play,* 'Tom thought to himself.

A final thrust from Slater remained.

'By the way, Tom, I must inform you that last evening, I received a letter of resignation from the Chair of Governors. She says that she cannot maintain the level of commitment we at Southwich desire of her. You'll be greatly disappointed, I know. I intend to engineer the Governors' election of Jacqui Erne as her successor.'

This intelligence hit Tom like a haymaker. His most enthusiastic supporter, on the Board of Governors for the Headship of Southwich High upon Slater's early retirement, was out of the ring. He suspected that the resignation was the culmination of a protracted strategy by his superior in order to foil his succession. And Jacqui Erne hated him. Just at that moment, Jennifer Bird walked in with Slater's coffee.

'Columbian Rich Roast… tastes a bit bitter, but we'll soon get used to it.'

Disconsolately, Tom took his leave, inwardly fuming at the calculating malevolence of Slater and his own impotence to redress the balance.

CHAPTER SEVEN

Friday, 15 May, 1992.

Phoebe Spong entered the staffroom with her usual flourish, the door slamming behind her. Her face matched the continuing, raging storm outside. She held aloft in her bony, manicured hand the note of apology which Tom had helped Lesly Atherton to compose during the remainder of his Year Eleven lesson that morning. Her long, blood-red, talon-like fingernails were furiously, piercing and shredding it like some ravenous raptor dismembering its unsuspecting prey. She marched, almost goose-stepped towards Tom, her left hand thrust forward holding out between her finger-tips, the letter, resembling a white handkerchief spattered with droplets of fresh blood. In the Staffroom's tiny kitchen area, the preparation of his break-time coffee came to an abrupt halt as she appeared at the doorway waving, in a fury, the offending note. Sensing an explosive outburst, and intimidated by her look of unredeemed malevolence, the babble of staff voices descended suddenly to silent anticipation of the activity that was about to occur before their eyes.

'No doubt, you're feeling pleased with yourself, you jammy bastard. I don't know… if you fell off a roof, you'd land in soft shit,'

Phoebe yelled at him, with eyes wide, jawline taut and neck-veins throbbing and swollen. Tom returned the look with raised eyebrows, eyes twinkling in amusement.

'Don't roll your eyes at me, Madam, and do you intend to let the whole of Southwich in on your insane rantings?'

He spoke calmly, his manner the exact opposite of the harpy who stood before him. She began to behave hysterically, as if performing in a hammed-up stage melodrama, and spat out at him,

'Once again, you've pulled the proverbial out of the hat, and made me look like a liar in front of Slater and your usual arse-licking of the gullible, men-crazy office staff has produced their adoring support in the matter. I'll get you yet, you wanker!'

'Promises, promises! ...Anyway, Phoebe, you said it...I made you look like a liar. Well, it's true...you are a liar. Now, buzz off and let me have my coffee in peace.'

His absolute calmness, unaffected by her frantic performance, only incensed her more and she became uncontrollable as she continued her ranting,

'I'll get that whore, Lesly Atherton, too. But it hasn't been total victory has it? Your soul-mate Chair has been superseded by Jacqui Erne. I bet that news has made you pig-sick!'

That was true. Jacquie Erne was more likely to support anyone rather than him. Any response to Phoebe's outburst seemed superfluous. His colleague's demonstrations of fatuously exaggerated anger one second and patent glorying in Tom's disappointment the next were common enough. Further attempt to bandy words would conclude in her inevitable, frustrated tears at her inability to rouse him to visible anger. She really wanted him to strike her but he never took that particular bait. She so desperately wanted some evidence of sexual harassment that it seemed that she would stop at nothing to reach her goal. Not this time, however. Coffee in hand, a half smile on his face, with a deep sigh, he simply walked past her.

    He re-entered the staffroom, from the kitchen, where the hush evaporated as eavesdroppers to the outburst pretended to engage in nonstop, frenetic conversation. In one corner of the room, a group of women, comprising his detractors were pouring coffee from a capacious thermal jug, their backs towards Tom, their heads unnaturally close together embarked upon an excited babble of confidential conversation. They pretended not to notice his exit from the kitchen as he strolled across to his usual chair in the work-room amongst a group of men.

    In another corner, Alan Bairstow sat huddled up to the young, attractive Sian Waite, their heads together in animated conversation. Neither chose to acknowledge him as he approached. Nor was it likely. Bairstow had an eye for any young woman. How he had attracted the amorous attentions of a sequence of female colleagues and parents during his eleven years at the school, Tom was at a loss to understand. Currently, it had become obvious to Tom and the staff as a whole, with whom it was a matter of amused but prurient titillation, that Sian Waite was the latest to have fallen for his Don Juan-like charms. Tom had warned the Head again, that Bairstow's sex life included another woman other than his wife, Charmaine. His sexual dalliances were common knowledge and he was the talk of the staffroom most of the time. Slater had told Tom not to be so suspicious, to forget about it and to remember that Ms Waite was the niece of the County's chief Education Officer and hence one whom they would be obliged to treat with extreme caution, even if she were a 'jumped up little madam'. Tom had reminded the Head that since the caretaker and the cleaning staff were highly excited by this illicit liaison, it was only a matter of time before the pupils, and the community knew of it, with dire consequences for the school's image.

'School's image be damned', Slater had responded. 'There's nothing there. He's just a man like you, Tom, who likes talking to the women. They can hardly be said to have objected to his attentions.'

Bairstow did not fit the accepted pattern of eligible men. He was married to Charmaine, a tough, careerist teacher in another of the County's schools. Most likely, her career ambitions had been the primary reason for her husband to seek his sexual thrills elsewhere. Not particularly tall, slim in a flabby sort of way, with fine, pale gingery, receding hair, and a mass of ginger facial stubble, surrounding a prominent fleshy nose, pale eyebrows and lashes and a ruddy complexion. However, he possessed large hands and his feet, a size eleven were massive for his general body shape and size. He had that suave charm and a quietness of voice and above all the vital manly tackle that appealed to all of his numerous conquests.

Bairstow disliked Tom intensely. Tom considered him to be effeminate, and he thus avoided Tom's company and that of his other male colleagues in favour of the women staff. Tom also had shown his disapproval of Bairstows's way of life. In Tom's opinion, he was destroying the lives of the young and possibly innocent women for his own sexual gratification. In the early days, when Bairstow was a relatively new member of staff, he had been given a lift home, after some kind of emotional breakdown in school, by Tom. He had taken Tom into his confidence about his troubled home life. Tom had never made any reference to this confidential information divulged to him by Bairstow, but Bairstow was suspicious that Tom would take a hostile view of him since he was so antipathetic towards modern marital fragility. On numerous occasions in staffroom talk and in his Assemblies, Tom had emphasised the value of stable relationships, preferably legal ones, in which to bring children into the world. Bairstow knew that he was attractive to women and this bolstered his self-confidence and encouraged an air of arrogance and self-love. He would admire his reflection in whatever mirror or glass partition he passed, touching his fine hair and grinning at his image. He was unaware of the amused and interested glances made by all and sundry, so engrossed was he in his personal vanity.

Tom, as Deputy in charge of the curriculum, disapproved of the disorganised methods he used in the running of his Mathematics Department. In his view, a subject such as Mathematics, which dealt with matters largely of a finite nature, required a methodical, rational, systematic method of organisation and teaching. It required a teacher with a high academic achievement at degree level, but Slater had seen fit to appoint Bairstow on the advice given by one of his Ichthus-bearing inspectors of schools. He had yet to prove himself as an efficient Head of Department and an effective purveyor of good examination results. Yet, incredibly, blinded by false promises to his advantage, Slater insisted that Bairstow would make it to Headship with a few years of experience behind him. Tom was appalled by this often-stated opinion as he, so able and desperate for promotion was likely to be left standing by the obnoxious, incompetent, ill-experienced junior colleague. Bairstow's staff, mainly women, seeking his approval, protected his image by working diligently but ineffectually because of his lack of knowledge and guidance. He pretended to have respect for women but patently he used them to enhance his own narcissism. He regarded them as cherries to be plucked when ripe, or tender green shoots to be ravaged by locusts. The macho men in the staffroom were agog at the hold he seemed to have over most of the women, even those who should have known better, but Bairstow was only interested in the young, often unpractised members of the opposite sex, whether they were married or not.

One such female was the pretty, precocious, conceited niece of the Director of Education for the County. Ted Slater had been on many a committee, nominated by this important member of the County Establishment. They both attended the same place of worship and Ted had anticipated some help from him in his application for the Ministry on his retirement. He had appointed the young Ms Waite, ahead of other more deserving, academically well-qualified candidates as a sprat in his angling for the Ministry. He was prepared to ignore her ineffective efforts in academic performance and her developing, rather unsavoury relationship with the Head of Mathematics because her primary quality was her relationship to her Uncle Bertie. As a disciplinarian, she was better than most of her age group, giving her an air of self-assurance , confidence and complacency which was seen as a powerful weapon in her ascendancy over colleagues who were more academic but less able than she in classroom control. She was not universally admired. The women, out of jealousy, disliked her good looks, her family connections, her natural ability in the control of her classes and her cavalier disregard for the rules and regulations of the school as they pertained to staff. The men disliked her youthful denial of all authority and especially her relationship with Alan Bairstow whom they mistrusted. Phoebe Spong, like many of her female colleagues, did not care for Sian Waite who had more than her fair share of favourable attributes for Phoebe's liking. Her main distaste was Sian's disregard for authority, in particular, the authority of Phoebe Spong. There was no love lost between them. Sian was aware of the power that Spong appeared to exert over the other women but she was so full of self-confidence as a result of her looks, her discipline and her family connections that she rode rough-shod over whomever she chose. An early flouting of Spong's authority was when she appeared in black, slim-fitting, leather trousers with an equally figure-hugging cashmere jumper. In Spong's opinion, it was quite unsuitable attire for school attendance. Indeed, she had hauled Waite out of her Science lesson to tell her so, but Waite had stood her ground, threatening to invoke the County`s Equal Opportunities machinery. The other women were in awe of her audacity, and in spite of their dislike of the woman, they had a degree of admiration for her opposition to the distasteful Phoebe Spong. Slater had instructed Spong to drop the matter. He could see no reason why a woman should not wear trousers if she so wished. Spong had denounced his response to Tom,

'The pusillanimous bastard... He's shit-scared of upsetting Uncle Bertie'

Tom had been non-committal on the matter. He was not prepared to support either Spong or Waite. Female staff dress code was not his concern. He had enough problems of his own where Slater was concerned and he was not prepared to increase the load unnecessarily. Let Spong get on with it. He was content to watch proceedings from the side-lines. As Tom passed the pair, almost canoodling, in the corner, it was obvious that they were completely unaware of him, so totally engrossed with each other as they were. The sight of them filled him with revulsion but another altercation was not on his agenda. They were not harming him by their activity. Let the rest of the staffroom exert any pressure for the cessation of their amorous antics if it so chose.

Longstaffe greeted Tom with a knowing smile which acknowledged an awareness of the unpleasant episode which had been overheard throughout the staff room.

'Sorry you had to leave the Assembly this morning', he observed sympathetically. 'Have you heard of the Gaffer's latest gaffe after you left?'

Tom had to admit that he had not. The restiveness of the pupils as they exited the Assembly Hall now seemed to take some meaning.

'He announced that Philip Johnson had died of leukaemia whilst Johnson was sitting right there in front of him, as large as life! I was obliged to interrupt him with the correct information that it was in fact John Philpott who had sadly passed away. I know the names have a certain similarity but, hey, it's a blunder he should not be making. He's under pressure for some reason. God knows why…he's hardly ever here…attending some committee or other and then lunch at the rate-payers' expense. Have you noticed how nervy he's got and absent-minded and I'm sure I could smell alcohol when I last spoke to him?'

Tom agreed that he had noticed all these odd changes in Slater's behaviour. He congratulated Vernon on his brave intervention and passed into the staff workroom which doubled up as a smokers' corner. Immediately, he was aware of a totally different ambience. Even to Tom, a life-long people watcher, it was a continuous source of wonder that the staffroom could exhibit such strident dichotomy. It was as though he were passing from a dark subterranean tunnel into the welcoming light such as described by those describing near-death experiences. Despite the suffocating fumes from smouldering cigarettes and the odd pipe, the room appeared brighter, the occupants infinitely more relaxed and the buzz of conversation greatly more genial and unforced. The occupants were predominantly male in this ante-room. Naturally, the sounds were more raucous and less restrained. No-one seemed aware of Tom's recent embarrassment and he consciously relaxed as he moved, lighting a cigarette as he went towards a group of men whose natural bonhomie and unsophistication attracted him as does a mass of squirming tadpoles the inquisitive child.

Tom joined a group of five men who hardly noticed his taking a vacant seat. They were listening intently to one of their number, David Southwich, coincidently bearing the school's name as a surname, tell one of the subtly blue jokes in which skill he excelled.

'Hi Tom, I'll start again. Have you heard the one about the Liverpool University Anatomy lecturer who so insisted on telling blue jokes that a particular prudish set of female students threatened to boycott his lectures if he persisted?'

No-one acknowledged having heard it. As he proceeded, the other groups of staff halted their conversations and turned their seats to listen intently to David's joke. As a comedian, he had no equal in the school where he was a most popular figure. He was perpetually witty and an immensely entertaining colleague who claimed the attention of pupils in the classroom by constant hilarity. Laughter could be heard on a very regular basis emanating from his classroom. All Southwich pupils adored the wit of David Southwich. His fund of humorous anecdotes seemed endless. He was a natural raconteur and a sportsman of some distinction, having played cricket at a junior level for the county. Rarely did he arouse envy or spite. Tom was in awe of his laid-back approach to life. There was nothing of Tom's intensity and career ambition. He taught German with the ease of an accomplished linguist but he made the subject vibrant and alluring to all comers.

'When the lecturer happened to be dealing with the topic of the male sexual anatomy, the old temptation got the better of him and he alluded, with a wink, to the widely held view of the

West Indian's superiority in that department. As one, the young women stood up in their places and moved towards the door. The lecturer announced, 'Ladies, there's no need to hurry...the next boat to Jamaica doesn't sail 'til next Wednesday!'

Chaos ensued! The room exploded with side-splitting, guffawing from all the men and women. Tears of laughter ran down their cheeks as they looked round at each other in their shared amusement. Paul Sawyer with evident glee slapped Southwich on the shoulder saying,

'Good 'un, that, Dave!'

Keith Dawson, the Head of PE rolled in his seat like a tickled child. Irma de la Haye guffawed, Lucinda Terry-Smith, the animated and avant-garde Art teacher stretched out her multi-coloured, legging-covered limbs in unaffected hilarity. The rather sober Henry Gill looked around sheepishly, sniggering softly, unsure whether or not to give vent to the laughter he felt inclined to express. All merriment subsided as Monica Dickinson raised her voice. No-one had noticed her arrival at the edge of the group. Where she hovered, leaning against the door jamb, like a spider waiting to ensnare an unsuspecting fly. With ostentatious prudishness and dramatic expostulation she issued forth,

'You lot ought t'bi ashamed o' yersells; yer mek him wuss. Such laddish 'umour 'ud bi more apt t' th' lads' smokin' corner at t' back o' t' bike sheds. Typical o' men, that. In attemtin t' tek wimmin down, all they show is the'r own psychological 'ang-ups.'

'Come on, Monica', David playfully retorted, 'you look as if you're about to follow the students to the boat yourself!'

Another wave of uncontrolled hilarity rocked the workroom as all had their own mental pictures of Monica Dickinson, her bosom leading the way, running in her ridiculously high-heeled boots, lime-green coat and violently bottle-enhanced red hair, flowing in her wake as she rushed to board the ship, shouting,

'Wet fer mi will ya? Am cummin as fast as a can.'

Monica was left speechless. There was little point in any further castigation. She was patently in a minority of one. But she was offended. David's jokes, she considered to be in thoroughly bad taste. Why was it, she pondered, that members of her own gender, such as Irma and Lucinda, were prepared to encourage men like David Southwich to indulge in joking and conversation which were so intimidating and dehumanising of women? This was behaviour which she must bring to the attention of the Secondary Schoolteachers' Association representative along with Phoebe's likely complaint about Tom's behaviour that morning. Feminists like she would have to stick together and eliminate all such forms of sexual harassment from the workplace. Little wonder, she thought, that girls suffered so much when the male staff were so misogynistic. The bell signalling the end of beak brought a sudden cessation of their ribald mirth and raucous laughter.

'What's that ringing I hear in my ears?' David asked as yet another of his throw-away lines.

'It's called tinnitus.'

Harvey Gill announced to anyone who might hear, in a futile attempt to get in on the act. But the observation was lost.

Members of staff were going their own ways to their various lessons, still tickled by David's performance and variously appalled by Monica's graceless response, at the same time chuckling over visions of her graceless dash to catch the boat before it sailed. Tom was aware that Harvey Gill had recognised instinctively that he would have been better advised not to have attempted to cling to the coat tails of David Southwich's comic genius. Had he related the lecturer joke, no-one would have laughed.

    '*Still*', Harvey had satisfied himself, '*I did manage to avoid allowing myself to be tarred with the brush of Monica's complaint.*'

It was a matter of personal determination in Harvey Gill to sit on the fence in all matters controversial, whether in staffroom banter or formal meeting. Tom considered him to be the archetypal educational careerist. Never one to 'rock the boat', a 'yes man' to the *n*th degree, without an ounce of personal charisma. In possession of a 'Mickey Mouse' degree, he elevated non-entity and unoriginality to a level of notoriety. Yet, in Tom's opinion, knowing the way in which the establishment's wheels turned, this pale shadow of a fellow would inevitable find his way to a lucrative niche in the educational hierarchy, probably in an Advisory capacity where his intellectual dullness and conformity would be welcomed with open arms. Tom could understand the facility with which educationally inadequate products like Gill made career advancement only in terms of the Establishment wishing to appoint professional nondescripts as a means of ensuring their own ascendancy. The same tactics applied, apparently at school level. Many had been the occasion when he had supported staunchly, after interview, junior candidates of spirited intelligence, only to have Heads of Department pour cold water on his recommendations. Tom was unable to fathom the motivation behind such reluctance. For himself, the more lively the intellect, the more likely was his intellectual stimulation of the pupil. And that was what Tom considered his reason for being in the profession. It was a motivation which appeared to attract few imitators.

Tom left the staffroom and made his way contemplatively towards his own office where he intended to make a start on the following year's timetable. He walked quite jauntily twirling a rubber band which he had found littering the floor, around his finger, relieved that the storm had passed before break, enabling the pupils some freedom to expend their energy in the fresh air. Following a wet break, pupil behaviour deteriorated, often resulting in his being called to lessons to intervene in the teacher-baiting activities caused by their confinement within the four walls of their classroom. As he walked, he reflected on the craziness of that morning's events and wondered what other occupation could provide such a variety of experience in a matter of three hours or so.

'*We are really going to have to watch this dreadful women's lobby,*' he thought, '*Monica and Phoebe are going to be the backbone of a clutch of women who will stop at nothing, however unacceptable, in order to establish their own superiority.*' He was suddenly reminded of an old favourite sketch from *The Two Ronnies* entitled *The Worm That Turned,* a nightmarish, dystopian, comical serial in which leather-clad women exerted control over the men who were forced to wear frocks and do all the housework. Surely, life in the future would not reflect this comedic parody. He dreaded the thought of women like Phoebe Spong, Monica Dickinson and their acolytes being in a position of authority over the likes of David Southwich and himself.

Tom settled into his comfortable Arts and Crafts style Carver Armchair that he had owned ever since his university days. It had been a fixture in his flat during the two years of his occupation of it. On graduation, he had begged his landlady to sell it to him as he had become so attached to it. Always a favourite with most ladies of senior years, she would take no payment from Tom but ever since that date, he had always, until her death, sent to her a huge bouquet of yellow roses.

He arranged before him all the information to get started on the intended task when the telephone rang. It was Ted Slater.

'Get down to my office, will you? We need to talk.'

There was no time for Tom to reply because the receiver had been slammed down. Tom, without further ado, jumped up, and responded immediately. It sounded urgent. Even the annoyance he felt at Slater's demand would not hinder his helping his boss in an emergency. He arrived at the Head's door in less than a minute. He knocked and heard a thin, breathless voice invite him in. Slater was draped over his chair his normally ruddy complexion had paled to an unhealthy shade.

'I'll have to go home, Tom. I feel dreadful. I must have eaten something, I think. No other cause that I know of. There's nothing urgent this afternoon. Just hold the fort, will you? See you, Monday, all being well.'

Tom waited and saw him to his car. He did look rather unwell so Tom was not suspicious of his leaving early before lunch on a Friday. He thought, *'Good riddance'*. He was now in charge, at least for the afternoon. He wondered what else would be thrown at him before he could head off home for a weekend's peace in the family home.

Not many minutes had passed when Jennifer Bird appeared. For some reason, Slater had not informed her of his need to get home. She enquired after his health. Tom was non-committal.

'Something he ate, he thinks. He'll be back on Monday, no doubt, giving us all the run around.'

'Why don't you come and have some coffee with us? She said. I've just made a pot and we won't drink it all. It'll only go to waste.'

He accepted the offer gladly. The task ahead of him required a clear head which he was sure her offer of a coffee would provide.

'It's a new blend', she said, 'Columbian Rich Roast'. I gave 'Sir', some earlier. I hope it has not upset him.'

'Well', said Tom. 'I'll have some and that will prove whether it was the coffee that upset his stomach.'

She poured him a large cup of the steaming, aromatic, black fluid and offered him the milk.

'No thanks, but I will have some sugar. I need to keep my energy levels up for this afternoon.'

They stood together, Tom and Jennifer looking out at the ravaged tulips when they noticed Phoebe Spong leaving the building.

' I wonder if she's just going out for lunch or whether she's got wind of Dr Slater's early departure, or maybe they've got a secret tryst going on?' she laughed.

No action of Phoebe Spong would have surprised Tom. But he would make it his business to find out if she was in school after lunch. He felt invigorated after the strong coffee. He gave his grateful thanks to Jennifer Bird and turned to leave as Jennifer spoke,

'Would you and Maudie like to come for supper next weekend? I know Harold would be pleased to see you both. It's been some time since you came for a meal with us. We can have a real good natter about things over supper. Come early and you can have a look at the garden. I know how interested you and Maudie are in plants'.

Tom, pleased with the prospect of some great entertainment the following weekend, almost skipped down the corridor to his office where he spent the afternoon busy with his time table. He rang Phoebe's office several times but there was never any answer.

That evening, it being Friday, the family indulged themselves in a take-away from the local 'Chinese Chippie' The order was always the same - Sweet and sour pork for Jack, cod and chips with mushy peas and curry sauce for Freddie, a special

Chop Suey for Maudie and a rump steak and chips for himself. He always called for them on the way home. The proprietor of the 'Hong Kong' would be expecting him with the order already for collection. Maudie had prepared hot plates and iced beers for themselves with a *Coke* for the boys. After supper, they settled down to watch TV with a bottle of wine and the boys retired to their bedrooms to attend to their own entertainment. Maudie asked Tom how his day had gone. Tom felt so comfortable and well fed that he did not want to spoil his pleasant evening recounting the events of the day. He did, however, repeat David Southwich's joke, which once more gave rise to much laughter.

They retired to bed tired and a little drunk. Tom did not sleep well. He dreamt. Nightmarish images filled his mind, different from those of the previous night. The jack-booted Phoebe and Monica were frog-marching David Southwich and himself to the outfitters where they were to be dressed in floral frocks of an unbecoming design. They were then issued with short handled shovels and brushes and ordered to sweep the horse manure from the streets. Employed as a supervisor, was the fence–sitting Henry Gill who had ingratiated himself into their good books. As he dreamt on, the images changed. Phoebe and Monica now took the form of a pair of leering, praying mantes threatening to impale David Southwich and himself on the lethal barbs of their vicious mouthparts as they prepared to devour them whole. Overseeing the whole proceedings was the self-satisfied grinning face of Ted Slater, surrounded by a halo of raging flames.

CHAPTER EIGHT

Monday, 18 May, 1992.

Following a restful weekend with Tom's deliberate refusal to consider school affairs, Monday dawned. Always, the first task of the morning was to open the curtains and view the weather which these days affected Tom's humour more and more. At least, it was bright with some cloud covering the sun, but he had the impression that the sun would shine at some time. He looked forward to an uninterrupted day in his office where he would try to break the back of the following year's academic timetable. Ensconced in his office, he located some of his favourite pieces of music to provide some prolonged tranquillity as he started to piece together the jigsaw that would become the next year's timetable. He played lilting melodies that acted as a cocoon to protect him from the extraneous sounds of school life and which would act as a sponge to absorb some of his troubled, inner thoughts. He immediately started to listen to the gentle *Pavanes* of Ravel and Fauré. It was his usual practice to play light classical music at such times when concentration was vital. He glanced at the photograph of his wife smiling down on him and felt suddenly calm, knowing that she would have selected the same soothing pieces as he. Their tastes in music were the same like everything else, shared treasures which symbolised their union. Neither could abide those composers whose works were predominantly strident; opera was lost on them as was modern Jazz. Hardly had he time to sort out his documents, when there was a subdued, deferential knock on his door. He reluctantly pressed the pause button. Although he was generally genial, his response at this moment was that of feigned affability,

'Come in, please'.

To his utter amazement, it was Phoebe Spong who stood there. Deference was hardly a characteristic he had ever associated with this colleague. After her behaviour on the previous Friday, a conciliatory approach like the one he was witnessing had seemed a million miles distant. She had an apologetic demeanour. Tom was immediately suspicious.

'What's she up to?'

He merely looked at her to announce the reason for her intrusion.

'Look, Tom, I have come to apologise for my totally unwarranted response to your intervention on Friday and for my fatuous attack on you in the staff kitchen. I really am very sorry.'

Tom was momentarily disarmed. He knew in his heart of hearts that she was not to be trusted, that he ought to give her the cold shoulder and to tell her what a malicious old bitch she was adding that he disbelieved her perfidious disingenuousness. But Tom, ever the hopeful believer that no person was totally wicked and like Paul on the road to Damascus was able to change for the better. He was prepared to listen to her and give her the benefit of the doubt. Sensing his dilemma, Phoebe re-opened her utterance, sitting as Tom gestured her to do so.

'I take it all back. I have been to see Slater and have acknowledged the same to him. I have seen Lesly Atherton again and I have accepted her apology.'

Tom was not convinced about her motives. Yet, he so desperately wanted to believe her and to be on good terms with her.

'And what about the staff?' Tom felt constrained to add, but he choked on the words as he swallowed them. If he were to make the most of this opportunity, rubbing salt into her wounds hardly seemed appropriate. He was an eternal optimist and he fervently wanted to devise an opportunity to heal the widening gulf between them. So he responded,

'Good, I'm pleased. Now what in Heaven's name is goading you into such suspicions as were evident in your allegation about me?'

'Oh, it's nowt that you've done, Tom',

She assured him disingenuously in an attempt to deflect any suspicions he might have about her ultimate intentions where he was concerned. She was occasionally given to relapses into her local dialect. Unlike its use by Monica Dickinson, it was an affectation. She imagined it as some kind of compliment, a kind of familiarity which signalled trust on the one hand and an acknowledgement of common working class origins on the other.

She was the only daughter of northern urban stock. Part of her trouble was that she had been idolised by parents for her cleverness and a perceived attractiveness in her youth. They had increasingly seconded to her, so that she was inured to a lifetime's view of herself as someone special. It seemed to Tom that parents of only daughters had a lot to answer for in this indulgence. She continued, tears by this time, welling up in her eyes causing mascara to run, like muddy streams down her pale, puffy cheeks.

'You know the bruise which I regretfully alleged had been done by Lesly Atherton. Well, you will have guessed how I came by that. It's Steve again. We'd had the most awful row. He came in about midnight, pissed out of his mind. He got hold of me by the hair, shoved me to the floor and kicked me in the forehead. Ugh! I can't bear to think about it. He only ever does it when he's drunk. But it's happening on a fairly regular basis nowadays. You know that he knows about my affair with Alec don't you? I thought he'd managed to come to terms with it. We ought to split up. We've certainly talked about it. But he won't admit to his cronies that anything is wrong. He thinks they'll call him *cuckold* or something. You'd know all about that being an English specialist like Steve. He threatened to kill Alec if he got hold of him. He called me a tart. He's even told the boys. 'Your mother's being shagged by a lawyer'. He does talk like that you know. Nobody would believe it if I told them. He's such a joker and a really good Head. I must tell you that his staff think the world of him. He's not like our plonker. He really knows what he's doing at school. But... ugh! Tom. I'm sick of him. I'm at the point of ending it all. I can't see any way out of it. I even bought a bumper bottle of aspirin this morning and have been thinking about taking the lot with a bottle of whisky.'

By this juncture, she was sobbing uncontrollably. Her narrow shoulders were hunched. She wrung her handkerchief in her hands at one moment and dabbed jerkily at the flooding tears the next. For all of his dislike of the woman, Tom forgot for the moment that she might have been indulging in some very clever acting, but why would she tell him all that information? He felt the prickling of tears of sympathy welling into his own eyes in response to the abjectly pitiable creature before him. Extraordinarily sensitive to others' woes, Tom usually felt moved to tears by their misfortunes. It was not unusual for colleagues, whether male or female, to want to share their troubles with him. He could not understand why they chose to unburden themselves to him with the frequency with which they did. He liked to think that they chose to do so because of their instinctive recognition of his empathic qualities and sureness of his confidentiality. But it had been a constant source of surprise to him that he should be elected as school counsellor-in-chief. After all, was not he equally criticised as cold and aloof, a typical concocter of the time table, unyielding and somewhat arrogant?

'Please dismiss such thoughts from your mind, Phoebe. But, you will have to do something about your marriage. Have you tried a marriage guidance counsellor?'

'We've mentioned it, of course, but Steve always says, 'Marriage guidance be buggered. Your stopping shagging with that fucker of a lawyer will do for me'

'And are you prepared to save your marriage by ending your affair?'

'No, I'm not. Alec and I have our share of rows you know. He's always on to me to leave Steve. And I say, 'I'll leave Steve if you'll leave Muriel.' She's a Junior School Head, you know. I want to set up home with him but he's not prepared to leave her. He keeps on about the effect of divorce on his kids. They're in their twenties, damn it! I tell him that they'll probably prefer their parents to separate rather than constantly witness the unhappiness in the home.'

'I'm afraid I'm not very capable of advising you any further. You know that I disapprove strongly of the modern tendency towards easy divorce, don't you?'

'Yes, I know. You do tend to go on about it too much. Half the staff are either divorced or having it on the side. You should tone it down a bit. You get on their wicks with your 'holier than thou' attitude.'

'I'm sorry they feel that way. I'm not trying to lord it over them, but, I can't help how I feel about things, Call me 'old fashioned', if you like, but, I won't change my thoughts on such matters that are important to me.'

'Yes, I know that. It's just that your experience of marriage seems to be thrust at other people as a kind of pattern which they ought to follow. Who else in this school, for instance, has photographs of their family slapped on the wall for all to see? You seem to be boasting about it. Please don't think I'm making that accusation. I rather envy you your domestic peace.'

Phoebe seemed to be calmed by the emotionalism of the conversation. Tom's first responsibility now that she was more composed was to see that she did not do anything stupid that evening. He would never forgive himself if he not taken steps to ensure that she was unlikely to take the suicide threat seriously. It was not the first time that she had threatened such action. In his heart, he suspected that it was an attention-seeking exercise. People, intent on suicide, did not keep on making threats. They just got on with it. But he could not afford to take that risk with her.

'Look, Phoebe, promise me that tonight, you'll try to be less combative with Steve. I know that you can be extremely provoking. Try to approach him with the air of someone who wants to make peace. And promise me that there will be no more talk of aspirins and the like.'

'Oh, Steve's no problem. He'll be out. We haven't slept together for over two years. I'll simply lock myself in my room. My mistake on Thursday was to be up when he arrived home and to ask him, with some spite, where he'd been. I'll just keep out of his way. He'll probably come home with flowers and an abject apology. He can keep 'em. I'll be buggered if I'm cow towing to him.'

'And the aspirins?'

'I'm sure that was only self-pity. I'll get over that. There's little danger of me topping myself in actual fact.'

At that point, the bell rang for break and Phoebe stood up, seeming ready to make her exit. She thanked Tom, an unnaturally, shy smile on her face, for his ready ear for which she expressed appreciation despite her behaviour the previous week. He was still confused about her.

'I tried to contact you on Friday afternoon without success...'

Her face returned to its usual frowning expression, for a moment, deep in thought, and then she remembered.

'I fell asleep at my desk, having developed a migraine after Thursday night's fight with Steve. I obviously didn't hear the phone. By the way, Tom,' she added as she was about to leave, 'there are three Year Eleven boys I want you to help me to interview this afternoon. They have been reported to me by two Year Eleven girls who allege that last evening they saw them 'gang banging' a Year Eight girl on the school field... juicy, eh? I thought you'd like that!'

On that note, without giving him the opportunity to deny her final assertion, she marched buoyantly, from his sight as though the topic of their conversation for the previous hour, had been the unseasonable, wet and windy weather, and the business of her marital problems had been totally irrelevant. Tom was uneasy once more. On his way to the staffroom, he went over the strange event which had occupied his first hour of the morning. He was at a loss to understand Phoebe Spong. She was definitely up to some devious activity and she had deliberately deceived him. He was in no doubt about that, but why? He would never understand how the minds of women like Phoebe worked. He was thankful that his own wife was straightforward and committed to him and so the antics which were apparently being played out in the Spong household he would never experience. All would be revealed, he supposed, before long. He rushed to get some coffee and a cigarette to calm his nerves before the bell went again.

He arrived at the coffee pot too late. All that was left at the bottom of the pot were some unpleasant dregs. There were Phoebe and Monica, heads together, enjoying some titbit of scandal, no doubt. Tom just hoped that they were not discussing how to fetch him down. He turned away and made his way to Jennifer Bird's little enclave where he hoped they might still have some coffee or even tea left. He was in luck on both counts.

'Which do you prefer, Tom? We've got the 'Columbian' or you can have the 'Yorkshire'.

He was spoilt for choice. However, he chose the coffee.

'I like this blend', he said. 'Is this the one you thought might be bitter?'

'Dr. Slater thought so at first, but he's got used to it. He likes it.'

'I do too. I must get Maudie to look out for it. Thanks, ladies, for the drink. You've saved my life.'

He returned to the business of timetabling. To him, it was not really a chore. He loved piecing all the various elements together so that they fitted like a well-made jig-saw. He knew he could not please everyone on the staff but he tried his best to make it fair as far as he could. The staff inevitably groaned when their commitments were announced but 'by and large' they knew that he did his best and that there was no-one more competent than he for the task. In short, they trusted him. He found concentration difficult. Even Debussy's *The Girl with the Flaxen Hair* could not massage his thoughts into the direction of his intended work. He decided to allow some time to revisit the earlier conversation so that he might take stock. The positives were that Phoebe had chosen to apologise and also, if she were to be believed, and, for the moment, he had decided to take her words as the truth, she had admitted her fault to Slater. But the negative was that the impression of his alleged sexual harassment or worse where Lesly Atherton was concerned would still be left with the women of the Monica Dickinson ilk. Then there was the allegation on which she departed. He was mortified by her foul assumption that he could derive any kind of prurient satisfaction from pupil sexuality. It was she, not he, who was warped. He was confused by her being wracked with inconsolable despondency and suicidal melancholia one minute and the next becoming almost exhilarated at the prospect of dealing with an incident so depressing as the one alluded to. He, generously, attributed it to female hormone imbalance, a subject about which he knew very little but was aware of it being a popular reason for certain of the women staff to take regularly a day or two off per month. His cynical view was that these 'extra days' holiday' allowed them to catch up with their housework.

    The prospect of sharing an interview with Phoebe Spong and sixteen-year-old boys allegedly guilty of sexually abusing a young female pupil filled him with apprehension. He had seen her operating in such matters before. As the Pastoral Deputy, there was no denying her responsibility in the issue. She did extract, however, an inordinate amount of unhealthy delight in delving into teenage misbehaviour of this sort. He would have to consider very carefully indeed over the lunch-hour, his intentions regarding the proposed interview.

CHAPTER NINE

Monday, 18 May, 1992.

Tom had not taken his usual lunchtime relaxation at the Bridge table in the staffroom – a serious sacrifice indeed! Instead, he felt the need to drink his coffee in his own room in isolation in order to think through the implications of Phoebe's suggestion. He had barely begun to string together his thoughts about the intense embarrassment which she would cause him by what would prove to be her deliberate attempt to shock the boys into abject acknowledgement of their crime, when his telephone bell sounded.

'Good afternoon, Tom Portland speaking.'

'Good afternoon my arse,' the misanthropic tones of Ted Slater bellowed down the line. 'I've just had Phoebe up here reporting sexual goings-on by Year Eleven boys on the field last night. What the blazes is going on? They're due to start their exams next week. This is precisely the sort of caper that will upset our results and damage our reputation in the community. I want you to interview the boys with her and get the truth out of them. This school's going to get the reputation of a bear garden. Get on with it, Tom!'

Tom could not help but recognise the extreme anger in the trembling voice of the Headteacher but before he could open his lips to reply, he could hear Slater's receiver crash down in a single violent action.

'So there's no way out for me.' Tom thought self-pityingly.

The only thing he could do was to attempt to minimise the inevitable embarrassment to the boys and himself. He must, at all costs, engineer the interview in such a way that Phoebe was obliged to let him take the initiative in questioning. He knew instinctively that her approach would be to oblige the boys to give graphically detailed accounts of precisely what their actions had been. Not for a moment did he condone their behaviour. On the contrary, he was sincerely appalled by teenagers' familiarity with adult conduct as presented tantalisingly through readily available X-rated blue movies. He was determined that he would not entertain for a moment the interviewing of the girl. That he would leave entirely to Phoebe. But he must necessarily gird his loins about him and enter an affair which his better judgement told him was foolish. He would have much preferred to deal with the boys alone. An admission of guilt alone, was all that he would have required, sparing both the culprits and himself the awful trauma which would occur if Phoebe were allowed free reign, her unnecessarily probing questions would only satisfy her unnaturally, perverted interest in the sexual activities of these under-aged pupils and would not lead to a satisfactory outcome for those possibly, psychologically damaged by the process.

'Perhaps, if I send for the boys myself and steal a march on her, I'll achieve the required results,' thought Tom. 'But that might be madness in view of the electric nature of the allegations. I need to protect myself.'

Tom was painfully aware that even a male teacher interviewing boys in a group, had to be constantly watchful in order to avoid the danger of malicious allegations being made against him. He knew of two cases where completely innocent teachers had been accused falsely of sexual misconduct by vindictive boys, with the distinctly tragic consequences of one committing suicide and the other dismissed from the profession...so a joint approach it had to be.

Tom was about to settle into an easy chair to take five minutes, in which to compose his thoughts, before the bell rang to signal the end of lunchtime when his own telephone bell raucously interrupted his reverie. It was Phoebe Spong ringing him.

'Ah, Mr Portland, I wonder, would you be so kind as to pop down to my office for a minute? I have with me three Year Eleven boys whom I wish you to hear giving an account of their behaviour which I know will shock you. I thought that obliging them to tell you in their own words precisely how they have let the school down and themselves, not to mention the effects on the younger female pupil, would constitute a start to their re-integration into the civil behaviours we expect of all Southwich pupils.'

'The infernal witch!' gasped Tom as he replaced the receiver.

He could feel the colour rising from collar level into his hairline. Beads of perspiration formed on his pulsating temples as he grew more incensed, and at the same time, frustrated by the outright nerve of this she-devil that was his colleague. His stomach felt hollow as ripples of butterflies in quick succession wracked his normal physical state of calmness. Clearly, the march he had considered stealing on Phoebe had been stolen on himself. She had been quick to take the reins whilst he was still thinking about it.

'That's Phoebe, all over,' he thought. *'When will I cease to let that conscienceless, cloven-footed harridan get the better of me and seize the initiative from under my very nose? Well she's not going to get it all her own way. If she thinks I'm going to lend a hand in the deliberate humiliation of boys, then she is mistaken.'*

He could think of no approach more inclined to arouse the bitterness of boys towards the school than the dehumanising procedure which Phoebe had conceived. His task was to invoke in the boys a sense of shame once they had admitted responsibility and to counsel them in favour of behaviour which was most likely to generate respect for themselves, for the opposite sex and for the school. To indulge in the lecherous, obsessional enjoyment of the boys' discomfort, in revelation, seemed to Tom a sacrilegious profanity. He would have no part in it. Phoebe was going to be enraged again but if that were going to be the incurred cost which he would have to pay, then so be it.

CHAPTER TEN

Monday, 18 May, 1992.

As Tom strode in the direction of Phoebe's office, he imagined the scene that would greet him. He was not far out. He entered Phoebe Spong's room and was confronted by three boys standing in manifest discomfort. Their faces were uniformly blushing in embarrassment; perspiration decorated each forehead like droplets of dew on a ripe Victoria plum on an autumn morning. Their heads bowed in shame, they looked to the floor and, on his entrance they quickly turned their gaze in his direction with a glimmer of relief showing in the sudden shift in their expressions. An unpleasant stench of sweaty teenage bodies hung ponderously on the atmosphere which was already clammy on account of the heavy, overcast, humid weather. Phoebe's ostentatiously overpowering perfume, more suited to a lap-top dancer in a sleazy night club, intermingled stridently with the body odours encouraging the silent request,

'Will someone open a window before we all suffocate?'

But no-one did.

The dejection of the boys was in sharp contrast to the purposeful animation of the female Deputy. She perched on the edge of her chair, ready for the offensive, like a taut, coiled viper ready to leap out explosively at the boys. Tom was sensitive to the exaggerated mobility of her sponge-like facial features. She greeted him with a feigned smile of welcome, her blood-red, lipstick-plastered, rubbery lips parting slightly, as she hissed,

    'Come in, Mr Portland'.

But her eyes, dark and unsmiling, would have pierced his heart had they been able. The jacket of the black suit which she had worn during her earlier meeting with him was now resting on the back of her seat. She was wearing an expensive, vivid red, silk blouse whose top buttons were casually unfastened to reveal a delicate gold chain which bore a gold, pendant in the form of a stylistic fish. Tom could not believe his eyes. She was wearing, for all to see, the ubiquitous *Ichthus*. His eyes were fixed on the emblem, for a few seconds, maybe, but which period seemed like an eternity. An onlooker may have wondered if he were some weirdo, searching for her underwhelming cleavage. As soon as he realised that he was gazing at her chest, he quickly averted his eyes, but the sight of Ichthus near the heart of devil-woman had upset his equilibrium. Whether the boys had also averted their gaze away from her provocatively unbuttoned blouse, Tom could not be sure.

    'Thanks for coming along, Mr Portland. I thought it would do these lads a lot of good to admit, frankly to a man, what they have been up to. They seem reluctant to spit it out to me.'

Tom's brain was now racing in overdrive. He had to forget his shock at the sight of Ichthus on her bared throat and get his thoughts back to the matter in hand. As he had anticipated, his colleague was determined to put these boys through the mill, and to squeeze out of their discomfort, as much salacious pleasure as she could from the graphically, libidinous accounts of their exploits, with the under-age girl, which she hoped would be forthcoming from their naïve mouths. The boys' guilt was evident enough to Tom. He did not require a step-by-step account of what precisely had occurred. To have demanded it seemed to him not unlike the motivation of the voyeur. He did have to prevent the voyeuristic Phoebe from making that demand herself. How could he ensure the boys' and his own release from this ensnarement without giving cause for further professional recrimination from his embattled colleague? As the skies darkened further and torrential rain hammered against the window, it seemed as if an ultimatum was being delivered. Tom thought to himself,

'If you don't seize the initiative now, Tom, mi old son, the cause is lost'.

He looked directly at the boys with just enough seriousness in his gaze to convey a view of the heaviness of the allegation and yet a slight movement of the eyes and lips sufficient to indicate a sympathetic demeanour. As he was attempting to formulate the wording of his opening question, he became aware of a light footstep outside the door. The sound went unheard by the agitated boys and the transfixed Phoebe. Tom was alert to the fact that there was an eavesdropper at the door. Furthermore, his intuition told him that the listener would be Ted Slater whose common practice it was to creep up to closed doors to be a party to potentially explosive conversations, sometimes barging in in feigned innocence of the circumstances but more frequently to slither, silently away having witnessed the proceedings unnoticed .

For now, it suited Tom to keep that intelligence to himself but in the event of his need for an escape route, the Head's surreptitious approach offered the golden opportunity. He looked intently at the boys and said,

"Now, boys, look at me. Here's a simple question. Listen carefully. Are you responsible, as reported by some of your Year Eleven fellows, for sexual behaviour on the school playing fields with a Year Eight girl?

The directness of Tom's question and the non-threatening manner of its delivery prompted the accused to look up from the carpet, with its intricate patterns like spiders' webs…webs in which they were enmeshed, waiting for the fangs of the Black Widow Spider in the form of Mrs Spong to destroy them…and they looked directly into Tom's compelling gaze. He appeared to possess the authoritative capability of sounding challengingly emphatic in his demand whilst permitting the captives the realisation that truthfulness would receive a non-condemnatory response. Instinctively, the boys knew that their salvation lay in frank admission and that Mr Portland would rescue them from the perfidious clutches of the morbidly prying 'Sponge-face'.

'Yes Sir', the boys replied in unison, their anxiety, apparent.

'Ah,' interjected a somewhat thwarted Phoebe Spong, now visibly excited by their admission of guilt. Her eyes glittered and her tongue flicked out from her mouth where saliva had dribbled from the corner, in her eagerness for some explicit description of their offence. 'Let Mr Portland know exactly what you did. Did sexual intercourse take place, for example?'

The boys looked pleadingly at Tom, each set of eyes imploring him to end their misery. Their eyes locked. Now was the moment to swing open the door to introduce the ghoulishly, meddlesome Slater into the melting pot. With a swiftness and dexterity which alarmed Phoebe more than it did the boys who were familiar with Tom's utilisation of dynamic, physical movement as a shock tactic, Tom swung open the door to reveal a strained-faced Slater, head exaggeratedly forward, about to fall headlong into the room.

'Ah, Dr Slater, how fortunate it is that you happened to call on Mrs Spong at this very moment. I think that she and I will need your assistance in this problem.'

Slater stamped angrily into the room, livid that, once again, Tom had caught him red-handed. His embarrassment and fury caused consternation amongst the boys who were nevertheless relieved to anticipate delivery from Mrs Spong's indecent, rapt interest in the admission of their improper activity.

'What seems to be the problem?

Slater asked disingenuously, attempting to act the innocent - as if he had not been caught in a dubious act - that of listening at keyholes.

'These boys have just admitted their sexual misbehaviour, Dr Slater,' Tom replied with alacrity, pre-empting any intervention by his furious, cheated colleague. 'Such is the unsavoury nature of the misconduct, Dr Slater and such its unsuitability for a lady here to have to witness, may I suggest that we two relieve Mrs. Spong of the unpleasantness. I am sure she has enough to do in counselling the unfortunate girl'.

There was little Slater could do to deny Tom's suggestion. Entertaining a debate in front of the boys about whether Phoebe should remain on the scene seemed palpably inappropriate

'Right... you boys make your way to Mr. Portland's office. Wait there'.

Having delivered the order, Slater, turned abruptly to look at Phoebe Spong, standing with her mouth agape like some *Black Molly* gasping for air. He did not address her but Tom felt he saw a look of apology on his face. Ted Slater had also spotted the Ichthus charm nestling in her throat, and as he stalked off along the corridor he wondered if he should form a closer alliance with her in his continuing conflict with Tom Portland.

The three boys slunk, shamefaced from the room, mightily relieved, though they shared still a residual anxiety concerning their likely punishment. How Mr. Portland would deal with their affair they knew not. But since their escape from the maws of the fiendish 'Sponge-face' had been enabled, almost anything which the Head or his Deputy might come up with was infinitely preferable.

As Tom was closing Phoebe's door, he heard her expostulate self-dramatically.

'Fuck the bastard; he's got one over on me again. I'll get him. Pincer movement with Monica Dickinson'll do the job.'

CHAPTER ELEVEN

Monday, 18 May, 1992.

Greg, James and Kevin patiently waited for Tom to appear. They had very little to say to each other, as they were still recovering from the ordeal of appearing before Dr Slater, Mr Portland and Mrs Spong all at the same time. They were in agreement though that whatever happened, they would always be grateful to Mr Portland for his support in Mrs Spong's office. Tom strode along the corridor to his office where the boys were silently waiting. He said,

'Come in, you young reprobates.'

Slater had left Tom with the instruction delivered in the form of an implied threat.

'Get this business sorted out. I want nothing to do with it.'

'Will you please do me the favour of instructing Phoebe that the boys are in my hands and that she must confine herself to counselling the girl?' Tom had requested passionately. Slater had agreed. Even then, he had felt the need to add,

'Don't EVER do that to me again! I'm the bloody Head in this place and if I feel the need to listen at doors in the interests of the school then I'll bloody well do it.'

Greg Judson, James Waterson and Kevin Leyland moved dutifully into Tom's office, standing attentively in a line facing his desk. Gone were the physical evidences of abject trepidation and embarrassment. Instead, their mutual glances indicated unstated recognition that though they might be in for some retribution, at least there would be no attempt to humiliate them. Mr Portland, each knew, would strongly disapprove of their behaviour but there was an instinctive trust that he would nominate a resolution which would be just and still allow of some self-respect for them. Tom took his seat.

'Sit down, will you, boys? I need some moments to think things through. This is no easy matter. You're in a mess and if we're not careful, we'll all be in a mess. Police, under-aged sex, rape, parents placing charges – all possible consequences you know.'

The boys gulped in anxiety. Their faces became uniformly white. Each of them was a lively, athletic, socially popular figure in the school. Together as a group of friends, they had represented the school in the basketball and football teams. Their academic abilities were varied: Greg, Tom anticipated, had potential for University entry, James and Kevin would take apprenticeships locally. For now, their minds were a consistent blank. The possibilities which Tom had just suggested left them numb with a fear none of them was capable of articulating, even privately. Tom had no intention of permitting any of the mentioned outcomes. His veiled threats had been a deliberate attempt to shock the boys into the recognition of the gravity of their offence. Genuine remorse was his only thought where the boys were concerned.

But first he had to consider his modus operandi. Nagging at the back of his mind was the perennial question of whether to introduce a colleague to witness the interview. It was undoubtedly in his interests to do so. And yet he faced the same dilemma as he had in the interview with Lesly Atherton earlier. The boys deserved confidentiality. The desired outcomes of the boys' acknowledged remorse, their determination to avoid repetition and maintain their own self-respect were hardly going to be assured by the introduction of a third party who would be viewed by the boys as a way for Tom to protect his own back whilst exacerbating their own embarrassment. Disregarding his earlier deliberations about involving a third party…a witness… he decided to continue alone. This was no time to act self-indulgently. As usual, with Tom, the altruistic motivation took precedence. All the same, some record of the proceedings might prove ultimately invaluable. Tom covertly switched on the record function of his cassette player which lay conveniently at the back of his desk, his action going unnoticed by the preoccupied boys.

'You have already acknowledged that sexual misconduct occurred with Gillian Sumner on the playing field.'

Tom looked quizzically at the three of them making each feel himself the centre of his attention. Nervous, twitchy acknowledgement was returned. Greg Judson, looking directly at Tom, sat up in his seat and looked very much as though he was trying to make a cautious, prudent response. James and Kevin, following the lead of their peer, made a strident effort to emulate his attentiveness despite fluttering stomachs and stamina-drained muscles.

'I'm certainly not interested in a blow by blow account of the events.'

Tom smiled inwardly at the amusing potential of the double entendre. Such a verbal slip would have caused untold hilarity around the favoured staffroom table with David Southwich leading the raucous chorus of unrestrained laughter. It was lost upon the emotionally jaded group. He continued,

'Your acknowledgement is all I require. Tell me Greg, perhaps you could act as spokesman. What was Gillian Sumner's attitude to your fooling around with her?'

The opportunity to respond defensively allowed Greg Judson to shake himself free from the languid condition into which the three of them had sunk. Complete frankness was the only response he considered. There seemed little point in trying to minimise their offence. Mr Portland would not be shocked, nor would he be unnecessarily retributive. Greg's trust in Tom stimulated complete openness despite the possibility that he might be consigning all three of them to Heaven knows what punishment and public humiliation.

'Look, Sir, we know that she's very young but she's also very mature for her age and proud of it. She's always trying to get off with one or the other of us. We were playing football on the field when she came along with her mate. They watched us play for a while. When we sat down to talk to them, her mate had to go. What started off as a bit of banter... and tickling each other with some grass flowers... led to some much more serious touching. At no time did she object. She was willing to be...'

'That's enough, thank you, Greg.'

Tom warmed to the boy in his inability to select the appropriate vocabulary. He felt no such temptation to complete the sentence for him which was his acknowledged fault with Slater. To Tom, the boy's inability to select the right word showed his awareness of the inappropriateness of any but a pejorative term. Tom lingered over the memory of Phoebe's chosen expression of *gang-bang*. Greg to his credit had been too shamefaced to use even the terms *fun* or *games*.

Tom's thoughts drifted from the boys' predicament. In his heart of hearts, he knew beyond a shadow of a doubt that to entertain a punitive view of the boys' misconduct would make him as grave a hypocrite as his nefarious colleague. How could he countenance punishment for something of which he himself had been guilty when of a similar age? But what was there to feel guilty about? 'Guilty' had been his own term. Was it not likely that a sense of wrong-doing by himself at fifteen years of age had arisen not from an authentic regret for his premeditated exploitation of a teenage girl but from contagious mores reluctantly contracted from the evangelical atmosphere in his home? Tom's day dreaming was interrupted by an explosion of torrential rain which rattled like the ammunition of an automatic weapon against the window panes. That vague, early promise of sunshine had not been kept. Had he been superstitious, he would have believed that the continuing dark and squally weather was in some way linked to all the trials and tribulations that he had to deal with, currently, at Southwich High School. His recollections of his doubtful, youthful sexual misdeeds continued as the boys sat on the edge of their seats, their muscles tensed and rigid, waiting for Tom to complete his interrogation and to pass judgement. Tom was oblivious to their plight for a few moments as he recalled his own teenage crime.

He had been a newspaper delivery boy. On several occasions, he had plotted assignations half way round his delivery route with a plain but sexually precocious girl of the same age. She had been persistent in her pursuit of him so that ultimately he gave way and a relationship of sorts began. He avoided the usual haunts where he might invite a girl because he was ashamed to have been observed by his peers with a girl of such coarse features. Yet he had been prepared to use her for the satisfaction of his gauche sexual inquisitiveness. The boys watched him, wondering what agonies he was suffering on their behalf, as they observed beads of perspiration appearing on his forehead. The palms of his hands became sticky and he could feel his sweat-soaked shirt sticking to his back and chest, at first hot and clammy and then, cold. He shivered and involuntarily loosened his tie in his attempt to get more air. He was transported to the scene as though watching with some prurient titillation a triple *X-* rated film. Young Tom Portland with minimal niceties of youthful conversation in the darkness and privacy of an convenient arbour, put down his canvas delivery bag and embraced the trembling, expectant, but unlovely, female, whose name he had long since forgotten. It was an irrelevance that the girl was a living, breathing person with feelings. She was there simply as a landscape to be explored with its associated hills and valleys and underground caverns. With racing pulse, feverish temperature and weakness in the joints, he behaved totally out of his perceived character.

Without any preliminary pleasantries of caressing, kissing or stroking her body, because he was untutored, he slipped his hands under her jumper and managed in his inexpert fumbling to unhook the strap of her bra and attacked her ample breast with his frenzied groping .The girl's increased breathing rate encouraged his exploration of her willing body which she demonstrated by rotating her pelvic bone against whatever part of his body was available to her. Her moaning and rhythmic movement against him caused his young, but rampant male organ, to become massively engorged and fully erect. He remembered tugging at her regulation, thick, navy knickers in his desire to feel her juicy, swollen, passion-filled female inner parts with his enquiring fingers. She opened her legs to admit his entry to her clitoral area. He needed no further invitation. He rubbed her thrusting, female parts violently with the ball of his hand and thrust his fingers into her vagina so that she screamed out, whether in delight or pain he neither knew nor cared... She unzipped his fly and seized his throbbing penis, now outstanding in its erection and appearing to have a life of its own, and guided it clumsily and frantically towards her warm, moist, expectant vagina. Once inside her, he moved in rapid piston-like motion, using more energy than expertise, thrusting to and fro like a fireman loading the locomotive's boiler. He experienced an extraordinary thrill as every nerve in his body tingled. He had not known before this encounter that such ecstasy existed. He had devoured *Lady Chatterley's Lover* and the *Kama Sutra* many times, and whatever other steamy novels he could acquire at the local library, secretly, hidden behind plain brown covers or hiding behind a copy of *Devotional Readings* but nothing he had read could have provided the physical pleasure he was experiencing at this girl's hands. Suddenly, after reaching a crescendo of frenzied moaning, the girl stopped his thrusting and screamed out loudly, bringing him to his senses, frightening him and causing his erection immediately to be lost. He was anxious lest anyone should hear them. As her screams died away, she trembled and involuntarily shivered. This was followed by relentless spasmodic involuntary twitches of her muscles. All this unnatural juddering of her body almost caused his heart to fail. Whatever was the matter with her? What had he done to her? Was she going to die? It was a massive relief to him when she eventually calmed down. She grabbed his flaccid organ which she proceeded to stroke and tickle, increasing the ferocity of her movement in order to get another erection and he did not refuse her demands. Another wave of pleasurable ecstatic feelings engulfed his whole body until finally he arrived at the uppermost point of his first orgasm and sexual fluids exploded on to her skirt.

    And then it was over. She lingered over him wanting him to kiss and pet her, but he pulled himself from her. He offered his handkerchief to wipe away the semen and as quickly as could be managed, left her alone, in their secret hideaway. Filled with youthful elation he promised to return to her the following evening.

The boys looked towards Tom, watching his every bodily twitch and spasm, wondering what on earth was going on inside his head. He had little awareness of how long he had mentally withdrawn from them. Possibly only moments had elapsed before they had his full attention. He noticed that during the recollection from his teenage days, the promised sunshine had appeared, warming the air and illuminating his office with natural light. The heavy clouds had been dispersed and the stormy squalls had abated. The change in the weather seemed to beckon Tom towards expediting the resolution of the meeting. He assumed a determined posture as he signalled his readiness to address the boys.

'Okay. I've got a great difficulty in dealing with you. Anyone who has been young knows what you did was understandable and certainly not evil. But clearly, what you did cannot be condoned. You obviously took advantage of a young girl. The fact that it was reported by some of your female peers suggests that you gave offence to others. The school playing fields hardly seem the place to conduct your amorous affairs anyway. Remember, you are all ambassadors for Southwich. The school's reputation is spoiled by reports of this kind. Should the girl's parents make a complaint to the police, there is a danger of rape proceedings occurring. However, I have to tell you that the law concerning sexual consent is rather irrational. In all probability, though what happened to the girl since she is under the age of sixteen would be regarded as child sex abuse, you, as sixteen year olds, would probably not be regarded as criminally responsible. Let's hope that Gillian, realising her complicity in all this, feels disinclined to drop you in it. Let's also hope that Mrs Spong's counsel backs that up. I'm sure she'll feel the need to inform the girl's mother since, clearly, she's at risk – of pregnancy not least of all. In which case, I'll have to inform your parents in case they are contacted directly by Gillian's parents. However, provided I become satisfied with your responses, I'll advise the Head that

Gillian's parents should not be informed of your identity and I will promise to talk with your parents in a manner which saves your faces somewhat. In other words, I'll attempt to persuade them that you were not criminally motivated but guilty of indiscretion.

'Now, I must counsel you to avoid this kind of public display. You do bear an awesome responsibility for the welfare of young girls. A premature pregnancy may well ruin their lives. Teenage pregnancy and abortion are running today at epidemic proportions. Sexually transmitted diseases are also rife. There you have a responsibility towards yourselves.

'Will you trust me to deal with the matter sensitively with your parents? And do you feel at all sorry for the inappropriateness of your actions?'

James and Kevin looked nervously at Tom following the pattern of the more confident Greg. Each of them exhibited tearful, strained faces which nevertheless displayed relief that Mr Portland was taking a reasonable and understanding approach. They well knew Tom's reputation for dealing with parents in a manner which healed rather than exacerbated family tensions. Therefore, they were not greatly agitated at the prospect. Greg expressed their regret and assured Tom that no such occurrence would again take place. The other two mumbled their assent.

'Thank you, Sir, for what you have done for us. You've rescued us from a fate worse than death. We'll always be grateful. We think you're a great teacher, Sir. You should be the Headteacher, but please don't go anywhere else will you? Not yet anyway!'

'Thanks lads. You must also have a quiet word with Gillian and tell her that you are sorry about what took place, advising her, for her own safety, to avoid such adventures.'

Each offered a hand to Tom to shake as they left his office. Tom was fascinated by the fact that boys who seemed not to emulate their seniors' habit of hand-shaking should do so with alacrity when they felt the need to express their pleasure in his treatment of them as mature young adults. Tom wiped a tell-tale tear from his eye as soon as the boys had closed the door quietly behind them.

CHAPTER TWELVE

Saturday, 23 May, 1992.

Maudie had been up since six awoken by the brilliance of the sun's rays finding their way through chinks in the curtains. Tom slept on. She had crept downstairs silently so as not to disturb him.

'Poor lamb needs to catch up on his sleep after his trials of last week', had been her thought as she left the bedroom.

She was referring to the various interviews he had had to conduct with the parents of the four pupils involved in the reported incident of sexual shenanigans on the school field on the previous Sunday night.

She made herself some tea, and wondered out into the back garden. It was her favourite part of the day - sunny, warm enough to sit outside but not overly hot. A slight breeze made her perambulation round the borders more comfortable. After the peculiar weather of the previous weeks, it was pleasant to see the clear blue sky on the first day of the weekend. She wandered from plant to plant inspecting them for damage and dead heads, intertwining, newly grown stems of clematis among the roses to avoid their later breakage and checking her most recently planted specimens in order to ensure that they were thriving. The perennial sweet peas which she had grown from the seeds collected two years before were all growing well and were making their own way by means of tendrils though the existing framework of her planting. The Victoria plum tree had lost two of its branches, owing to the gusty squalls of the previous week, along with a third of its somewhat meagre crop. She would prune them the following month but in the meantime, she needed to remove some of the thin branches that were likely to be broken if the storms returned. She entered the garden shed to locate the secateurs with which to carry out the operation. As she sliced off each branch she uttered in turn,

    'Icky's left hand, Icky's right hand, no that's Tom, you need him,' she laughed out loud 'Icky's left leg, Icky's right leg, That should slow you down a bit !'

It was not the sort of chatter that she would let Tom hear her say. Although he was in a constant state of mental and physical fatigue throughout the week as result of the incessant demands made on his time by that slave driver, Ted Slater, his natural actions were not vicious or vindictive. Maudie's nature was more like that of a human piranha compared to Tom's Angel fish-like temperament. She returned to the kitchen where she emptied the dishwasher, prepared the breakfast table, and brewed more tea. It was half past eight when she re-entered the bedroom with tea for Tom. He was still asleep. She woke him.

    'We've a pleasant day in store...nice weather...time to potter in the garden...light alfresco lunch...then off to the Birds' for dinner - followed by a week's holiday for some lucky beggars. Remember you and the boys are on half-term all next week. I only get Monday then it's back to the grindstone for me.'

She joked. She did not mind going to work. She loved her job at the library.

'Anyway, I'll have to go into school next week and do some preparations for the exams. All that interviewing last week took up a lot of valuable time which I would have otherwise have spent on exam organisation.'

'Remember...Jennifer said to go early so that we can spend some time in their garden', she reminded him.

Jennifer and Harold Bird lived in a small, picturesque, highly desirable, chocolate box village in the rural hinterland of Longborough. Harold, who was quite a joker, would say to intended visitors,

'You can't miss us...we live at the dead centre of the village.'

Actually they lived adjacent to the dead centre which was Harold's parlance for the Church of St Michael and All Angels and its churchyard full of gravestones. It was a joke that Harold cracked so often, that some of his impatient acquaintances would complain, in a mock exasperated manner,

'For goodness sake, Harold, How many more times are you going to boil that cabbage?'

Harold was such a jovial fellow, kind and generous with not an enemy in the world. It was impossible not to love both him and his humour.

Tom and Maudie set off at three o'clock to drive to the home of the Birds, aptly named, 'Robin's Nest' at Crossechester. They had estimated a journey time of three quarters of an hour which meant, traffic permitting, they would arrive about four o'clock, giving them ample time to enjoy the garden in the late afternoon sun. The cottage stood on a narrow, cobbled street next to the churchyard with its silent occupants.

'We have very quiet neighbours, you know,'

Harold would tell new acquaintances. His face was deadpan but his eyes would be twinkling.

At the opposite end of the street was the site of the ancient wayside cross of Crossechester. The original mediaeval octagonal base comprising five steps now bore a modern cross. The church, the cross, in fact the whole street were tourist attractions. The double yellow lines on each side prevented their easy parking so they left the car a short walk away on the carpark of The Three Fishes gastropub. Tom knew that they had to pass the wayside cross on their way to 'Robin's Nest'. The cottage was easily located as it was the last one before the church. There was no front garden. The front door opened straight onto the street. At each side of the door stood enormous deep planters in which were growing, quite rampantly, a wisteria and a Morning glory vine in one and a *Madame Alfred Carriere* rose with scented, creamy-white blooms in the other. The front, east facing façade, of the house was in shadow, but the large rear garden would be bathed in sunshine at this time of day.

They stood for a few minutes admiring the row of eighteenth century, Georgian cottages. 'Robin's Nest' was double fronted, with a simple, Flemish-bond, grey brick-built façade, but embellished with ornamental brickwork lintels over the central front door and casement windows with leaded lights. The roof, thatched with weathered reeds, accommodated two dormer windows. They approached the six-panelled, black-gloss painted, timber front door with its brass letter box and doorknob, large keyhole and rapped on the door using the brass doorknocker which took the form of a woodpecker.

The shiny, beaming, bronzed face of Harold Bird appeared before them and welcomed them into the narrow hallway, where they were relieved of their coats and the various gifts they had brought...wine, flowers and chocolates which would appeal to most tastes. The doorways were all very low and as they proceeded towards the kitchen, they observed, with amusement, above the door, a board on which was painted a stylised game bird with the inscription 'DUCK OR GROUSE'. The Birds, both being of short stature, had an easy passage through but Tom and Maudie chose to duck. Harold led them via the living-kitchen into the huge garden at the rear of the cottage the rear boundary of which was the River Crosse. At this point, the river was clear and shallow with no hidden dangers and so on the hottest of days, Harold could be seen paddling in the cool waters looking for trout. It was so idyllic on the river bank that one of their several patios was located there, furnished with teak benches and chairs and a garden swing seat. It was to this particular spot that they made their way. Jennifer was lazily swinging on the seat, relaxing in the warm, spring sunshine. She called to them,

'Welcome. It's been some time since you last came.'

Her ample, motherly figure was draped in a loose, ankle-length, green cotton robe. She looked as cool as a cucumber. Her fair hair, as usual was pinned up in a chignon. She wore sunglasses. She rose from her seat to greet them and invited them to sit down,

'What'll you have to drink, Maudie? Tea... iced lemonade... fizz... G and T with ice and a slice?' enquired their host.

'Yes please, Harold, the gin sounds just perfect.'

'What about you, Tom?'

'Have you got a beer?'

'Only 4% continental'

'Sounds good to me. Thanks'

Harold, similarly rotund, dressed coolly in tailored, white cotton shorts and a green polo shirt and wearing a safari hat, set off up the garden to the kitchen. Whilst he busied himself pouring the drinks and serving some nibbles, Jennifer continued to swing on the garden chair, obviously deep in thought. Eventually she spoke,

'Sorry, Maudie, to talk shop for a minute... but how are things going for you, Tom? The girls and I haven't seen hardly anything of you this week?

'Let's put it this way...I was glad to see the end of school yesterday. I seemed to be interviewing boys and their parents then the girl and her parents nonstop. Next year's timetable is no further forward. It seems as if I'm running just to stand still'.

Tom looked at Jennifer as if looking for some words of comfort.

'The foot-fall past my door is on the increase. If it's not Phoebe Spong, then it's Peter Smalley. I don't know what's happened to Ted's system for seeing staff. I suppose if they bypass me and go direct to his door then there's little he or I can do about it. The system only works if people go through me to make an appointment to see him. I wouldn't trust that woman further than I could throw her...she's got a smug, determined, self-satisfied look on her face all the time now, it seems to me. Peter Smalley is almost as bad... Creepy so-and-so that he is!'

If Tom was seeking some comfort then he was disappointed. The combination of his enemies, Slater, Spong and Smalley, all wearers of Ichthus badges, getting their heads together was a recipe for his destruction, he felt sure.

'Here we are folks...something to cool us down',

Harold had returned to the river bank with a tray of drinks and some accompanying tasty nibbles of juicy black and green olives and mini garlic breads. He distributed the drinks and placed the nibbles on the table. Tom raised the glass to his lips and took a couple of gulps of the refreshing beer. His glass was immediately half empty.

'Bring your drinks. Let's have a wander round the garden before I need to think about dinner,' Jennifer suggested.

Tom was pleased that she had made this suggestion. While the two 'girls' and Harold were discussing their plants, he could get some of his thoughts together without seeming to be rude. The four of them stood for a few moments and looked down the bank at the clear mini-rapids caused by waters of the River Crosse, as it made its way over the stones and gravel on the river bed. The sun's rays, bouncing back in all directions as they were reflected from the water as it flowed erratically over the small obstacles in its path, gave the river the appearance of a sparkling, diamond-encrusted, shimmering, liquid silver serpent engulfing the group as it slithered silently by. They turned and looked back towards the house which was glowing as it was bathed in the late afternoon sunshine. The Birds' garden was a delight for their eyes. It was large enough to include all manner of interesting ideas which were denied most gardeners. Harold was a skilled craftsman who could turn his hand to most tasks. If Jennifer came up with a design, he could usually realise it for her. Even though it was a cottage garden, Jennifer liked to contain the informality in some kind of ordered formality. Nearest to the cottage was formal arrangement of four triangular outer beds, edged with box and filled to overflowing with a jumble of cottage garden favourites, with a central interesting feature which caught Maudie's approving attention. A central dominant post, with a circular seat, surrounded by shorter posts arranged in a circle, twelve in all, each connected to the next by a rope and similarly all connected to the central master post. At the base of each post, Harold had planted a climbing rose together with clematis. In another month, the display would be glorious. To Jennifer and Harold, it was a wonderful way to sit amongst their climbing plants in a confined area. To the religious, it might represent the disciples with Christ at their centre. To Tom, beautiful as it might be, he saw it as a secret society with Slater at the centre surrounded by his acolytes all connected by the bondage of the Ichthus symbol.

Jennifer reeled off the names of her plants as if she were reading from a plant catalogue:

'Aconite, aquilegia, autumn crocus, azalea, buddleia, clematis, cherry laurel, Christmas rose, euphorbia, everlasting sweet pea, foxglove, golden chain, hollyhock, hydrangea, lily of the valley, wisteria.'

She neglected to mention all the bulbs which had either bloomed and were finished or which had yet to appear above ground.

Jennifer went inside to refill their glasses. Tom, Maudie and Harold walked over to the greenhouse where Harold practised plant propagation from seeds and cuttings, and which also housed some exotic specimens amongst which were Anthuria, with its shiny, red spathes, so perfect in form, they looked as if they were artificial, a huge, *Brugmansia suaveolens* - 'Angel's Trumpet', a magnificent Calla lily with several blooms and a small selection of insectivorous plants.

'What's giving off that wonderful scent?' asked Maudie.

'It's the Datura...the one with the trumpet flowers, sometimes called 'Devil's Breath'

It gives off its perfume at the end of the day to attract moths for pollination.'

'Yes, that's right. I've heard of Datura, but why is it called 'Devil's Breath'? It's poisonous isn't it?'

He did not get the opportunity to answer her. They were interrupted by a commotion coming from inside the cottage. They could hear whoops of excitement from Jennifer. She dashed outside and shouted over to them,

'We've got one more for dinner… The eagle, no sorry, the Robin has landed.' Chuckling over her own joke, she rushed back inside. Robert Bird was unloading his tackle from the taxi and paying the driver.

The tour of the garden came to an abrupt end as Harold hurried into the cottage to greet his explorer son. Tom and Maudie looked at each other wondering whether they should excuse themselves in order to let the Bird family catch up with each-others' escapades without their intrusion, but Jennifer was adamant that they should do no such thing but stay and listen to some of Robert's stories over dinner.

It was now approaching six o'clock. The garden was still bathed in sunshine but having had a surfeit of sun and witnessing the unexpected arrival of the adventurer, they all felt relieved to go into the comfortable sitting room at the front of the house, where the cool, cream, leather sofas welcomed them to take their ease. Jennifer brought in more drinks, gin for Maudie but Tom contented himself with iced lemonade whilst Robert Bird tucked into a pint of Guinness to which he had been looking forward, for the previous twenty-four hours. Maudie offered her assistance in the kitchen but Jennifer assured her that all was under control and urged her to re-join the men in the sitting room. Robert had plenty of stories to relate about his adventures in Brazil and above his deep sonorous tones, Jennifer could be heard singing away just like the mother gathering food for her fledgling offspring.

Robert, now thirty three years of age, tall, broad, and fair and sporting an untidy beard, had been at the University of Manchester when he saw the first Indiana Jones movie, *Raiders of the Lost Ark*. He was twenty two. Just at the time when he should have been researching the market for suitable employment, he became mesmerised and hypnotised by the persona of Indiana Jones as portrayed by the actor Harrison Ford. His studies in Anthropology and Archaeology only added fuel to the fire of enthusiasm already raging in his belly, occupying his mind day and night and taking over his whole raison d'être. His parents knew better than to dissuade him. He had always displayed a stubborn streak. The best way to treat his outlandish schemes was to either ignore them or share and encourage his enthusiasm.

'Let him get it out of his system, he's only young; Let him do his travelling while he's fit and strong and has no ties to bind him. He'll settle down eventually', were the wise words of his father and they were echoed by his mother.

So Robert became an adventurer, an explorer, an eco-warrior travelling to those places which most people only read about or see in film or on TV. He had no fear. He was like the young Spitfire pilots in World War Two. The world was his to conquer. He was determined to experience as much of the unknown world as he could. He answered any and every advertisement which appeared in the Geographical journals and in the major daily newspapers and as soon as he became successful in his application, he was made aware of more and more opportunities. He had always been interested in South America. He was fascinated by the geography, the people and the myths and legends of the Incas and the Aztecs. The story of Indiana Jones in Peru was the catalyst for a reaction that was going to happen anyway; the process was simply speeded up. Ten years later, he was as avid as ever. Never had he lost the enquiring mind of the adventurer and explorer. Of late, he had been particularly interested in the Peruvian tribes who practised the shrinking of heads - the indigenous tribes who used curare on their hunting arrows, the discovery of new species of poisonous plants and the acquisition of their seeds which his father was anxious to try to germinate in his greenhouse. His latest expedition to the deepest parts of The Brazilian rain forest had resulted in some hair-raising episodes when the team had encountered a previously undiscovered tribe. It was a nerve-jingling task to communicate with indigenous natives who had never been in contact with any other human except for members of their own tribe. It was virtually impossible not to let the excitement of the discovery upset these people to the extent that the team might be targeted as enemies or even as potential food .

Robert's descriptions of his travels gripped the imaginations of Maudie and Tom who listened entranced and without a murmur.

'If you're interested, I'll show you my collection. It's only across the hall.'

They stood and he led them out of the sitting room to the door immediately opposite. They entered. In the original cottage, this would have been designated a reception room but Robert had taken it over to act as a repository for all matters associated with his travels. It was obviously a male preserve - dusty and in disarray. It was obvious that Jennifer left it alone. A central table was piled high with cardboard boxes of a variety of carved wooden artefacts and mineral specimens awaiting classification. Two walls were lined with cupboards and glass-fronted display cabinets, housing other, more delicate treasures. Tom saw a large collection of shrunken heads and remembered Jennifer's words about their home becoming swamped with such monstrosities. One cabinet was filled to overflowing with items of primitive jewellery. Another contained musical instruments – pipes of different sizes and drums. Displayed on the other walls, hastily mounted with Blu-Tack were photographs of Robert posing with the indigenous inhabitants – both human and other creatures of the rainforest. Robert's enthusiastic ramblings of his exploits were interrupted by the shrill voice of his mother announcing that dinner was imminent. His battered old suitcase had been hastily placed by the door. It contained packets of carefully gathered and labelled seeds for his father, who would be so pleased and excited at the prospect of working with a hitherto unknown variety of a plant from the rain forest.

    Everyone made their way to the rear of the house where the bi-folding doors were fully open. One of Harold's first tasks after purchasing their home was to seek planning permission to alter the rear elevation to its present state. The living kitchen occupied virtually the whole of the rear half of the cottage. It contained separate cooking, dining and lounging areas. Jennifer was in her domain between the island unit and the Aga range, at the ready to serve the first course - a cold starter of poached pear on a bed of lettuce served with a tarragon cream sauce. She followed that with herb-crusted roast leg of lamb, accompanied by red-wine gravy served with Jersey Royal potatoes and asparagus. Finally, she offered a school pudding of treacle sponge with thick vanilla custard.

'Would anyone like cheese? I've got some lovely ripe Camembert.'

'I thought that was Bobbie's socks I could smell,' joked his father, 'I don't suppose he's changed them for weeks.'

How could they resist the Camembert? Everyone found room for a taste of the creamy, odoriferous but delicious cheese. Everyone had enjoyed a plentiful supply of wine with their meal, except for poor Tom. He decided that he had enough on his plate with his problems at school without the possible addition of being breathalysed on the journey home.

Harold, Robert and Maudie retired to the front sitting room to relax during what was left of the evening, leaving Tom in the kitchen, where he chatted to Jennifer whilst she started to make the coffee. He helped to tidy up where he could. He was able to clear the table but left her to stack the dishwasher. He knew that everyone had their own system of stacking the dishes and in any case there was only room for one in the cooking area and that was the way Jennifer liked it. The evening had been a delightful affair and Tom was most grateful to Jennifer for all her work in the production of a most magnificent feast. He congratulated her on the beauty of her home and garden. She was pleased to receive such praise. She always regarded Tom fondly like she would a younger brother and it was painful to her to witness all the problems he was suffering at the hands of his boss - Slater and his fellow deputy, Phoebe Spong.

'You go through, Tom, and join the others. I'll be a few moments yet'

Early adventures with Ted Slater were remembered as she set about brewing the coffee. She, Harold and Tom had been students together in the mid-fifties at Longborough Central College. Harold and Ted were a couple of years older than she was because they had fulfilled their National Service commitment before starting their college courses whereas she had gone straight to college after completing her 'A' levels. Harold was a born craftsman and was pursuing a Higher Diploma in Woodwork and Metalwork whereas Ted had opted for the teaching training course enabling him to teach in a secondary school. She was specialising in secretarial skills. The three of them had become friends straightaway, but it soon became clear that she was planning to become more than just a pal to Ted Slater. A romantic attachment of sorts formed between the two of them, with Harold always there in the background, a good, solid, dependable friend when support was needed. However, when it finally dawned on Ted that she was getting too serious, he made it plain to her that his real love was at another college in another town. As she recalled this bombshell and the recollection that he had used her in the absence of Ayna or 'Anal' as she used to refer to her afterwards in spite, the knife she was handling slipped on the worktop, slitting her finger in the process. Carmine droplets of blood dropped like red teardrops onto her blouse and onto the floor.

'Rotten, bloody creep', she uttered, vindictively as she dashed for a plaster in the first aid box.

Harold had been there, as he always was, to console her. Of course, she realised eventually what a true friend he was, and what a cad Slater was. So their attachment developed and they married. However, much as she loved and revered Harold, and hated Ted to an equal and opposite extent, she had always been attracted by his flamboyant personality and self-confidence even though she believed him to be a rotten scoundrel to the core. Over the passing years, she had managed to keep track of his career by some means or other, eventually managing to secure a position as his personal secretary cum bursar at Southwich High School. He had been delighted to resume their acquaintance little knowing that she had planned it all along. And she of course, had feigned surprise at the coincidence of their meeting again after so many years had elapsed. She was now back as close to him as she could get without actually sharing his bed. They had worked as colleagues for at least fourteen years…Slater barking the orders and she responding like a faithful puppy. She had become aware of all the undercurrents in the staffroom, the illicit relationships which were constantly springing up between colleagues and Ted Slater's gradual succumbing to the addiction of whisky.

She had always been fond of Tom and his family, regarding him as a younger brother or even a substitute son, her own son being absent for months on end. She felt it personally when Tom was treated so abominably by Slater. That rat whose academic qualifications of teachers' certificate upgraded to B.Ed. and then a postal Doctorate paled into insignificance compared with Tom's B.A First class honours and Master of Education. Although she could not confess to Tom, she knew Slater to be a jealous, malicious task master. She knew that Tom would never have Slater's approval, because he would tolerate no-one being compared with him in a more favourable light. And the final nail in Tom's coffin was the scorn he poured on the religious cliquishness of the Ichthus-bearing so-called Christians in the staffroom and amongst the advisory service.

Jennifer wheeled her trolley bearing coffee, liqueurs and chocolates from the kitchen to the cosy sitting room at the front of the house. This room was situated on the north wall of the cottage and so never saw the direct sun so the window ledge was an ideal location for Harold's orchids, mostly in bloom, mainly *Phalaenopsis*, in various shades of pink. The soft furnishings typically suited the cottage, being chintzy and floral with lots of pink and gold. The ancient stone fireplace housed a dog grate in which a huge log continued to burn, giving the whole room a cosy glow as the flames flicked and the sparks flew up the chimney.

'Did you have to collect the beans too?' asked Harold, mischievously.

'No, but I had to grind some more', she laughed as she lied.

As the antique wall clock chimed eleven o'clock, Tom and Maudie exchanged looks signalling to each other that it was time to take their leave. Having thanked their hosts for entertaining them so royally, they donned their coats and set off walking to the pub car park.

'That was superb way to spend our day, lovely weather, good food and good company. Jennifer and Harold are a lovely couple aren't they? And Robert is so knowledgeable and entertaining.'

'Jennifer is a real brick!' Tom replied. 'She's about the only one I can depend on at school. She watches my interests when some are trying to take me down.'

'Did you notice anything unusual today at the Birds?' Maudie quizzed him.

'In the kitchen, after dinner, I noticed a shelf full of mortars and pestles. She must use them to grind her coffee,' he said.

'Maybe, she collects them. People do have unusual collections. I only ever collected stamps and first day issues. At least that didn't take up much space.' Maudie thought of her childhood collection of stamps lying in a cupboard, waiting for a crumb of interest to be shown by either Jack or Freddie.

'Hope Freddie has behaved himself for Jack. We've left them for a long time today.' She thought about their two sons and hoped that they would stay closer to home in their adulthood than had Robert Bird but she thought, philosophically that once the offspring are fully fledged, they have to make their own way in life.

'In the garden, did you notice the plants? There were a lot of poisonous ones and the flowers had not been deadheaded. They were all producing seed.'

'Harold's hobby is propagating from seed isn't it? That's what he uses his greenhouse for.'

They reached their car. There was no message on the windscreen 'politely asking them to refrain from parking'. All was in order. They would have been surprised to have returned to find it vandalised in such an idyllic village but in the current state of society, all eventualities were possible.

CHAPTER THIRTEEN

Monday, 1 June, 1992.

The sexual misconduct episode proved to be a nine days wonder. Tom duly interviewed the parents of the boys who were as ever, grateful for his pragmatic and unfussy handling of the matter. The girl's mother had been greatly upset by her daughter's involvement but wished to take no further action against the anonymous boys. This had been a considerable disappointment to Phoebe Spong who had attempted to persuade the mother that approaches to the police on the grounds of underage sex ought to have been pursued. Phoebe had seemed blissfully unaware that all parties, boys and the girl, had been underage. The confusion arose from the fact that she had found the circumstances titillating whilst confirming the justification for her own anti-male prejudice. Concerned for her daughter's reputation, the mother had resolutely refused to be moved.

'Another victory for the smarmy, smarty-pants Tom Portland - on the side of the men, as usual', had been her private reaction together with an enthused determination to see him brought down.

Phoebe Spong entertained a highly complex attitude towards Tom. On the one hand, she envied him his domestic peace and uncomplicated happiness. On the other, she suspected him of both naivety and pretence. Tom shamelessly maintained an unswerving admiration and simple love for his wife and sons, a confidence in the essential goodness of all humanity and a belief that Man might achieve personal goals without deliberate spoiling of others' opportunities. Phoebe's own relationships were in a state of such constant flux that she considered that anyone like Tom must be inevitably guilty of disingenuousness. She sought solace from her own marital disharmony and its antidote, marital infidelity, by imagining the condition universal, and that anyone avoiding it, must be either under-sexed or spiritless. Hence, she interested herself to an extraordinary degree in the relationship breakdowns of all whom she knew together with those in the public eye or in her chosen reading matter and TV and film viewing. Likewise, she envied Tom his undoubted linguistic skills. Her control of language she knew left much to be desired. In her imagination she was an accomplished public speaker – a skill which had been fostered self-consciously through membership of a Speakers' Club– a pastime enabling the opportunity for surreptitious investigation of others' dissatisfaction with marriage partners and their inclination towards extra-marital affairs. But she knew her control of language skill to be woefully wanting. Tom's ability to write and to speak with fluent control she suspected like one might the supposed extra-sensory perception of a fortune teller. While she envied his semantic expertise and rhetorical delivery, she felt obliged to attribute it to a kind of conjuring trick. A skill denied herself, she supposed must be false and therefore suspect.

      Tom was simply another male who stood in the way of her self-perception as superior to all, whether male or female. Perhaps, as a consequence of disappointments in her own relationships, she had taken an irrational dislike to all men. As an only child, her early contact with the male sex had been solely with her father, a figure of distant, male chauvinism with whom despite his tendency to idolise her, she had developed no meaningful relationship. Steadily, she had become the archetypal misanthropist without actually recognising it. Naturally, any male who did not revere her as had her father, was regarded by her as misogynistic. All men were considered thus since no man, not even her current lover, gave her the total respect which she craved. They were, therefore, to be defeated in competition. Their sexual availability was a biological matter of fact, there to be tapped like the male Black Widow spider. Though she did not actually consciously desire to consume her mate, consummation lay in its victorious entrapment and subsequent imprisonment rather than in her own personal selflessness.

    Men, she saw as inevitable competitors. She felt driven to prove to them all that in every circumstance she was their equal. However, she was disturbed by Tom, because she recognised in him an inner strength which commanded admiration but his apparent flawlessness with words and actions angered her immeasurably since her raison d'être, where he was concerned, was undervalued. Furthermore, after many hours of private conversations with him, he had not succumbed to her femininity but had treated her as a neutral entity. The female in in her had been spurned. Possessing an androgynous psyche accompanied by a natural feminine pride in her own perceived attractiveness, she felt both emasculated and defeminised by Tom's responses to her. In her conceited, high opinion of herself, retaliation was her only option. In dispute with her husband, her frustration and undervaluation led to physical combat in which she was always the loser. There was, in relation to the non-combative Tom, little urge to hit out physically, but to attack in a much more hurtful and subtle fashion.

An ardent feminist, she was no stranger to the clamour of the current age against sexual harassment in the place of work. Her own teaching union, The Secondary School Teachers' Association had recently submitted in draft form, discussion documents relating to model procedures for the handling of Sexual Harassment allegations in schools. She was excited by the potential which the material offered women to redress the balance of gender power relationships which existed in all workplaces, schools not least of all. If women could call upon allegations or sexual harassment each time a male hierarchically superior to themselves, issued unpalatable instructions, then women would be armed to the teeth in the battle of the sexes. Such armoury was all she needed in order to secure total equality of opportunity for her gender. She exulted inwardly at the thought of the forward strides women were making towards bolstering up their relative power through the various guidelines on sexual harassment, which in schools would inevitably arise from the draft document. Civil Case Law was establishing rape as a matrimonial crime and the courts were beginning to condone murder of husbands ostensibly guilty of physical abuse. She identified with the Suffragettes' elation when in 1918 a limited proportion of women were newly enfranchised in the gender war. The two males she perceived currently as opponents might be floored by weaponry hitherto no more than a forlorn hope. She was adamant that Monica Dickinson, a sympathetic feminist, who had her own grievances against Tom, would be a major comrade along with others with whom she had already begun to foment anti-Tom hysteria in order to bring destruction to the conceited Deputy.

Phoebe began to compose a list of the school's personnel who could be depended upon to join the conspiracy. Monica's name was first on her list. The two of them had shared frequent sympathetic conversations about male obtuseness and ineptitude whilst having authority and power in their imagined right of superiority. Monica's marital problems had been shared frankly with the volubly receptive Phoebe. During these cry-on-my-shoulder sessions, Phoebe had elicited Monica's contempt for Tom which, it had been reported, was a common feeling amongst a group of women who felt intimidated by Tom's attitude towards matrimonial instability... At least five of the staff were divorced; another three were indulging in extra-marital liaisons; their names were written on her list. Then there was Alan Bairstow. Because of his marital difficulties, Phoebe and he had found a natural affinity. They had spent long hours in mutual commiseration. It had also become apparent that they shared a mutual irritation with Tom on account of his tendency to preach a gospel that neither wished to hear- the sabotage of western culture by the subversion of family values through promiscuity. Alan would be a male counterbalance to any charge which Tom might assert, of attack by a group of jaundiced women alone. The same was true of Peter Smalley. As a divorced cohabitant, he, too, had felt intimidated by Tom's unashamedly public pronouncements about society's insouciance concerning domestic instability. He would be an invaluable support in bringing Tom down.

Alan Bairstow's current liaison with the young Science teacher, Sian Waite, could be used to good effect .Phoebe had, weeks before, squeezed out of him his acknowledgement of his affair with Sian. An inveterate observer of acquaintances' social relationships, her technique was simple. Observing a nascent amorous relationship, she would use an opportunity to admit to the suspected party her own domestic unsettlement as a catalyst to their own admission of an affair. By this stratagem, she had elicited the precise matrimonial condition of just about everyone on the staff. Flattered by a Deputy's preparedness to share such confidential secrets, junior colleagues were beguiled into sharing their own.

Being a young, attractive and potentially vulnerable female, Sian was conceived by Phoebe as the person best suited to act as agent provocateur in her plot. Furthermore, as the niece of the Authority's Director of Education, her witness against Tom could be calculated to arouse both the credulity of Ted Slater and the respect of the rest of the female staff, each of which was going to be crucial if Tom were to be successfully prosecuted for sexual harassment. The males on the staff, Smalley and Bairstow excepted, were bound to side with Tom. The trick was to outflank them by weight of opinion. So universal was the horror amongst colleagues at the prospect of sexual harassment that if she were able to gather together a heavy representation of females, supported by at least a couple of males, the rest of the men would baulk at intervention on Tom's behalf for fear of appearing to impugn the veracity of the complainants. If it could be arranged that the Head himself wished the prosecution to proceed, the invariable human reluctance to stand out against the hierarchical superior, together with the emotional pressure of a considerable group who articulated gross offence, would make intervention in support of Tom infinitely less likely.

The list was concluded by the addition of the Home Economist, Vivienne Lowther, Smalley's cohabitant, Trudie Long and the English assistant, Sharon Crabtree. Phoebe counted them upon her fingers- two men and five women; if she added herself and the Head, then nine people stood ready to dislodge from his self-constructed pedestal, the self-righteous Tom Portland. One collateral advantage of Tom's disgrace formulated prominently in Phoebe's mind- the way would be laid open to her own succession to the Headship once Slater applied for his early retirement. The recent appointment of Jacqui Erne to the Chair of Governors had made this a more likely outcome. The notion of probable victory caused a witch-like cackle to escape from her distorted lips shattering the studied silence of her room. With pleasure, she contemplated her own professional advancement at the heart of the convoluted web of intrigue she was about to weave. Tom would need more than Ariadne's thread to escape this particular labyrinth; she would make sure of that. Her own outburst was accompanied by a dramatic, brilliant flash of forked lightning which illuminated her gloomy office followed immediately by the roar of a thunderclap; the storm had arrived overhead. Phoebe considered it a suitably good omen for her despicable plan.

Having composed her list, Phoebe felt the nervous thrill of conspirators down the ages. Not one jot of remorse at the ethical impurity of her proposed course of action did she experience. Portland was the personification of the male enemy- an individual who arrogated to himself a charismatic correctitude which cried out for a retributive *blitzkrieg*. Her face was contorted with lips moving manically from right to left with each stroke of her pen. She was like Satan in female form as she scowled and smirked, her thoughts switching from her distaste of Tom to her plan of action against him.

The steps to be taken would require the exercise of the highest levels of her conspiratorial skills. Clearly, Tom had to be lured into a confrontation with a woman, there being a witness to give corroborative account, in which it could be shown that he was behaving with characteristically sexual harassing intimidation. The whole group would then be persuaded to write reports of Tom's conduct over the years which would substantiate the contention that he were unfit to continue to wear the mantle of educational manager. Pupils would be persuaded to give critical accounts of his handling of their affairs. Phoebe was convinced that Tom's Achilles heel was his imperious refusal to follow the advice he so liberally distributed to all other colleagues – never to interview pupils of the opposite gender without a third party witness. In addition, was he not much given to tactile contact with all and sundry? In her confused memory, Phoebe's imagination recalled recalcitrant girls shrugging off his contact when he had touched their arm during a disciplinary intervention. Was it not a consistent characteristic of Tom when addressing anyone to seize their attention in dramatically flicking or tapping them? Had she not already alerted the Head to this feature of his conduct with pupils? Was he not equally anxious to see Tom brought down?

Phoebe drooled lovingly over the text of the Draft Model Procedures on Sexual Harassment. As haltingly she re-read the first page, she experienced the rapturous response of a young ingénue reading a *billet-doux* from her beau.

SECONDARY SCHOOL TEACHERS' ASSOCIATION.

DRAFT DOCUMENT

ON THE HANDLING OF ALLEGATIONS OF SEXUAL HARASSMENT

For the purposes of this document, sexual harassment is defined in terms of unsolicited sexual interest or unwanted advances, physical or verbal. They may be deliberate and persistent but will always be unwelcome and unreciprocated. Its most serious manifestation will be actual sexual assault.

In schools, sexual harassment may be evident in:-.

1. Comments
2. Salacious jokes
3. Verbal abuse
4. Sexual teasing
5. Sexual innuendo in conversation
6. Unwarranted 'touching'
7. Invasion of private 'space'
8. Sexual assault
9. Suggestions that sexual favours are a condition of the retention of employment or a pathway to promotion
10. The open or covert display of sexually offensive or pornographic material in the workplace.

A villainous leer became etched on her face. In a frenzied, though private display of fiendish glee coupled with guileful determination, she exclaimed,

'Fuck it, we've got him. The bastard will be mastered!'

CHAPTER FOURTEEN

Tuesday, 2 June, 1992.

The first day of external exams, entirely due to Tom's meticulous organisation, passed without any hitches. Having taken the Bank Holiday Monday off with the family, Tom was back at work. He had spent a large portion of the half-term break in the school office with only Jennifer and the office staff for company. Ted Slater and Phoebe Spong were noticeably absent. He had been in and out of the strong room checking every last detail concerning the examination papers, the lists of candidates and the staff invigilation rota. The girls in the office had kept him well supplied with cups of caffeine-loaded coffee which had maintained his energy levels, enabling his total concentration on such an important task.

     Tom started off the first English paper at nine thirty that morning. The candidates included his Year Eleven English set. He looked around to ensure that all were present. He was relieved that Lesly Atherton had arrived in good time. He wondered how much domestic work and child –care she had been obliged to undertake before presenting herself for the two hour English Language paper. He looked reassuringly at her and she smiled back at him. Her manner appeared to be bright enough. He took the opportunity to observe Greg, Kevin and James as they beavered away at their answers. They seemed to be coping well. Greg caught his eye and gave him a broad smile as if to say,

'Thanks again, Sir, for getting us out of that hole before half term.'

Those staff who would normally teach Year Eleven found themselves either invigilating the examinations in the Assembly Hall, or able to take their ease in the staff room. For them, the period of external examinations gave more free time whilst for the staff whose teaching commitment was with lower school pupils, it was business as usual.

At the end of the school day, most members of staff stayed on the school premises either involved in extra-curricular activities or just winding down over a cup of coffee in the company of their usual cliques before having to make the inevitable journey to all points of the compass to face the realities of their out-of-school lives.

Phoebe Spong was much in the habit of joining the women's corner of the staffroom where she played out a pretended role of friendly mentor to the female staff. Highly officious in all her formal dealings with staff, she took, nevertheless, time out each afternoon in order to dramatize a persona of social acceptability. Most of the women on the staff kept their distance but some favoured the practice of cronyism when it suited their purpose and she was no different. On this particular occasion, she was determined to introduce into the conversation the topic of gender discrimination which she had decided would serve as an effective launching pad for her assault on Tom Portland.

'Did anyone pick up the news, yesterday, about the woman who got life for stabbing her husband to death?'

'Ah bloody did', was the immediate response in the jarring local dialect of the opinionated Monica Dickinson. 'I thowt it were a soddin' aberration. 'Ow much torment are us wimmin s'posed to tek at th'ands of bleedin' blokes?'

'You're dead right', agreed Vivienne Lowther, the short, chubby, bespectacled Home Economics teacher. 'The poor woman must have been putting up with Hell for years. How can the Law support women's causes one minute by establishing rape as a matrimonial offence and then condemn a woman for justifiable self-defence another?'

'Come off it, Viv,'

Anne Jones who was not part of this particular clique, interrupted. She just happened to overhear this snippet as she was packing her brief-case at a nearby desk.

'Let her off with a mild tap on the wrist and what happens? Nobody's safe. What women need is equality of treatment before the Law. There's no room for positive discrimination where the law's concerned. Murder's murder; gender doesn't enter into it.'

'Bollocks!' Monica exploded. 'Yer 're a traitor t' t' cause, Yer spend t' much time fraternising wi' them bleedin' fellas o'er there, who sit like a whoop of chimps, cracking jokes at ower expense, ad infinitum. They're just typical, that shower, of men in general. They tret wimmin like shit. Course the law's got t' protect uz. I'd stab th' whole bleedin' lot of 'em, given t' chance. That woman, charged wi' murder should a bin given a sainthood, ne'er mind life. And so should t' lot of uz, just havin' t' tolerate t' filthy bastards!'

Phoebe sat upright, giving her full attention to Monica's ranting.

'Hackles rising nicely', she thought.

Phoebe liked nothing better than to stir up angry and recriminatory debate among the women. Monica was proving to be a useful stoker of the fire which she had started and which was beginning to engulf the imaginations of this group of enthusiastic man – haters. She felt that it was an appropriate time to introduce the matter which was consuming her so.

'How, in the name of Heaven can we women expect men to treat us with the respect we deserve if the dice are loaded against us?' Anne countered.

'Dice be b-b-buggered.' Phoebe, her voice strident and loud, stuttered out her words. The colour rose in her jaundice-tinted cheeks, her eyes began to water, their pupils suddenly dilating and her wrinkled, rubbery lips, quivered in her fury. 'Which of us is safe whilst fellas are allowed to treat us like chattels?'

The group's rising emotions inflamed the normally contemplative Sharon Crabtree, who with tears welling in her eyes, causing black rivulets of mascara to slip from her lashes onto her cheeks and downwards towards the crease lines around her mouth, painfully acknowledged,

'It's true. You're right, Phoebe. I sent Joe packing last night when he eventually arrived home at midnight, reeking of beer, after a night out with his rugby cronies, expecting to get his end away with me. I told him to sod off and not to expect me to be at his beck and call when it suited him.'

'Good on you!' Trudie Long congratulated her. 'Catch Peter behaving like that...well...he wouldn't, but if he did, that would be it. Last one were a sod though. And that's why I kicked him into touch. Tek my advice, Sharon, love. Have nowt to do with blokes like Joe. Find yersel' a fella who'll put you first. Mind you, do like me and find one who can do the business.'

'Sounds as if Joe can do the business, if he's fit forrit after a night on the booze.' Monica observed.

Knowing winks and stifled ribald laughter rippled sheepishly around the group of otherwise invigorated women except for Sharon who was still coming to terms with her dismissal of her fiancé, Joe, the previous night.

'I'm off; I've heard enough. You're a load of hypocrites, you lot,' barked an incensed Anne Jones. 'In the same breath, Trudie, you've condemned the majority of men, boasted about your own superior catch and then, without being aware of it, admitted that women have, after all, something to thank men for.

You know damn well that without our fellas, we women would be reduced to a load of wankers.'

Anne wanted to remind Trudie that although she had netted Peter, her landing of the catch fell short because she hadn't got him, yet, to marry her. But she thought she'd said enough. Her name would henceforth be mud as it was. Instead, she tossed her head, flicking the hair from her eyes and raising herself to her full height, she marched towards the door triumphant in having had the last word before departure. Her parting remark had quashed momentarily the self-conscious fervid zeal of the group. She left, exulting in the shocking effect of her parting salvo, inwardly smiling at the contrast between the misanthropic tone of the conversation she was leaving and her own mindfulness to nurture the respectful relationships enjoyed between herself, her husband and her two teenage sons.

'Well, we could have done without that kind of filth. It's just the sort we have to put up with all the time from men. When it comes from a woman, though, our cause is in jeopardy,' Phoebe tutted in disgust at Anne's remarks.

'Forget her, Phoebe,' Monica said. 'She's one of yer actual idolising sort. Every institution has 'em; that's where they should be…in institutions! She's a friggin' prig. She seems t' tek a particular delight in waftin' 'er lovey-dovey life under ower noses. She's another Tom Portland. Like 'im, she imagines 'erself superior on account of it. Uz divorcees are s'posed t' feel we're to blame for the ills of the modern Society. Well, screw that! Let her piss off to her lovey-dovey mate. Don't give her another thought.'

Phoebe was cock-a-hoop. Without having to introduce the topic, the hated name had arisen quite naturally. Now was her opportunity to move in for the kill. In subdued tones, she invited the present company to accompany her to her office where they could continue their conversation in a more private space, away from the eyes and ears of the likes of Anne Jones. She had already made preparations by buying extra coffee and milk and ensuring that she had sufficient cups and saucers to offer refreshments. Monica, Vivienne, Trudie, and Sharon duly followed her from the staffroom. Sian Waite appeared at that point and, as Phoebe had in mind a major role for her to play in her intended destruction of Tom Portland; she invited Sian to join them.

CHAPTER FIFTEEN

Tuesday, 2 June, 1992.

Though it was only a quarter past four, Phoebe was obliged to switch on the light in her office. It was not an hospitable room. Situated on the north wall of the building, it lacked natural warmth and light.

'Crikey! It's going to get dark early tonight', she observed to the group of women as they shuffled, conspiratorially and self-consciously, behind her.

A fluorescent strip light fully illuminated the room which was furnished minimally to the extreme with a desk, two stand chairs, although extras had been brought in for this occasion, an occasional table and some bookshelves on which a coffee percolator gurgled and spluttered like a simmering volcano. The walls were bare and there was no family photograph on her desk. The entire ambience of the room was cold, stark and most unwelcoming to even the dullest of dimwits. The temporary, sole colour, apart from the dingy brown carpet, was in the form of six, azure blue, fine china coffee cups and saucers placed in a circle on the table. The strong aroma of coffee assailed their nostrils. The collaborators took their seats accompanied by mighty crash of hailstones rattling against the window panes, causing them all to shriek in unison and at the same time to shiver involuntarily.

'Oh, do close the blinds. Let's shut out this dreadful weather.' Phoebe issued the order to which ever one might obey.

She poured out the black, pungent liquid and began to hand round the cups of steaming coffee. Monica, meanwhile, was studying the titles in the bookcase. As she extended an arm to extract *The Female Eunuch* from its housing between *Sexuality and the Teenage Girl* and *Gender Stereotyping in Britain Today,* so concerned was she to articulate a comment but one that was not obvious and trite, that she knocked out of Phoebe's hand a cup which was being passed to Sian Waite. The brilliant, blue glazed, fine china cup shattered into tiny fragments spreading widely onto the intricately patterned, brown carpet, giving the illusion of many iridescent bluebottle flies trapped in the web of a cunning and rapacious spider. The contents of the cup disappeared into the dark, deepest recesses of the fibrous snare.

'Oh. Bugger!' exclaimed Monica.

'Forget it, Monica. It was my fault, not yours. I simply wasn't watching. Anyway, what's a cup between friends?'

The pieces were extracted with great difficulty from the clinging grasp of the carpet's fibres by Sian Waite. She was not too bothered about missing a coffee as she was a tea drinker by preference. Phoebe was secretly pleased by Monica's faux pas; she would be all the more disinclined to baulk at the proposition with which she and the others were about to be presented. The sight of the myopic Sian kneeling on the carpet, in the search for the china fragments, with head down and bottom up gave rise to a certain amount of forced humour from the still mildly, uncomfortable group of plotters.

'Pity we don't have any men here with us to clear it up.', Trudie Long tittered. 'They do have their uses you know.'

'Some hopes,' Vivienne added. 'From my experience of men…they'd let us do it and simply take their opportunity to ogle our gussets as we scrambled about the floor.'

'Wouldn't you be the lucky one?' giggled Sharon.

Some raucous, unkind laughter followed this remark accompanied by knowing winks, and nudges. Although they shared the common hatred of Tom Portland, they were not averse to jealousy or criticism within the group. The image of the bespectacled, ball-on legs form of the unmarried Vivienne, revealing her gusset to ogling males was too much for them to contain their laughter.

Vivienne hated men because she had never married. No man had ever been attracted by her looks or her personality. Frumpish and old fashioned in appearance and long-winded in the extreme, she invoked such unkind comments from her female colleagues as 'the only way Viv will ever get near a man's tackle is by boring the pants off him.'

Anxious not to be diverted, and to get to the point of the meeting, Phoebe launched her proposal. In deliberate dramatic tones, with whispered implications of confidentiality, she started to instruct them in her proposed plan of action.

'Something Monica said in the staffroom a few minutes ago prompted me to invite you down here. We've got to do something about the burgeoning sexual harassment we women are being subjected to in this school. Not only us, but the girls too.'

''Alleluia, sister! And how! T' bastards 'ave 'ad their way wi' us fer just abaht long enuf. I'm pig sick t'back teeth o'er men lordin'it o'er us. 'Ow many times 'ave wi 'ad t' put up wi' sexual innuendo and unwarranted pawin' by men like Tom Portland. I'm sorry, Phoebe, since he's yer colleague an' all that, but he's the wust on 'em – and I can produce several gels who'll tell yer they're sick on 'im touchin' 'em too.'

A beatific smile beamed from Phoebe's jubilant face. She sat on the edge of her seat leaning forward so that the faces of the attentive, trembling posse were in near contact. The red gash of scarlet opened and she exhaled a long sigh of stale coffee-breath in their faces, saying,

'No need for apologies, Monica, I know you're right. Sod professional niceties! If he's the prime offender, then so be it. A little bait will catch this big fish. If we can snare him then the rest will be caught in our net. We'll ensure the emasculation of the contents of their codpieces for good.'

Squirming on their seats like a knot of frenetic frogs with butterflies in their bellies, a thrill of excitement rippled through this alliance of animated women; a quickening of the pulse and a sudden surge of sweat in their armpits made them eager for the chase to begin. Each was aware of heightened sensations of the sort allegedly experienced by each hunter, shooter or fisher pursuing a quarry.

Phoebe was rejoicing in the enthusiasm being displayed by her acolytes. She saw them hanging on her every word. She had them entirely on her side. Like ripe pears, they were ready for the plucking. Her facial muscles started to twitch, involuntarily and uncontrollably. Her neck and throat started to glow and she began to itch all over as sweat trickled over her flesh, making her shift, repeatedly, her seating position. She was positively orgasmic.

'Now, I have here our Union's guidelines on sexual harassment.'

Standing erect, with imperious, dramatic formality, she pushed a copy of the document into the hands of each of her supporters, a look of victory on her face as she handed out each one. She embarked on her oft-times rehearsed monologue, barking out her instruction,

'I'd like us to consider the definition of sexual harassment and the form such incidents take.'

Each obedient member of the cabal studied the document with intense concentration. Knowing looks and nods of agreement passed between them as they read and reread the official guidelines.

'Now, I needn't emphasise to you, but I must and I will, the extreme delicacy of what we're about. If we are to cancel out the general masculine tendency towards sexual harassment, then we're going to have to nominate a particular offender. And we're all agreed, aren't we, that Tom Portland's fall would create the greatest effect for us? But let me remind you, he's as slippery as an eel. He's a smarmy bugger too. There'll be a lot of support for him. What we have to do is to ensure that he's assailed by so many watertight accusations, that he's caught like the eel in the fisherman's net.

'I propose that each one of us lures him into delivering one of his characteristically, high handed bollockings. Another will be a convenient witness to what then must become an altercation. The offended woman will then write a letter of complaint. This will be corroborated by the witness. You all know how he touches people's arms in conversation. Well, we'll easily make a sexual harassment case out of that... The witness will confirm that he had his hands all over the victim. I know the Northern area Union Rep. She's shit hot on sexual harassment. We'll get her to make an approach to the boss demanding that he conduct an enquiry into sexual harassment by Tom Portland. Then the rest of us will put the boot in with a barrage of such complaint about his intimidation, inappropriate touching, sexual innuendo and the like, together with half a dozen or so corroborative complaints. I'm pretty sure we can concoct between us some complaints from some of our naughtiest girls. He'll be dead meat as sure as eggs are eggs.

'What I want you to do tonight is to write down individually each occasion you feel that you can substantiate the allegation that he's had a go at you - his griping about the accuracy of your register, Vivienne; his constant preaching 'the Ills of Society' sermon to those of you, eh, Monica, who are divorcees and those of us with marital problems - that's you Sharon and me, insinuating that we and our ilk are personally to blame for the increasing dissolution of Western Culture or some such crap. What's your gripe Sian? I'm sure we can set you up with one if you're struggling to think of one.'

Sian had not been harassed in any way by Tom Portland. Her only gripe was her belief that he disapproved of her relationship with Alan Bairstow.

'There are two incidents which come to mind immediately. We can easily massage their details so that they fit our criteria for complaint. We can start the ball rolling with them. A year seven girl, Amanda Crawshaw, some months ago, told me that her friend, Jane Pilkington, had reported to Mr Portland that her leg had gone numb and that he had touched it. No doubt he was just checking that it had not just gone to sleep because of the way she had been sitting...goodness knows why she did not report it to me rather than to him...anyway, apparently the numbness persisted for a short while then pins and needles followed...so there was no cause for alarm...but we have a witness to the fact that he touched her leg. There was another girl. I think she was called Elizabeth Richey, in year eight. She was injured slightly in PE and couldn't walk properly, so he carried her out to a supply teacher's car. I'm sure we can make some capital out of that incident as well. These two will do for a start. Let's see what other snippets of his dealings with the girls we can manipulate to our advantage. There must be lots. We've all seen him, many times, handling girls' affairs. They do go to him rather than to me. I suppose they think he'll be more sympathetic to their minor ailments than I am.

Anyway that's his bad luck. His care for them will now be his undoing. The big headed sod thinks he's too clean to be accused of any impropriety where the pupils are concerned. But there are bound to be some adolescent girls to whom he's not the flavour of the month, who he's had cause to tell off. And you know how girls can hold a grudge against someone for years, sometimes. Just see what you can come up with.

'There are just two other important issues. Firstly, we're all women. We desperately need at least two men to join us. Otherwise, it is going to be seen as a feminist plot.'

Sian raised her hand to speak. She stood. Her manner was quietly diffident and at the same time determinedly assured. She spoke with trembling voice and absolute conviction as might a convert at a Billy Graham campaign.

'I know without a doubt that Alan Bairstow will be prepared to speak out bravely against Tom Portland. He's disgusted with him at this very moment since the boss has just told Alan that the swine has made allegations about his conduct in the management of the GCSE coursework. Portland has virtually accused Alan of allowing the pupils to rewrite their corrected work so that they can get a better mark. Slater has called in the Maths inspector about it.'

Sian spoke with such disdain about Tom and with such palpable admiration for Alan that the women were left in no doubt whatsoever as to her emotional entanglement with the Head of Maths. Phoebe latched on to this suspected liaison with the smile of a salacious Cheshire cat which slowly disappeared, unnoticed by the rest. This young, attractive science teacher might prove to be a valuable pawn in her game.

'Good,' the Deputy responded. 'I'm pretty positive also that Alan will have a word or two to say about Portland's perpetual preaching about the prurience of today's society and his fondness for sexual innuendo.'

'And I know of one guy at least who will second that, Phoebe. I'll make damn sure he writes it all down with incidents and dates to back it up,' Trudie added with a smug grin.

'Great stuff,' Phoebe rejoiced. 'Assure Peter that his help in this matter will go down very well with the boss. I've a little more work to do on him yet. I know he'll be a bit reluctant to take on such a massive undertaking as our proposal will necessitate. He really hasn't got the balls for it. But I'll push him hard. He's a bit under the weather just now so I'm quite confident he'll be glad to agree with me just to get me off his back. He has such contempt and suspicion for Portland that he'll be pleased to go ahead with an investigation and the Disciplinary Procedure which will follow for sure.'

The fact that Bairstow and Smalley would be on board was a great relief. Phoebe could count on Sian and Trudie to make the necessary effort to get the men's complaints made in writing in accordance with Phoebe's requirements. It would save her a job and they would be more willing when the demand came from their own women rather that from the female Deputy Head. So far, her plotting against Tom was proceeding nicely, at least in theory.

'Finally, ladies... the jewel in our crown is the new Chair of Governors – Jacqui Erne. She detests Tom Portland. I have spoken to her frequently about him. She knows all about my suspicions. She, too, finds him arrogant and patronising and she'll be delighted by our action and will be a staunch support for us. She's a dedicated feminist, a divorcee who's furious about Tom's bigoted social outlook and of course she's a prominent churchgoer... at the same one that your uncle attends, Sian.'

Phoebe caught Sian's eye and nodded with enthusiasm.

'Jacqui Erne absolutely resents Tom's unashamed atheism.'

At the vague reference to her Uncle Bertie, Sian, feeling awkward, gave a small embarrassed smile in acknowledgement. She did not want it known by every Tom, Dick and Harry that she had an influential relative in County Hall.

'Right girls, does anyone want more coffee? Don't forget, you all have some homework tonight. For Christ's sake, do a good job. Let's stitch him up good and proper. But, not a word to anyone. Remember, we risk some backlash for malicious complaint so we have to make it stick. If we do our job right, there's no danger of that. So, mum's the word.'

Phoebe felt elated as the women, buoyant in their chattering about the moral crusade upon which they were about to embark, trooped out of her office. But, she was no fool. She did not dare to believe that Tom could be undone so easily. She had not to be tempted to assume that their methods were going to be infallible. It required constant concentration and attention to detail if they were going to achieve success in their venture.

She was glad that the meeting had finished with the desired outcome. There had always been the chance that these complainants might have had cold feet and would be unwilling to put their heads above the parapet in the fear of damaging both their reputations and their careers. She was, now, looking forward to a secret meeting with her lover, Alec. She picked up her telephone receiver to give him a quick call, as Sharon Crabtree dodged back into her room, leaving the others still in an animated, volubly loud, conversation in the corridor.

The battery of excited women, totally engrossed in and eager to chat about their impending campaign, were unaware that the cacophony of their shrill voices had caught the attention of Irma de la Haye, who in all innocence was at that minute approaching from an adjoining corridor. She was instantly suspicious that something untoward was afoot and she slowed her step to a standstill while she eavesdropped on their cacophonous hubbub and heard the loud announcement in the thick accent of Monica Dickinson.

'Don't concern yersels t' much wi't' truth, girls. Just let's mek sure we nail that bastard Tommy bloody Portland. T' circumstances yer write up will 'a' bin either witnessed by somebody sympathetic t' ower cause or not witnessed at all, certainly not by anybody sympathetic t' 'im.'

Phoebe, meanwhile, engaged with the loquacious Sharon, was unaware of the enemy - a Portland supporter –overhearing vital information concerning the nature of their attack.

'Excuse me, Phoebe', Sharon interrupted as the Deputy was about to dial her paramour's office number. May I talk to you about the anxieties I acknowledged in the staffroom? It's about Joe, you see.'

'Certainly, Sharon, by all means come in and tell me what exactly your problem is and I'll be glad to listen and to advise you in any way I can.'

As she ushered Sharon Crabtree into a chair, and offered her more coffee, a lascivious smile crept over her fleshy, rubbery scarlet lips and her eyes glinted with the prospect of some tantalising glimpses into the private sexual problems of Sharon Crabtree and her fiancé, Joe.

'Just drink your coffee while I phone my bloke and tell him I'll be late.'

'Oh, I wouldn't wish…

'Hush, Sharon, dear, it's alright. It'll make me all the hornier if I have to wait a bit, and that's how he'll want me this evening! Now about this fella of yours…'

The gaggle of chattering women agreed to go into a huddle at Monica's flat the following evening. 'We'll strike while the iron's hot, girls, whilst it's all fresh in our minds what we have to say to satisfy Phoebe's brief.'

'Shall I bring a bottle and have a good time while we do the dirty. It might loosen our tongues a bit more about the nasty remarks he's made to us,' Vivienne suggested.

'I'll bring one too,' said Sharon.

'...and so will I. Three bottles should be enough,' added Trudie.

'OK, I'll bring crisps and nuts, said Sian Waite, not wishing to impose on the others' generosity.

Sian Waite did not leave the building immediately. She walked to her teaching laboratory in the Science wing, passing through the Maths suite on her route. She hoped that she might see Alan Bairstow. She was anxious to tell him all about the meeting she had just left. But she was out of luck. He had already left.

As she drove home in her old, dark red Renault 5, she thought about what she could write about Tom Portland. He had never really done anything to offend her. It was just that she felt that he was critical - of her friendship with Alan, her clothes and her relationship to Uncle Bertie.

Vivienne Lowther, a teacher of Home economics, thirty-five years old and unmarried, caught the service bus home. She lived in a one-bed flat in a block in the centre of the town. The urine-infused lift was out of order and so she had to trudge up the two flights of concrete steps to the open balcony from which she accessed her front door. She entered her dark living space, cheerless even on the sunniest of days. She switched on the light and the TV at the same time. From the tiny freezing compartment in her fridge, she took a frozen, ready-to-eat dinner which she proceeded to 'cook' in her microwave oven. With her plate of food in one hand and a fork in the other, she sat down at the table in front of the north facing window, where only her purple Phalaenopsis orchid prospered, and began to eat her meal for one in the solitary confinement of her tiny flat. The spiky, yellow-haired Bart Simpson raced about and shouted from the TV screen as she considered her grievances against Ted Portland.

She wrote down the heading, 'Grievances against Tom Portland' and underlined it. Chewing the end of her pencil, she put in order, mentally, her complaints starting with the most serious.

    1. He grumbles about my messy register.
    2. He caught me eating sardines from the tin and told me to set a better example to the girls.

She had to admit that these were not exactly offences worthy of attempting to deprive a man of his career. Vivienne was hopping onto a moving bandwagon in order to gain a little notoriety in her otherwise drab existence.

Trudie Long popped into the staffroom where she hoped to find Peter Smalley. He was not there. She started walking, some paces behind Sian Waite, along the Maths corridor to the Science wing, where she found Peter busily preparing for the next day's work.

'How much longer, Pete?'

'Nearly there – couple of minutes; that's all.'

'OK. I'll wait outside.'

She could not escape from the laboratory fast enough. The stench of the Kipp's apparatus, even though it was enclosed in the fume cupboard, always made her feel ill. She had dropped Chemistry at the earliest opportunity in favour of Modern Languages.

Trudie, petite, pretty with dark brown curly hair, had been an able student, the eldest of three children, borne to parents who themselves were professional educationalists. In her first year at University in Leicester she had become totally engrossed in student life to such an extent that she failed her examinations and so had to repeat the year. During her second year, when she should have knuckled down to serious study, she had a brief, intimate relationship with a fellow student whom her parents would have described as 'undesirable'. She became pregnant. To be saddled with an unwanted child, especially having already lost a year through a wild social life was the last thing she wanted and so at the earliest opportunity she sought an abortion. She was finally successful in gaining the necessary qualifications to become a teacher, but her experiences had left their mark and she seemed unable to forge a lasting commitment to a man.

While she waited, she considered how she might proceed with her conversation about the proposed assassination of Tom Portland's character. She had to acknowledge that Tom Portland had done nothing to sexually harass either of them. He just had a different point of view. He was lucky to have had a good relationship with his wife whereas she and Peter had not been so fortunate and were, in effect, still searching for the perfect match. She just wished that Tom had not made his disapproval of them so blindingly obvious. She knew that she had to tread carefully because Peter was a devout Christian and needed to be seen to be squeaky clean even though he had left two failed marriages and three children in his wake.

CHAPTER SIXTEEN

Wednesday, 3 June, 1992.

Monica Dickinson lived in Southwich town centre in a small, untidy flat which she had purchased with the proceeds of her divorce settlement from Bernard Dickinson. Before the breakup of her marriage, she and her husband had lived in a new house on the outskirts- where town met country. They had known each other since their school days. After leaving school, she had gone to teacher training college while Bernard had become apprenticed to a local decorator. She was a clever woman who never forgot her roots. So loyal was she that she deliberately spoke with a broad rough accent which frequently offended her colleagues. She was proud of her striking physical attributes, but she was not proud of her house. Flamboyant in the extreme in her dress, she was slovenly in her habits both personal and domestic. Ultimately, Bernard, who by then had set up his own small painting and decorating business and who was well respected in the area, could not tolerate the extreme aspects of her personality, found a replacement partner to share his bed.

Monica did not take kindly to being thrown over for a younger, less attractive woman. She took her revenge in a number of ways. She attacked with a screwdriver his newly acquired, top of the range, Toyota saloon, which was parked on the street outside the house. All tyres were punctured and deep scratches were gouged in the silver metallic body work. She sabotaged his stock of paints, by mixing the colours on the bonnet of his car and tipping the rest of the gloss over his shirts and suits. Stories detailing her revenge, some of which were further embroidered, spread rapidly through the local community. Monica was a woman to be avoided at all costs. Any man who took her on did so at his own peril and was generally regarded as a fool. She was left alone...becoming bitter and twisted and a hater of all men, with the exception of Ted Slater – the man who had ignored her rough accent and had given her a job. She was an ideal second-in-command of Phoebe's squad.

They met at half past seven. Monica ushered them into a tiny sitting room. She had made no attempt to prepare for their arrival other than to provide a selection of glasses - a mixture of cheap tumblers and wine glasses which she had obtained from petrol stations in exchange for vouchers. At least they were clean and free from chips. All conspirators arrived; the first few found a seat on the sofa or a chair. The rest had to be content to sit on the floor, so tiny was the space.

'Do you think we should have asked Phoebe to join in,' asked Vivienne Lowther.

'No way,' said Sharon. 'Anyway, she's seeing her solicitor bit-on-the-side. She told me after our meeting this aft.'

'I don't think it would have been a good idea even if she had been available to come,' Monica added. 'There's no way I want to socialise with her. Actually, I can't stand the woman. I've no time for her. She's useless in dealing with the girls. They wouldn't go to her in a month of Sundays for advice. She does little or no teaching...she always has some excuse why she can't take her class. She's earning money for old rope. God help us if she gets into a position of real power...which she might...if Tom gets the elbow and the Head keeps going off sick. I bet she'll have forgotten all about our connivance in this episode in her life.'

'I suggest we worry about that if and when the time comes. Meanwhile, let's have a toast to our success in ridding Tom bloody Portland from our lives', suggested Trudie.

They spent the following couple of hours, nibbling, quaffing, making ribald comments and jotting down their evidence against the Deputy Head. Monica suggested that each describes to the rest what her particular objections were.

'Me first,' said Monica. 'Ever since I came to the school, he has stared at my breasts. He can't speak to me without putting his hand on my arm. He's always going on about people, like me, in difficult marital situations being the cause of the decline in society. Pupils have complained to me that he's always talking about sex in his English lessons. I'll have to stop; I could go on about him all night.'

'Ditto, largely, but not the bit about the breasts,' said Trudie.

The others sniggered. Monica's breasts had been the subject for discussion on many an occasion in her absence. She was proud of her firm, ample bosom, wearing the kind of fine-knit jumper to display it to best effect She was a firm believer of – 'if you've got it, flaunt it' – but woe betide anyone who stared at her.

If Tom had been guilty of that offence then he was not the first and neither would he be the last. The staffroom gossip was that her husband had replaced her with a less ostentatious model. Trudie added,

'He's got it in for me and Pete. It's none of his business how many blokes on the staff I've shagged before setting up home with Pete. But you can tell what he's thinking...the way he stares at you....'

'He's always telling me off about my untidy register with all the crossings out...says the office must spend hours trying to decide whether a kid is present or absent,' interrupted Vivienne. He caught me on one occasion at lunch time in my kitchen. I was setting up the materials for the afternoon's lesson with some girls from Year Ten. I was eating my lunch...sardines out of the tin with a fork...says I should put my sardines on to a plate...says I should show a better example to the girls. I don't think they were taking any notice of me eating my lunch. They were too busy with their heads together, laughing and joking as girls of that age do.' The rest looked at each other, eyebrows raised, while she was talking and stifled their laughter at the mental pictures they had of the rotund, rosy-cheeked, bespectacled spinster munching her way through a tin of sardines during the lunch break, with girls laughing at her behind her back.

Sian Waite waited for silence then spoke,

'I don't like the way he looks at me as if I'm in the wrong. He was not in favour of appointing me and believes that it's only through Uncle Bertie's influence that I'm here at all. He always looks askance at me and Alan. He should realise I'm a grown woman and can please myself who I associate with. Alan's offended about his interference in the Maths GCSE course work. Portland claims the children re-wrote their corrected work before handing it in. He says the evidence of malpractice by Alan and his staff was ignored by the Maths adviser'

Sharon Crabtree piped up,

'It's the way he looks at you, as if he's blaming you for the way you live. He's never really done anything to me I can put my finger on. It's just an impression I've got.'

'Ok girls. Let's wind this up. We've all had the chance tonight to get things clear in our minds. Let's just get it all down in writing, now, and nail the bastard. Just make sure that you give a copy to each one of us so that we can corroborate each other's testimonies if asked.'

Monica was anxious for them to leave. She'd heard enough of their prattling. It was time for them all to get on with it.

CHAPTER SEVENTEEN

Wednesday, 3 June, 1992.

Hardly had he settled into his office after administering the first examination of the day when there was an urgent knocking at Tom's door. It was the Head of the English Department, Irma de la Haye.

There were various words to describe Irma – Bohemian, hippie, unconventional, free spirit - the list seemed endless. She was a tall, gaunt woman of about forty years of age, casually dressed with ankle-length flowing skirt, African seed necklace, unkempt hair, Jesus sandals on her un-stockinged feet, and her face bare of any makeup. Irma was not the archetypical head of a major department. She was the most, erudite and best qualified individual, having taken a first from Cambridge in English followed by a distinguished result in the Graduate Certificate in Education. Plain speaking with a southern counties drawl, she had a sharp mind. Ted Slater was frightened of her. She was too clever for him. She could argue him under the table. He would never have appointed her had the decision been up to him but the county policy was an inclusive one and all sorts had to have their presence on the staff.

On graduation, she had reinvented herself by changing her name by deed poll from plain Marie Halliday to the rather more exotic Irma de la Haye, believing that an interesting name was more likely to catch the attention of a prospective employer. Mild mannered for the most part and on first sight, a probable easy target for obstructive pupils, she was instructed, during one of her lessons, by a future delinquent to 'Fuck off'. Her calm response to him had been 'Fuck off yourself'. She had gone, in tears, to Tom to report her inadmissible behaviour towards one of her pupils. However, he had laughed out loud at the image which she had created in his mind's eye, and had been comforting - banishing her fears. He reassured her that the matter would go no further and that the particular boy would not cross her again, so astonished would he have been by her response to his insolence. Irma was firmly in Tom's camp. She was his greatest ally, aware of the staffroom chatter from the clique of misandrous women, she was determined that she would keep him informed of any relevant intelligence.

'Have you got some time, Tom? I need to talk'

Irma revealed, in as much detail as she could, the conversation that she had overheard on the previous afternoon in the corridor adjoining Phoebe's office. She named the enemy - in total - six women. There were a couple of men too but they had not been identified by name by the babbling women- just 'our blokes'.

Tom listened intently. He had had no idea that there was such a feeling of hatred amongst the staff against him. His whole being had been totally consumed by the Slater problem. He raised his hand to scratch his head and his face became contorted into a frown. He was lost for words but he did manage to thank Irma for her information and for looking after his interests in the staffroom. At least, he had been forewarned of any malicious gossip or action on their part. He would be more observant in future during any situations in which he might find himself when in contact with any of them. However, he was rather blasé about the matter as he contended that any allegation they might make about him would be dismissed because he was a caring, sympathetic teacher whose sole interest was in the wellbeing and success of the pupils in the school. On what grounds could anyone criticise him?

Irma left him to contemplate an uncertain future as he gathered his teaching materials together for a Year Ten bottom-set English lesson. He would have no further time to worry about his own affairs for the forthcoming eighty minutes. The pupils would demand his total attention for the duration of the lesson.

At lunch time, he went, as usual, into the school canteen. He was determined to exhibit his normal pattern of behaviour to anyone who might be watching him. Afterwards, he walked down to Jennifer Bird's office where the aroma of freshly ground coffee assailed his olfactory organ. He entered the office.

'Any chance of a brew?' he asked.

'Any time for you', Jennifer replied with a beaming smile. I've just made one for his Lordship. She jerked her head towards Slater's door. Just a sec. I'll be back in two ticks.'

'How are things with you, Tom', Jennifer quizzed him. She too had been aware of certain female heads being close together and a cessation in their conversation whenever anyone approached them.'

'Comme ci, comme ca,' he replied.

'What's new re Ted,' he asked. 'He's not looking too well these days...been off sick once or twice.'

'Once or twice?' she exploded. 'Here for two days then off for three! He's got a bobby's job, sat in that office all day or out for lunch in a fancy restaurant, no doubt... at someone's expense, knowing that you are here to see that things tick over peacefully. However, you're quite right, he does look a bit peaky and his hair's getting quite thin. That's upsetting him the most. He's drinking more on the job as well...always nipping out to his car for something...that something being a bottle of vodka, I'm sure of it.'

Just as Tom was about to leave, the telephone rang. It was Jill Field, ringing from the staffroom, hoping to find out the whereabouts of Tom.

'You're in luck, he's right here.' Jennifer handed the phone to Tom.

'Hello, Jill. How can I help you?'

'I'm just letting you know that Monica has gone home with a bad migraine. She's got classes all afternoon.'

'OK. Thanks. I'll see to it.'

Back in his office, Tom considered which available staff could take Monica's classes that afternoon. As luck would have it, most of the likely relief teachers were Monica's buddies. Perhaps that was a good omen, he thought. Sian Waite was free all afternoon. Vivienne Lowther and Sharon Crabtree were free for two periods, but he had called on them both the day before. Anne Jones, similarly, was free for two periods. That clinched it. He would ask Sian and Anne to fill in for their colleague.

As time was of the essence, he moved off quickly in the direction of the staffroom to break the bad news of the sudden need for lessons to be covered. The staffroom was almost deserted as several staff had already gone to their room to be ready to receive their form for afternoon registration. This was a duty which neither Sian nor Trudie had and so they had an extra five minutes or so to chat in the staffroom. Anne Jones was studying the notices. He approached her first with his request. Always affable, she was quite happy to agree to his appeal. She would be able to use the time to get some marking done. She gathered her belongings together and had soon disappeared out of the door. Sian Waite was sitting at one of the tables, where she had laid out her work for the afternoon. She had her back to Tom who approached her and touched her shoulder. She turned her head slowly to greet whomever it was trying to get her attention, but when she saw that it was Tom, she jerked her body away from his touch, snapping back in a voice loud enough for all to hear.

'Will you kindly take your hands off me? What do you want? Can't you see that I'm busy?'

His call for her agreement to cover for Monica fell on deaf ears.

'Why me? Why can't you ask someone who's not as busy as I am? You're always giving me classes to cover. I've had enough of it. Cover the class yourself.'

Trudie was in the far corner chatting to her partner, Peter Smalley. They stopped their conversation to watch the altercation unfold on the other side of the room. Tom put his arm out in an attempt to calm her. He touched her forearm. She shrugged him off. She was the very opposite of calm, becoming more annoyed and pronouncing quite categorically,

'Please yourself who does the cover. It's not going to be me.'

Without waiting for any response from Tom, she collected her books together and stalked off towards the door. Tom, in an effort to discuss the matter rationally with her, put his hand on the door handle. Sian saw this as an intention to prevent her escape. She flew into a rage and screamed at him,

'Get out of my way, you wanker and don't you ever lay your hand on me again!'

Trudie's face broke out into a broad grin which she hid behind her hand. The destruction of Tom Portland had begun. She nudged Peter and said,

'Hey, Pete, did you see what happened then? Portland touched her arm again after she'd told him to take his hands off her.'

Peter Smalley was not *au fait* with the conniving in which his partner was a prime mover. He agreed that he had witnessed the incident. That was what she wanted. She would now go and write it down, date and sign the statement and so start the dossier on Tom.

Tom, taken completely by surprise by this turn of events because never before had Sian reacted to him like this, could do nothing but watch her back view as it disappeared out of the door. He decided that it was too late to find another replacement. He had better do the cover himself.

Later that evening, over dinner, Maudie enquired about his day.

'Just the same as usual. What about you?'

'OK, thanks. It's been a good day,' she said.

Then she addressed Jack,

'How's the Latin revision going?'

'Well, thanks.'

Tom had no intention to comment on the day's events in front of their sons, Jack especially. He would do nothing to upset Jack's equanimity while he was preparing for his next examination.

CHAPTER EIGHTEEN

Wednesday, 10 June, 1992.

Phoebe Spong arrived in her office feeling frustrated. Frantic to meet with Ted Slater and to move forward her intended destruction of Tom Portland from the planning to the delivery stage, she felt as if she were walking on a mass of sticky tarmacadam, unable to make any progress. Ted Slater seemed to be hardly ever on the school premises. He had not made an appearance since the previous Thursday. The burden of his work naturally fell to her and Tom. Not that she was overworked by his absence. Tom was so efficient that he could carry both jobs. She was amazed that a Headteacher like Ted could earn such a fat salary for apparently doing so little.

    Her cabal of conniving men-haters had done their work well. They had watched Tom at every opportunity, observing his body language when talking to both men and women on the staff, listening to the words he uttered, noting his attitude to pupils and whether he laid hands on them. Selected pupils had been interviewed and persuaded to make statements which were not strictly truthful. Pupils had been manipulated - they had been asked the questions which would give their inquisitor the answers they were seeking. Between them, a complete dossier had been compiled. Having read, reread and thoroughly digested the contents, Phoebe knew that there was much massaged information. There would have to be some severe editing of any report since much of the dossier was not damning in the slightest. The fact was, for the most part, that he behaved to others much as others behaved towards each other. The group of complainants, if the truth was told, had some personal grievance which had become so magnified that in their eyes, it was sufficient to condemn the man to an unpleasant ordeal which could destroy him completely.

She spent the first hour of the day rehearsing her forthcoming conversation with Ted Slater about the Tom Portland problem. She was unaware of the ongoing problem between Tom and the boss. The bell rang for break. Phoebe walked to the Head's office and to her surprise, he was at his desk. She noticed immediately that he was suffering from some malady. His face was too red and too gaunt. His usually immaculate silver hair was too long in an attempt to hide the fact that it was thin and wispy and it clung unpleasantly to his sweaty brow. He coughed into a tissue, a pile of which were evident in the waste basket. He reminded her of a living scarecrow.

'Have you got time for a chat?' She asked, in a perky manner as if all was well.

'Just see Jennifer. She'll find a time for you,'

Slater answered, wearily and unsmiling as he continued to study a document on his desk. This obvious signal that the conversation was over was not lost on her. She did not care. It gave her a bit more breathing space to get her spiel absolutely word perfect.

Jennifer found a convenient slot after lunch but added with pursed lips,

'That's if he hasn't gone off sick again. He's coughing and wheezing as if he's got an attack of asthma.'

Phoebe turned on her heel and disappeared out of view.

'At last,' she said to herself. 'The show's about to go on the road. Look out, Tom Portland. We're coming after you.'

She strutted along, smiling at pupils who in the past had only seen her frowning or glowering at them for some minor misdemeanour. As she caught sight of her fellow conspirators, she gave the thumbs –up sign to them, in a casual manner so that she did not draw attention to herself. She did not set eyes on their quarry.

Lunch time came and went and she became impatient for her appointment with Ted Slater. She reported at the allotted time to Jennifer Bird who told her that she had better make it a quick chat with him as she thought that he would be heading home as soon as he could. Phoebe was more than satisfied with that piece of information. This would mean that he would be more likely to listen to her without interrupting and he would agree to her demands without much hesitation just so that he could end their meeting quickly.

The phone rang three times.

'Dr Slater will see you now. Please would you oblige me by taking his coffee?'

Jennifer held out the mug of steaming coffee to Phoebe. She took it and marched into the Head's office. She was correct in her assumptions, making her prepared speech. Ted Slater listened. He was well enough to realise that this was a means of ridding himself of the turbulent Tom. He thought,

'Supposing she pulls it off and Tom gets the push. Then what? If my health continues in this downward spiral...and I take even more sick leave...then she'll inherit this place and I know that she's not up to the job, but I don't have the energy to be bothered. Let her get on with it, the vile cow and good luck to her!'

'I would like to invoke the official grievance procedure against Tom Portland on a number of counts of his sexual harassment of female staff and pupils. All the relevant facts are here, in writing, in this dossier. Are you in agreement?'

She fingered her Ichthus pendant as a reminder that they were both on the same side. She pushed the dossier across the desk towards him. He picked it up, glanced at it as if it were a periodical in the doctor's waiting room. He pushed it across the desk back to her, saying in a weary, uninterested voice,

'Just get on with it.'

'YES, SIR. Thank you. I will do just that.'

She was off down the corridor, heart thumping in her chest, pulse racing, perspiration beginning to bubble up on her forehead and a broad leer on her scarlet gash of a mouth. In her office, she threw off her jacket, poured a large Scotch, sat back in her chair and raised the glass in a toast.

'Phase two now starting. Here's to you, Tom Portland! GOTTCHA!'

CHAPTER NINETEEN

Monday, 29 June, 1992.

Ted Slater, sticky with sweat, feeling cold, woke up. It had been another humid night. He sat on the edge of the bed in which Ayna, his wife, was still sleeping. He clasped his aching belly. He glanced at the clock. At least it had turned six o'clock. For several days, he had wakened earlier, always with the same chronic pain in his gut. He stood and stumbled his way, flat footed, to the bathroom, using whatever came to hand to steady himself. He approached the lavatory, still holding his abdomen. No sooner had he dropped his pyjama bottoms and sat down on the cold, white, plastic seat, than he it felt as if the entire contents of his abdomen had gushed down the pan. And he still had the pain.

Now at the age of fifty eight years, Ted Slater looked ten years older. The strong, athletic body of only a few weeks before was becoming pale, thin and gaunt. The perspiration, which had started to form in droplets on his forehead, formed tiny trickles of salty fluid which were finding their way along the meandering lines which were now much in evidence on his sunken cheeks. The much prized silver locks, now in need of a trim, were plastered with sweat onto his cranium. He was a shadow of his former self. His eyes rolled upwards towards the heavens. He closed them and he screamed, silently,

'Oh, God, when are you going to relieve me of this torment?'

He sat, for a few minutes longer, his pyjamas in a heap around his ankles. The pain had subsided a little. His urgent request to the Master appeared to have resulted in the easing of his suffering. He crept back to his bed and found it cold and damp where he had been lying, and sweating. Ayna continued to sleep, snoring quietly.

There was little he could do other than to go downstairs and make some tea. He hoped that a hot drink might aid his recovery. He would take Ayna a cup of tea at a more reasonable time, in the expectation that it might improve her attitude towards him. She continually found fault with him of late and he failed to understand the reason for it.

Ayna, his wife of thirty-five years, had maintained the slim body of her youth. Her hair, still dark, with few grey hairs, cut short with a straight fringe giving the correct impression of a strict, severe personality, framed her small, bird-like face with its short, pointed, beaklike nose. In her waking hours, she habitually held her head in such a manner that she could look down her nose at any and all of her interlocutors in a supercilious, dismissive, offhand way and would speak to them as she would address her pupils. She had worked on and off all of their married life and was now employed as a permanent part-time teacher of six year-olds in the local primary school which was within walking distance of their home. She was constantly aggrieved that she did not have the convenience of a car as befitted someone as important as she regarded herself in the community. It was a continual bone of contention between her and Ted.

The image of his wife encouraged his comparison of her with the other woman in his life – Jennifer Bird. What opposites they were in every respect of their appearances and personalities. The only trait they had in common was their gender. It had been obvious all those years ago that Jennifer had loved him, almost worshipping the ground he walked on. He had been flattered and had encouraged her attentions. After all, she had been on the spot – available at short notice – always ready and willing and able to agree to his every whim. He had enjoyed that attention. But he had always known that she had been there for his convenience. He realised what a cad he had been in his youth, taking advantage of a lovesick young woman, when all the time he had no real feelings for her. Finally, at the culmination of their student days, he had rejected her in favour of Ayna whom he had subsequently married and who had borne him a son and a daughter and who had treated him with distain all through their married life. Ayna who grumbled and groaned at his every move squawked out her criticisms in the condescending way with words that she had. She had never revered him as Jennifer had done.

'Why, in God's name did I choose her?' he asked himself.

He knew that it was too late to alter the course of history. He had made his bed. Jennifer was happily married to Harold. He just had to get on with his life, unhappy as he was. It was hard. He could do nothing right for Ayna. Never a practical man about the home, the smallest repair or replacement seemed to be beyond his capabilities, giving Ayna the opportunity to scowl and to be critical. Jennifer, on the other hand, was pleasant. Jolly and always smiling at him, even in his bad temper, she was ready to pacify and calm him with a hot drink and words of encouragement in his increasing depression.

He sat drinking his tea as he watched the sparrows fluttering around the bird feeder and the starlings making their jerky movements on the ground. There was no other sound. The trees were still. There was no breath of air. He laughed at their frantic antics. He was envious of their energy and apparent wellbeing – always full of life, constantly searching for their next morsel of food; they were never off colour. Grateful that he was feeling somewhat improved in both body and spirit, he decided that it was time he returned to his post as Headteacher. He had an important task to perform that morning. He anticipated a difficult meeting with his Deputy, Tom Portland.

The pattern of his recent attendance had been three days of work followed by two days off sick. How long was his malady going to last he wondered. The unsympathetic Ayna suggested quite sensibly,

'Go and see the Doctor. That's what he's for. Don't moan about your pain if you're not prepared to do anything about it. I get fed up of you constantly moaning. For goodness sake, do something about it!'

He knew well enough that she was correct, but he hated the business of attending the surgery – waiting for the officious receptionist to finish her phone call or to look up from her paperwork to give him a bit of attention, The waiting room appalled him, with its rag, tag and bobtail collection of folk from all walks of life and levels of society with a multifarious range of symptoms, all in brooding silence, waiting for the call. And, then, finally, the intolerable position of having the doctor - a so called expert – a mere mortal like himself – make a decision about his medical condition. No, he would avoid the visit to the GP until he could stand it no longer. He trusted in the Almighty to get him through his current ordeal.

He absentmindedly brewed the tea, his mind drifting to and fro between the infights of Tom and Phoebe, the ongoing battles of himself and Tom and the relationship between Ayna, himself and Jennifer. He poured the tea and put a spoonful of sugar in each cup, stirring slowly as he continued to watch three fledgling jackdaws on the bird feeder and to think about the other Bird in his daily life. He presented the cup of sweetened tea to his wife, wake and alert. She took a mouthful and spat it back out declaring,

'This tea has sugar. You know I never take sugar in my tea. What's the matter with you, Ted? For goodness sake, get a grip!'

He mumbled something about his mind having been elsewhere when he made the drinks. She flounced out of bed and poured the rest of her drink down the sink in the bathroom uttering not another word and totally ignoring his presence in the bedroom.

Alternating between sighs and silence, Ted went through the routine of washing and dressing. He went without breakfast. He would get Jennifer to make him some coffee later. He unlocked his car, a silver grey, top-of-the-range BMW, which was parked ostentatiously on the drive. His face contorted with pain, he entered his own, totally masculine, space and set off on his journey to Southwich High School where he believed that the turmoil at work was less onerous than that at home.

CHAPTER TWENTY

Monday, 29 June, 1992.

Maudie Portland had been up since six o'clock. It was so hot, sticky and silent with no breeze, like the calm before the storm. She never slept well in the summertime, usually waking as soon as the early light hit the bedroom windows. Tom and Freddie were still asleep. She was amazed how Tom could sleep so soundly, considering all the problem pupils and awkward staff (as well as Ted Slater) with whom he had to cope on a daily basis. He deserved his extra half hour in bed.

Jack Portland, unlike most other youths of his age, was also an early bird, especially on that day as it was the last of his A-level papers. He had a good feeling about the exams he had already taken. His father, a well-respected teacher of English, had been a great support to his understanding of the English Literature course and similarly, his mother had helped with the Latin. For the final A-level examination paper – Psychology -he was batting alone. He was not unduly worried. He had been a diligent pupil from the onset of Year Ten – the commencement of the O-level work. His parents could not have asked more of him. His only form of relaxation of late had been membership of the Judo Club at the local Sports Centre and the occasional game of table tennis where he had a struggle to beat his father who still maintained a high standard in the game. Strongly built like his father, he was tall with broad shoulders. He had taken readily to judo and had recently attained the rank of brown belt. His rate of progress had levelled off somewhat during the two years of his A-level work, but as soon as he became established at Warwick, he intended to pursue the sport seriously to achieve the highest ranking of which he was capable. Popular with his peers, with good looks and an attractive personality, he did not have a steady girlfriend any longer. His former relationship had ended because of his single-minded attitude to his studies – his target being a set of A-grades to ensure his first choice of university.

Over the previous few days, whilst taking a break from revision, he had been gathering together the items he would need for a brief holiday he was taking with his school friend, Duncan Rae. Always pragmatic and meticulous, he had a list. He checked each item into his backpack, ticking his list as he did so. They were not taking a tent on this occasion and so travelling would be light. Duncan's father, Fraser, a Scot from Fort William, had some business in Carlisle for a few days. Their plan was simple - travel in style, with Fraser Rae, to Carlisle - hitch a lift northwards to Fort William, where they would stay with Duncan's grandparents overnight - travelling by bus and Shanks's pony, they would head for Glencoe for some walking and sight-seeing– return to Carlisle via Fort William – back to Southwich with Fraser Rae. This was going to be their form of relaxation after their weeks of preparation for 'A' level examinations. All necessities were packed and ready to be picked up later. After dinner, he would spend the night at Duncan's home, ready for an early start the next day.

He had showered and dressed and was in the kitchen already when his mother appeared from the garden where she had been pegging out the washing, even though the sky looked stormy. Together, mother and elder son enjoyed the first cup of coffee of the day. The aromas of toast and coffee must have drifted up to the rooms where the other two members of the family still slept, diffusing through their nostrils to stimulate the nerve cells in their brains. Soon, they were up and about and in the kitchen. Freddie was already dressed in school uniform, but with jogging bottoms and trainers ready for the pre-school kick about.

'Just remember to change into your school trousers and shoes after your game,' his mother instructed.

Tom, as always, wore a suit, believing that smart dress was vital in the workplace. The family was a close-knit unit as they ate their breakfast of fruit, muesli and toast all the while indulging in lively conversation about what lay in store for them that day. Breakfast eaten, the two older menfolk were dispatched with shouts of, 'Good luck, Jack, stay cool', sounding from the kitchen.

Tom delivered Jack to the bus station where he would board the service bus to carry him to the Grammar School in Lancaster. Freddie, in his last year at the local primary school in Southwich, had another half an hour or so before he would set off walking to school with his friend, Dan, from next door, tossing the ball between them as they strolled along towards the school field. Freddie, in his twelfth year, was physically still immature. Of average height for his age group and with a slim, athletic body, he was designed to be an athlete of some sort. Like the majority of young boys, he loved to play football and to go with his father to watch their team play in the league whenever there was a home match. Come September, he would be moving to the school which Jack was about to leave, where rugby was the main sport for boys. He would find himself travelling by bus to Lancaster, on his own, since Jack, all being well, would be making the journey south to Warwick in order to embark on his Law degree.

Maudie was the last to leave the house. She limped slightly as she walked to Bessie, her car - an old, well-loved, blue Nissan Micra, which she had purchased from new, seven years before and in which Jack had been taught to drive by his father. She sat down in the driver's seat a look of pain on her face and took a sharp intake of breath as she said out loud,

'This damned hip, I'll have to get it fixed before I'm much older.'

She was referring to her left hip joint which was becoming increasingly painful due to an arthritic condition that she thought must run in her family. Now in her mid-forties she was rather young to be developing arthritis. She decided that she must make more of a determined effort to lose some weight which inevitably would ease the pressure on her joints. Her fair hair, worn simply in a short pony tail, showed a few silver streaks. Never having worn much make up, her skin was clear and blemish free, but crows-feet had already started to develop round her pale, hazel eyes. There was constant, good-humoured banter amongst colleagues at the library as to who would develop the first turkey neck and every day, with much laughter; each would inspect the others' throats for signs of the onset of crepiness.

On her arrival at the branch library in Southwich, her boss handed her a brown, official-looking, envelope with her name typed on the front. With a fluttery feeling in her stomach and an increased heart rate, she read and reread the contents. It was a concise letter and to the point. The shock it gave her was substantial. She learned that the branch was scheduled for closure at the end of the year. The lease on the building in which it had been housed for many years was due for renewal but the owners had decided to sell the property, along with several others, to a development company who planned to demolish everything on the site and rebuild new affordable housing, most likely blocks of apartments.

The usual daily routine of neck-checking was abandoned as Maudie and her colleagues contemplated their futures within the Library Service or not as the case might be. The most elderly would probably be offered an early retirement package but she did not fit into that category. Redundancy was another option to be considered. Throughout the day, as she carried out her library work, her agile brain was working overtime thinking of all the possible avenues that she and Tom could pursue. Perhaps, he could escape the dreadful Ted Slater once and for all by obtaining a sideways move somewhere...anywhere! She had a genuine concern for his wellbeing and contentment and was prepared to follow him to wherever he could find the post he wanted. Perhaps they could change direction altogether, and embark on a different sort of lifestyle - one in which they would avoid the petty jealousies of colleagues – the stress-induced anxieties and sleepless nights and an increasing dependence on the nightly bottle or two of wine to aid the winding down process. People made life-changing moves all the time. Only the previous week, someone from the Bridge Club had announced that he was moving to the Isle of Skye to be part of a self-supporting commune.

Over her solitary, packed lunch of home-made vegetable soup, kept hot in a Thermos flask, and an avocado and sweetcorn salad, with some sour dough bread, she reminisced about her life to date and anticipated the future. Maudie Portland née Trenoweth, an only child, was born to middle aged parents. She was brought up by her Doctor-father and practice-nurse-mother in the tiny hamlet of Rosecarn on the North Cornish coast in the area known as West Penwith. Her father, Doctor Ralph Trenoweth, now retired, had worked as a GP in nearby Penzance where her mother had also been employed as a practice nurse. Maudie had attended the local primary school in the ribbon-settlement of Pendruan, moving at eleven years of age to the Mount school for Girls. She left Cornwall behind, at the age of eighteen years, for the big city of Leeds which boasted one of the largest redbrick universities in the country. There, whilst studying for a degree in Latin, she met Tom Portland, a student of English Literature. She never returned to Cornwall except for holidays, travelling all the way home on *The Cornishman*, where, for the last twenty minutes or so of the journey, she stood at the open window of the train breathing in the delicious scent of the sea air and listening to the gulls screeching overhead. It became the place where her parents had their home, where she and Tom and later the whole family would descend at major holiday times for a family get together. Perhaps the loss of her job at the library and Tom's persistent search for a change of scene was a God-given opportunity to return to Cornwall physically because in her heart she had never left.

She thought about all the aspects of Cornwall she had relished - the cluster of low, grey, but sparkly, granite, tin miners' cottages, housing those grown men and youths who had laboured in the hot, dirty, uncomfortable, claustrophobic conditions down the local, last-remaining tin mine, now sadly closed, only a year before. The family house, as befitted a doctor, was the most opulent in the hamlet. Built of dressed granite, it had a square frontage with a central front door, on either side of which there was a sash window. Three similar, symmetrical windows occupied the upper storey. It was sort of house which every child could draw. The back of the house faced south west enabling, on a clear day, a distant view of Scilly at the point where the sea meets the sky. In the evenings, there were brilliant sunsets with fiery-red and marmalade-orange streaks melting into coral wisps permeating the massive aquamarine sky. But there were also days on end when the regular, mournful, whine of the foghorn at Pendeen Watch could be heard as the thick, sea mist hugged the coastline.

As a child, she remembered long, hot, sunny summers and mild, frost-free winters without snow, which allowed her father, an accomplished gardener, to grow an extensive variety of flowering plants and vegetables. She used to follow him around, helping him and learning from him the skills of raising plants from seeds, taking cuttings and the controlling of garden pests. He always carried his hoe and every now and then he would use it to disturb the earth and put an offending weed out of its misery. Maudie soon learned to recognise a weed from a cultivated plant.

Regular visits, with picnic baskets, were made to the deserted Pendruan beach, in those days, accessible by mountain goats and nimble footed locals only. Would she ever again pick her way down the cliff, following the stream, hampered by her dicky hip, she wondered. Her father, even in his mid-sixties, weighed down with fishing tackle had managed the walk. Tourists could never find the beach although it was plainly visible on the Ordnance Survey map. This meant that she had, on many an occasion, a beautiful, deserted beach all to herself. But nothing lasts for ever. During a storm in the early sixties, a cargo ship ran aground off the beach. All attempts to salvage the cargo were ultimately abandoned because of the inaccessibility of the site. But the damage had been done. Great, wide tracks were hewn out of the cliff top to enable heavy plant to access the beach and so this hitherto Eden suddenly was accessible to all and sundry. The magic of Pendruan beach had been lost for ever.

As a teenager, she had enjoyed simple pleasures offered by the locality – the drama group organised by the vicar's wife, culminating in the Christmas pantomime in the church hall, the procession up to the top of The Carn on Christingle Sunday, everyone carrying a lighted candle, the cromlech betwixt Madron and Morvah where she had played with her friends, the potato picking excursions on the back of a lorry to the farm at St Buryan for an evening of back- breaking labour and the monthly dance at the austere hut where the Women's Institute held their meetings. It was to one of these dances that she went with one youth and left with another. She was not proud of her behaviour that night, but at that age, a man's shoes were important, and she had not taken to her date's green, crocodile winkle-pickers. Her favourite activity had always been walking with her mother and their faithful, black Labrador, Sally. They might spend a morning collecting blackberries along No-go-by or, picking their way along the cliff paths, sitting amongst the cushions of thrift-like lollipops of pink froth, yellow bird's foot trefoil and blue sheep's-bit. They would lay back on the soft grass enjoying the warm sunshine and drinking in the spectacular coastline vista.

Naturally, there was plenty of time available for reading. She had made full use of the mobile library service operated from the main library in Penzance. She had read anything and everything and had developed an eclectic taste in her reading matter. Eventually, her love of the printed matter had led her to her present, but soon to be cut short, beloved job as assistant librarian. The memories of the delights of Cornwall now made her determined to seek out more information from the local Penzance newspapers - the *Western Morning News* and *The Cornishman* and she would scour the *Times Educational Supplement* for posts which might be of interest to Tom. Such were her fond memories of her home county that she ceased feeling depressed about the impending library closure and she relished the idea of a new direction in their lives.

CHAPTER TWENTY-ONE

Monday, 29 June, 1992.

The journey to Southwich took longer than usual. Road surfacing on the main thoroughfare, where temporary traffic lights were in operation, caused the inevitable delay. Tom thought how typical it was of the council to carry out this work in the kind of heat they were experiencing at that time. The heatwave was causing the tarmacadam on the open roads to become tacky so what hope was there for the new surface to solidify? But, philosophically, he understood that there was a schedule of work to be undertaken whatever the weather conditions. He wished, however, that it were cooler. His car had no air conditioning and there was no breeze. It was stiflingly hot as he waited for the lights to change from red to green.

Arriving later than he would have wished, he was surprised to see an envelope addressed to him on his desk. A sudden attack of nerves overcame him. The sight of this unexpected letter caused his legs to lose all their strength. He sat down quickly. Even in the high humidity of the morning, the accumulated sweat, which could not evaporate from his body due to the high humidity, felt cold. There was a feeling of nausea in his stomach, a dry, bitter taste in his mouth and an uneasy sensation in his bowels. He could feel the rapid thudding of his beating heart in his chest. He felt dizzy. These sensations were new experiences to him. Never before had he felt as he did at that moment.

He tore open the envelope to see an official note from Ted Slater demanding his presence at nine o'clock. He slumped back in his chair, in a state of shock, in the belief that this was Irma's prediction coming true. They had been out to get him and it appeared that they had succeeded. However, sensibly, not wishing to tempt fate, he washed his face in cold water in an attempt to calm his nerves then he looked at his watch. It was almost time to go to the Head's office. He was determined not display any discomposure during the events of the forthcoming half hour or so. His usual, unworried, phlegmatic persona would be obvious to Ted Slater and Tom believed this image would be the most productive.

Jennifer Bird opened the door to admit Tom to Slater's office. She patted his shoulder in support. Tom could not believe that a man's health could deteriorate so much in the matter of a few weeks. Slater was obviously unwell - haggard, gaunt, red in the face and his hair unkempt. He started to speak,

'It is my reluctant duty to inform you, Tom, that I am obliged to suspend you from duty on full salary pending investigations into allegations of sexual misconduct. I would be obliged if you would collect your belongings, speak to no-one about the matter, leave the premises and remain out of school until you are informed of the outcome of my enquiries. I must further inform you that suspension does not constitute disciplinary action. That may or may not follow, as the outcome of the investigation dictates. I would advise you to contact your

Union as soon as possible after leaving the building. I have been obliged to ask Phoebe here to attend this meeting as witness.

'With regard to the timetable for the forthcoming academic year – I understand that you have virtually completed it. I will ask Paul Sawyer to tweak it where necessary if you will be so kind as to liaise with him if appropriate.'

Tom stood in front of Slater's desk as though transfixed. The periphery of the room had merged into a halo-like image around the predominant form of the now self-consciously imperious Head. Ted Slater had delivered his speech whilst standing behind the chair at his desk, leaning slightly forward, his hands resting on the back of the chair, his face adopting the features of a highly charged turkey cock, his wattle-like jowls, flabby, blood-red and dangling from his face. Perspiration was evident on his forehead and on his upper lip. His normally immaculately coiffured hair appeared dishevelled. It was longer and thinner of late, clinging in lank clumps to his scalp. Deep furrows lined the brow of his gaunt face. He seemed to have dissociated himself from the situation and appeared unconnected with the object of the accusation standing before him. The enlarged print of Jacob Epstein's *St Michael and the Devil* hung prominently on the wall behind Slater's head. It was at such a level that the triumphant form of St Michael seemed to be almost totally eclipsed by the Head's bent figure. As Tom studied this superimposition, he was troubled by his ironic recognition that Slater appeared to be taking the role of the avenging angel whilst his own piteous predicament mirrored that of the vanquished Satan. A morsel of relief was afforded Tom when closer scrutiny of this fantasy indicated that the knuckles on the outstretched hand of St Michael behind Slater's head, took the form of horns budding up from Slater's forehead - not unlike those on the head of Epstein's Devil.

Try as he might, Slater had been unable to look Tom straight in the eye as he delivered his statement. Tom had been amazed at the fluency of its delivery; gone was the usual stumbling over vocabulary and impression of insecurity, but he sustained a cowed bodily posture. Tom continued to look at Ted Slater directly. Tom was not intimidated; he simply lacked his usual erect, commanding stance. There was not the slightest urge to avert the eyes or to lower the head; however, he felt a weakening of the knees, a hunching of the shoulders and a sensation of numbness throughout his whole body except for his stomach in which he could feel the fluttering of butterflies.

After some moments of preoccupation with the horror of his present circumstance, coupled with his fantasy of Slater as St. Michael, Tom quickly internalised his position. Slater's embarrassment, Tom imagined, arose from an instinctive awareness of his own dishonesty. Slater knew however much he disliked Tom because he was a threat to his own ascendancy in the school, that Tom was unlikely to be guilty as charged. He knew too that complicity in the lie perpetrated by the other Deputy would stain his reputation like the Judas Kiss. But to have rejected Phoebe's allegations as the monstrosities he suspected them to be, would have left him wide open to the charge of partiality. Favouritism towards Tom was not his preference. He knew only too well, as did the community, of Tom's stainless reputation.

Tom would undoubtedly extricate himself from this predicament but not without blemish. The inevitable stigma attached to the allegation, even if untrue, would be sufficient to make his easy passage to the Southwich Headship far less likely – a conclusion much to be desired.

For his part, Tom's usual clarity of thought required to navigate through these troubled waters had escaped him. The Head's statement had hit him like a thunderbolt and yet he could not deny that the likelihood of this occurrence had entered his imagination. Without a glance in the direction of Phoebe Spong, he turned abruptly towards the door. Then, like a flash of lightning, a memory from his youthful participation in Bible study inspired him to turn back. Suddenly darting forward towards Ted Slater and glaring accusingly at him, with racing pulse and guiltless aggression he spoke in commanding tones.

'Are you familiar with this quotation concerning Judas Iscariot, Headmaster?

'*Now this man purchased a field with the reward of iniquity, and falling headlong, he burst asunder in the midst, and all his bowels gushed out. ACTS 1. Verse 18.*'

What I wonder, Ted, will you purchase?'

Slater slumped into his chair, apparently exhausted, clutching his aching abdomen. The words uttered by his blameless Deputy seemed oddly ironic. He experienced a feeling of solemn wonder. How could Tom, a professed atheist be able to quote from the Bible so proficiently?

As Tom walked from the room, Ted Slater, his face racked with pain from his gut and from his action looked across at Phoebe Spong hoping for a glimmer of support. But Phoebe ignored his torture and smiled at his troubled face saying,

'Well, Headmaster, that went very well, I'm sure... I mustn't delay any longer. I have some important work to do now. If I were you, I should see a doctor – you don't look too well.'

The excessively high humidity had now subsided as the sound of thunder could be heard in the distance. Torrential rain rattled against Slater's windows as he continued to ponder on the likely consequences of his action. He reached inside the desk drawer for his trusty aid – his flask of whisky – which he drained in a couple of gulps.

CHAPTER TWENTY-TWO

Monday, 29 June, 1992.

'You were quite right , Irma', Tom confirmed disconsolately to the school's leading Union Representative and Head of English upon whom he felt he must call for solace before leaving the premises. He must necessarily pass her teaching room on the way to his office. He found her preparing her next lesson, enjoying the peace of a non-teaching period.

'Tom, do sit down. Whatever is the matter? You look as if you've seen the Devil!'

Not wishing to be self-dramatic, he declined to take the bait of her observation. Instead, he flopped down heavily into a chair. Irma was warm, maternal and comforting. She sat beside him, placed her hand on his arm in her usual avuncular manner and asked him first to compose himself and then to unburden himself.

'When you warned me that Monica and her cronies were 'after' me, I couldn't bring myself to take the warning seriously. But it has happened. I'm suspended pending investigation into alleged sexual misconduct. Slater has instructed me to leave the school premises immediately.'

'Oh, no! Tom! What a nightmare. I knew they were up to no good. I did hear the rump end of a conspiracy as I told you but I can't believe that they've succeeded to this extent.'

'Indeed they have, Irma. I'm going to need your witness in my defence.'

'You can be sure of that, Tom. They're an evil bunch. It is as I had thought. The publication by the Secondary Schoolteachers' Association of the dreaded Sexual Harassment Guidelines has inevitably thrown up the need for a scapegoat. I'm afraid you're it. It's happening, rampantly, nationwide. My own Union admittedly have been consulting about appropriate steps on sexual harassment guidelines too but we must have anticipated the danger of too precipitative a move leading to just this kind of silliness.

'Don't worry, Tom. You're OK. By far the majority of staff and all the parents revere you. The kids adore you. They'll never bring this off and you will be able to counter-charge malicious complaint. I can't believe that members of our profession and my own gender could stoop so low!'

'Yes, I know. Irma. You renew my faith in the sanity of the profession despite these rampant feminists.'

Now, Tom, don't go tarring us all with their brush. There are feminists and feminists you know!'

'Yes, I know, Irma. I'm sorry to lump you all together so. And thanks for your comforting words; they're much appreciated.'

'Keep in touch, Tom,' Irma added amiably as, with a heavy heart, he trudged from her room.

He had few items to collect from his office – the family photographs, his Renoir print and his carver armchair were the only possessions he kept at school. Every other item was school property. He was in his car ready to drive away before the bell rang for break. He turned his head to look back at the school façade before finally passing through the large green-painted, iron security gates. He saw Jennifer Bird and the other girls from the office watching him go.

Arriving home, Tom stopped his car on the drive and turned off the engine. His head flopped on to his chest. He marvelled that he had got home without having had an accident. He recalled little of his homeward journey. He drove, robot-like, unaware of the weather and road conditions even though there was a great deal of stopping and starting due to the road surfacing work which was now well under way. The rain was pouring down and the storm was getting nearer. The men, in bright yellow oilskins, continued to lay the tarmac.

He came to his senses, feeling the heat and listening to the rain beating down on the roof and windscreen of his car. He switched on the car radio for company while he waited for the rain to abate. There was no rush to get into the house. There was no-one to talk to. He might just as well sit in the car for as long as he wanted. He tuned the radio to listen to the last half hour of *The Jimmy Young Programme*. Rarely had he had the opportunity to listen to this exceedingly popular, eclectic piece of radio broadcasting, but there was strong possibility that he would get to hear it a lot in the forthcoming few weeks.

He glanced at his watch - noon - *The Jimmy Young programme* was just finishing. The rain kept coming but the violence of it had passed. He decided to brave it and dashed into the house. How strange it seemed. He had never been first to arrive home. It was only midday. He had been alone in the house at midday on many occasions but it felt very different this time. He looked in the fridge, wondering what to eat. He needed something tasty to regain his lost appetite. There was nothing he fancied. He took some bread and toasted a couple of slices, then spread each with a good helping of butter. He made a mug of tea and sat down at the table with his meagre but comforting lunch and skimmed through the post. The usual junk mail was in abundance but there was also a large white envelope addressed to Maudie. Lunch over, he settled into his favourite armchair and was soon asleep, so fatigued was he after that morning's troublesome business.

Maudie's shift at the library finished at four o'clock. She had called at the primary school to collect Freddie who had been involved in a team practice for the Summer Junior Football League. She had not realised how skilled he had become during the previous school year. The session was still in full swing when she arrived so she was able to chat with the other parents who were waiting for their sons. One of the waiting parents smiled at her recognising her as a librarian and also as the wife of the Deputy Head at Southwich High School across from which she lived.

'Saw your hubbie this morning, in all that rain, driving out of school – looked as if he was leaving town, his car seemed full of furniture', she said.

'How odd, he never mentioned anything at breakfast', she thought to herself. She replied,

'He was probably doing a good turn for someone... especially in the pouring rain... it must have been pretty urgent.'

She thought nothing more about the conversation as Freddie was heading in her direction, his football strip full of mud from the sodden pitch.

'I'm not having you in my car in all those muddy clothes. You'll have to strip off to your briefs. Take your boots off first.'

Home was only a few minutes away. As she neared their drive, she had a clear view of Tom's parked car. As she pulled alongside, she could see the furniture, referred to by the observant parent at the football practice, on the back seat. It was his favourite carver armchair from his student days.

'Come on, Fred, look sharp. There's something's up with your dad', she said, hurrying her younger son out of the passenger seat. 'We'll get your kit later. Get straight into the shower, please.'

Freddie scuttled off to the bathroom and Maudie, white faced and trembling, entered the sitting room where she found Tom asleep. She touched his shoulder and he woke up in a panic - wide-eyed –

rigid – faraway – silent - a pained look on his face. It was obvious that he was in some sort of severe trouble.

'Whatever is it Tom? What on earth has happened? Are you in pain? What's happened at school?'

Tom, suddenly realising that he was safe, at home, with Maudie, relaxed somewhat. He looked up at her. His face spoke volumes, leaving her in no doubt that Tom had troubles to relate. She wrapped her arms around him to attempt some comfort.

'I'm afraid that Irma was right when she warned me about Spong, Dickinson and Co. Icky had no choice really. Either he had to suspend me or tell Phoebe to drop her accusations. He wasn't likely to do that was he? If he had, I think he'd be more frightened of what she'd do to him. The upshot is that I've been suspended from duty on full pay whist they investigate the allegation of sexual misconduct. I suppose that means the sexual harassment of some women. At least, I hope that's all it means. These women are a vicious lot. Given the insinuations of Phoebe Spong over the years, though, and the fact that I've been suspended, I'm afraid, love, we must expect the worst. They'll have persuaded some of our naughtier pupils to make equally malicious allegations.'

Maudie reflected on Tom's relationships over the years - with men, women, neighbours, colleagues and acquaintances; he was a regular 'Mr Marmite'. People either loved him or loathed him. There was nothing in between. He was always honest to the point where it hurt and outspoken too. He had a whisper which could be likened to an aside in a melodrama on the live stage. He was an atheist with 'Christian' values who was politically incorrect. The people who feared him were insecure and vain and Maudie could understand the likes of Phoebe Spong, Ted Slater and their ilk finding him a great irritant, but these must be truly evil people to make such dishonest allegations about him.

Maudie made soothing comments in an attempt to bolster his spirits. Her insides, however, were in uproar with fury at the outright audacity of this bunch of bitter and twisted women to make such accusations against the love of her life who, although he had his faults, would never harm the hair of a pupil and if the women had had some grievance against him then they deserved whatever chastisement he had delivered. She was desperate to advise him that he should have played the political game to get to his goal. But now was not the time to rub salt into the wound. She just had to accept the fact that Tom was an apolitical soul who would climb the greasy pole by hard work and not by sycophancy.

'Trust Icky to support the women – they're doing just what he wants, aren't they. The blood'll be on their hands, not his. He's simply the go-between - the pusillanimous creep. Anyway, we must trust that justice will prevail. We must stay calm and keep our minds sharp for the forthcoming ordeal in whatever form it takes. What's the next step?'

'I'll have to get the Union involved. I'll ring the Rep now. We'll take it from there.'

The Union Secretary on his case and the meal ready, Jack breezed in.

'Hi Guys.',

Tom frowned. He would have preferred the words 'Mum' and 'Dad'

'Hello, Son, How did the last exam go?'

'It could not have been better. Everything I prepared came up. I think I'll get a top grade.'

'What about you? How have your days gone?'

Both parents were non-committal. They each had endured a terrible day but it was not their intention to spoil Jack's euphoric mood that evening. It seemed that the massive black clouds blocking their own sun that day was being alleviated by the silver lining of their son's performance in his last exam paper.

Jack in his exhilarated state had not noticed his father's unusually early appearance, so excited was he about his forthcoming trip to Scotland the next day. The talk over dinner concentrated on Jack, his exams and the trip to Glencoe. Tom and Maudie, both good actors, were able to mask the problems which, just yet, they were unwilling to share with their elder son. After dinner, Jack ran upstairs to collect his backpack. He said,

'OK, I'm ready. Just off to Dunco's. See you in a week. A quick brush of his lips on his mother's cheek and a hug for his father and he was gone.

Tom, although feeling personally violated and sickened by the accusations of sexual misconduct with minors by such deviants, philosophically concluded that although they were about to experience a rough patch in their lives, they would survive it and be the stronger for it.

Maudie was making plans for the family's future. She realised that they may never come to fruition but preparedness for every eventuality was vital.

The letter, which had arrived on the day of Tom's suspension, had lain unnoticed and undiscovered for a week. Maudie anticipated, correctly, its contents – documents related to the closure of the library. She had already decided to take the redundancy option. Her job at the library was secure until December. Whatever fate had in store for Tom, she would be out of work from New Year's Day 1993. She spent her time, whilst not working, researching into the various aspects of life which would affect them. She kept a close eye on The *Times Educational Supplement* for suitable posts for Tom – hoping that Cornwall would provide one. She wrote to schools in the county to ascertain the best establishment for Freddie and to discover their admissions policy. She started to take the *Cornishman* - the Friday publication, to reconnect with the news and events taking place in the county of her birth. She approached, with their housing requirement, all estate agents in the major towns of Truro, Falmouth and Penzance and requested a place on their mailing lists. She approached all the local agents in Longborough and Southwich for valuations of their home in readiness for its marketing, should that be necessary and she began to do some redecorating and she got Tom busy repairing and repainting the fabric. Maudie kept Tom busy during his enforced sabbatical. Her main task was to keep up Tom's spirits which she did by organising a variety of weekly get-togethers with their closest allies.

Jack, anxious for his father's state of mind asked to be allowed to study the documents from the various complainants, and had held discussions with Tom about the personnel involved and their assertions. All of this debate within the closeness of his family buoyed up Tom's spirits and enabled him to think clearly about his responses to their claims when interrogated at the Hearing.

CHAPTER TWENTY-THREE

Wednesday, 8 July, 1992.

The bell rang signalling the end of break. Sian Waite was in the staff room finishing her coffee. She had checked the cover list at least three times that morning. As she passed the notice board, she glanced at it again. Her name had not appeared. It meant that she had a free period until lunch time. There was no rush. After a period of ten minutes she left. She walked purposefully towards the Science wing. As she strode down the corridor past the Maths teaching rooms, in her figure-hugging, finely-woven jumper and pencil skirt, she deliberately swung her hips in the knowledge that she was a perfect specimen of the female form. She carried her lab coat casually over her arm so that should any one pass her, her magnificent body would be appreciated fully by the observer. Now that, the Blot on her reputation, Tom Portland, was off the scene, at least for the time being, if not permanently, she felt emancipated and quite reckless. However, as she approached Alan Bairstow's office, her manner became more stealthy and careful. This was the first time he had asked her to stop by and she felt a little nervous. The door to his office was locked. She knocked on his door in an officious manner and called out,

'Mr. Bairstow, are you there?'

Silence... She waited... The door opened without a sound and his arm was extended. In no more than a second, he pulled her in, pushed the door behind them and turned the key. The suddenness, rapidity and fluidity of his actions took her by surprise so that she gasped in astonishment. He gently put his hand over her mouth, and removing a stray hair from her cheek, he brushed his lips over her closed eyes and forehead. They stood close together in the darkness of his office, each feeling and hearing the rapid heart-beats of the other. As they clung to each other, with their bodies in close contact, each responded to the other's touch. She could feel the immediate stiffening of his penis against her leg and she encouraged him to make further advances by rubbing her pubic bone against his groin. She felt like crying out at the urgency of her desire to gain access to the contents of his trousers.

The private office of Alan Bairstow doubled up as a departmental store, but in the midst of labyrinthine corridors of bookshelves was a nest of easy chairs, a tiny sofa and his desk. Alan loved his private lair. The arrangement of crowded shelves was purposely organised to lend extreme privacy to his inner sanctum. Windowless walls and a cloistered distance from the door allowed the inhabitants complete protection from immediate visibility by a chance entrant. Alan had used this convenient bolt-hole on many occasions to practise his seductive techniques on a succession of female colleagues and parents.

He had practised his technique many times. He would begin with quiet, almost inaudible whisperings in her ear, allowing his lips to brush against her cheek, or eyes, or hair. He would gently sweep stray hairs from her face, and with his fingertips he would stroke her face and her hair. He would let his hand stray to her arm and he would run his fingers from her shoulder to her hand, where he would massage the palm of her hand. All these slow gentle caresses demonstrated that he was in no hurry to push her for immediate sexual intimacy. Such gentle caresses drove the women wild with desire for him. They understood the implication that he was no lothario, out for what he could get and be quick about it. It only made them hungrier for more of his attention.

Tom had not been alone amongst the male staff in his inability to comprehend quite what it was that some women – some very attractive women – found so tempting about this man. He was hardly good looking and his personality could not be described as magnetic, and his sense of humour? Did he have one? Maudie, Tom's wife had found him singularly repulsive. In her job as a librarian, she had access to all manner of manuscripts, documents and collections of academic theses. She had made it her business to conduct some private research into the appeal of positively ugly men to very obviously, exquisite young women. From her reading, she came to some conclusions which she shared with Tom over their nightcaps of hot milk laced with whisky for her and a glass of red wine for Tom.

    'From what I've read, it boils down to four possible explanations. It's certainly not his looks. He's always got a red face, his wispy hair is gingery and receding and he has that stubbly beard. He's rather flabby to say the least. His available spending power won't be great – he has a wife who'll make sure of that! Has he a sense of humour? No, I thought not. Well that leaves two possibilities – he's kind or he's got a big prick.'

'I'll confirm that last one', Tom said.

Alan and his young conquest stood for several minutes breathing heavily and perspiring freely. Sian could feel her underwear becoming sticky as her female fluids flowed freely from her cervix, soaking her scant panties. Her legs became weak with her fierce desire and she was about to faint with the knowledge of what was about to take place between them. She sank, powerless, into his gentle embrace as Alan's strong arms and his massive hands lifted her as if she weighed no more than a feather and cradled her whole frame in a gentle, unyielding, passionate embrace, carried her swiftly through the serpentine maze of bookshelves to the exclusive intimacy of his den. He set her down on the sofa and began to kiss her hair, her eyes and her lips. His hands found her shoulders and he began to massage them, pressing his thumb into the muscles of her back. His hand wandered up to her neck and he stroked and tickled her neck. He kissed her throat and her chin and her lips and then his tongue forced an entry into her open mouth and her body jerked forward involuntarily against him. He stroked her hair, her face, her arms, her legs and his massive hands found their way into her juice- drenched cotton panties. She opened her legs willing him to push those massive fingers into her receptive female opening and to stroke her pulsating, throbbing clitoris. She shifted her position continuously, groaning with pleasure as she felt his welcome invasion of her secret, feminine places.

Alan was not like other lovers she had known. In all previous relationships, she had been attracted to young Adonis-like, sex-hungry animals whose interests had lain in pursuing their own self-gratification at her expense - handling her roughly in their domination of her body, squeezing out her individuality and showing off their physical superiority by leaving their physical imprint upon her. She had felt bruised and contaminated by their preoccupation in their muscular manipulations of her whole being. She had likened her encounters as to being akin to rape. In Alan she had found someone who worshipped her as a goddess, who sought to give her sexual thrills without thought for himself.

    She lay draped unclothed on the tiny couch next to his fully clothed body and he nibbled her toes and ran his hands the length of her outstretched shapely legs. She pulled him towards her, kissing him repeatedly and grasping his trousers searching for his elusive penis. He shivered and let out an unintended cry of delight.

Phoebe Spong was in good spirits. She was in charge at last. That creep - the self-righteous Tom Portland was out of the way; she hoped that it would be for a long time; possibly she had scuppered him for good. The stupid, whisky-soaked Ted Slater was off work - sick. Too much booze she thought. He had complained to her whilst rubbing his gut,

    'Phoebe, I'm suffering with these terrible stomach cramps and my belly aches all the time. What am I to do? Can you hold the fort if I take a few days off sick?'

    `Lay off the booze, you idiot', she thought, but said to him,

'Ted, you go ahead. Take a well–deserved rest. You've had a hard time and it's taken its toll on your health. Things will run smoothly here. I'll take care of everything. Don't worry about a thing.'

She was feeling on top of the world as she surveyed her, albeit temporary, domain and patrolled her corridors during lesson time. All was quiet. All Year Eleven pupils had departed some weeks before and so the Maths suite was virtually deserted. She walked briskly towards the Science wing. She knew that Sian Waite was not teaching at that time and thought it would be a good opportunity to go over a few details regarding Tom Portland's suspension and its potential consequences. Her route took her through the silent corridors of the Maths suite. She arrived in the vicinity of Alan Bairstow's office when she thought that she heard his voice. It was an unusual sound. She was about to knock on his door when she noticed that it was actually ajar. So engrossed were the pair, cocooned in the middle of Alan's soundly constructed bookshelf maze that they were unaware of the sudden, silent, momentary, intrusion of a bright shaft of light in the otherwise darkened room.

Phoebe had observed that the key was in the locked position but the door itself was unlocked. She had deduced that whoever was in there was under the impression that they were safely locked inside .She looked around to make sure she was not being watched by some miscreant pupil standing outside a classroom in the corridor. She tentatively, with great care so as not to advertise her presence, pushed the door open and listened. She could hear muffled voices coming from the depths of his office. She could see nothing. All was in darkness. But she knew that there was something afoot in the dark recesses of that room. She tiptoed inside and like the spider, she waited, patiently, noiselessly and unmoving. Predicting more action, she had pulled the door to behind her so that she would be undetected from the corridor. She could not afford to close it fully because the turning of the key might be heard by those in the room and she wanted to remain incognito. Her eyes grew accustomed to the darkness and she could make out the mass of bookshelves lining a narrow passageway along which she was desperate to navigate but to do so would disturb and alert those in the room. So she had to play a waiting game. She listened intently, her eyes wide, with pupils dilated, to try to catch any glimpse of whatever questionable action was taking place.

As Sian Waite straddled Alan Bairstow's prostrate body, he lay motionless on the tiny uncomfortable sofa, he, stroking her thighs as she leant backwards to enable his further exploration of her body. He reached up and grasped her firm young breast with its erect, pert, puckered nipple. He squeezed it gently causing a torrent of liquid to flow from her innermost parts onto his trousers. She yelped with pleasure. She leant forward and their lips met gently at first and then with an increasing ferocity as they explored with their tongues the other's lips and throat. Sian was in a state of expectancy. She adored him and wished that these moments of anticipated ecstasy would last forever. She was prepared to do whatever he wanted of her. She wanted to give herself to him absolutely. She realised that with him she could achieve those sensations that she had only read about. She began to tremble violently, as a wave of excitement rippled through the core of her body making every part of her tingle with her desperate need to have him totally inside her.

    Phoebe Spong could not believe what she was hearing. Never before had she been in such an exquisite position to witness such real life activities at first hand. Sian unzipped his trousers. He adjusted his position to make her entry easier. She felt inside, groping for his male organ. She wanted Alan to penetrate her hard and fast and immediately but his male part was not co-operating. Her words of encouragement were having no effect. It was not in a state of erection as she has supposed and hoped. If she was disappointed, she hid her feelings well. She took hold of his generously sized, though flaccid penis and fondled it at first gently then with more vigour in her resolve to bring it to life so that it was capable of penetrating her, as that was what she wanted now more than anything. In a state of frustrated, heightened, personal, sexual demand she threw herself forward and opened her mouth wide in her desire to take into her body the dark pink phallus. To Alan, with his eyes closed, this was an action totally unexpected and he jerked forward and groaned out loud. Sian was frantically sucking and licking and nibbling him to try to get some life into this lifeless piece of his living body which she now started to rub as well in her craving to achieve an erection for his sake as much as for her own satisfaction. She began to rotate her pubic bone slowly against his flaccid genitals. Her excitement was increasing, her pulse was racing and her heart was thumping yet not a jot of response was forthcoming from Alan's loins. Try as she might, she could not get the response she desired so eagerly.

'Alan ', she whispered, 'What's wrong? Why have you lost it? Are you worried that the bell might ring? Don't you want me anymore? I'm ready to burst with all the love I feel for you. Why don't you respond?'

'Sian, you must help me! I've imagined this moment since you walked into school. Of course I want you too. I do love you. I want to give you my best but...'

She continued in her various endeavours to tease him into some activity. His mind was elsewhere as he remembered a jumble of disjointed memories from his past sexual experiences, rather like the disjointed pictures in a 'What the Butler Saw' machine, His wife, Charmaine's tearfully embittered face as she had worked on him, with increasing frustration, in order to procure some marital action from his disobedient organ, the hazy images of adolescent sexual games played in the school dormitory. He remembered the fascination with which he had viewed others' facility in wanking matches, the envy he had felt as they guiltlessly indulged in mutual masturbation and finally the abject terror he had experienced as they recognised ultimately that he was not joining their sport.

He pulled her head forward again towards his aching phallus and thrust her head down so that she was forced to take his penis once more into her mouth. Her licking and sucking movement together with the teasing, exciting feeling of her teeth on the delicate tip now started to have the desired effect and he regained his erection. She quickly grasped the engorged organ and manoeuvred herself without hesitation and lowered herself against him and directed its head into her throbbing vagina. As she felt his entry and the subsequent thrusts of his member through the extent of her vagina, she began to move to and fro in order to intensify the sensations for each of them.

Alan was exultant. From the moment of entry into her blissfully, receptive slit, he felt a total loss of bodily awareness. The throbbing sensations gave him a feeling of extreme well-being. He had fantasised this moment repeatedly. Sex had always been a psychologically painful experience for him because he could never manage to maintain an erection for long enough to satisfy his wife, who had eventually lost interest in the sexual side of their marriage. Dozens of liaisons in his forty one years had rarely produced a satisfactory response from his body. The women still adored him, however. He fulfilled their other needs by demonstrating his desire by gentle talking and caressing and worshipping them, treating them like Goddesses on pedestals. His satisfaction came from the chase, rarely in the capture which would inevitably result in disappointment for both parties. He would always back off from an intimate encounter if he thought he would be unable to give satisfaction and that had been, invariably, the case. Most of his women did not want penetration. They were satisfied in the knowledge that they could get their desired orgasms from an easily purchased vibrator but the ultimate act of penetration was denied them even if they had wanted it.

Perpetually, he sought titillation in pornographic magazines and videos. He had been a lifelong voyeur. Sound of lovemaking in adjoining hotel rooms and Peeping Tom excursions which he had practised for many years drove him to frenzies of sexual explosion, but in personal, intimate confrontation, arousal was severely limited. And he thought he knew the cause. The sexual counselling he had sought at the behest of his frustrated wife had permitted recognition of mother-fixation and guilt complex about his own sexuality derived from his manse upbringing. Here sex had been denounced as a mortal sin. His Evangelical pastor father had perpetually denounced sex as the pastime of the vulgar. Alan had been caught by his mother, as he peeped at his sister undressing as a thirteen year old. He had been beaten unmercifully by this father, cane in one hand and the Bible in the other. Little wonder that he had identified his fascination with female sexuality as incitement from Satan. And yet, fascinated as he was, urgency to witness others' sexual behaviour drove him with the intensity of religious zeal. But, satisfaction in voyeurism had left him ultimately drained and frustrated. Enormously stimulated by his night-time excursions to peep through gaping curtains and by his repeated viewing of blue movies from the three sex shops which he patronised, he was simply reminded of his own inadequacies and his impotence consequently became further exaggerated.

'Well I'm jiggered! They're actually copulating, here in the Maths storeroom in front of my very eyes. The little minx...pretending she's an innocent!'

Phoebe did not need to be Sherlock Holmes to deduce that the participants in this covert act of sexual intercourse were Alan Bairstow and that young flighty piece, Sian Waite. She strained her eyes and ears to see and hear more. She could make out the shapes in the darkness as she peered over the books lined up on the bookshelves which formed his carefully constructed screen. She was relishing this unexpected treat. This act of voyeurism had produced some sexual stirrings in her lower abdomen, which she might make use of on her date with Alec later that day.

Sian continued to move upon him with athletic tenacity. Alan had ceased to exist for her much as she idolised him. Her body was a seething mass of wildly pulsating sensations. Alan moved little. The slightest exertion on his own behalf, he knew would bring a premature ejaculation and Sian's disappointment. As she quickened the pace of her movement further, gasping for breath, sweat pouring from every pore of her body, shrieks of delight escaped from her lips, her eyes rolled towards the heavens and uncontrollable muscle spasms ensued. Then it was over. Alan exploded inside her. His erection vanished and her continued thrusting became useless. Her brief moment of total abandonment was over. She relaxed against him. She had experienced excitement greater than she had known existed and she felt drained. But she was ultimately disappointed. She had wanted this sensation to go on for ever. She had felt denied the ultimate explosion of ecstasy for which she had aimed. Now there was anti-climax. She was certain that there would be other opportunities and hopefully they would achieve that elusive climax together. She pressed her smiling face to his chest in contentment. They lay for several minutes, enjoying the warm sticky glue-like fluids that were binding them together.

'Alan, my darling', she felt moved to whisper. 'See how great you were. I've never known such ecstasy. You were brilliant. I felt as if by whole body would burst in my excitement. You were fantastic.'

Bairstow knew that she was saying what she thought he would like to hear. He said nothing. His mind wandered to the scene he had witnessed a couple of nights before. His wife had retired to bed at 10.20pm. Under the usual pretext of taking the dog for its evening walk, he had crept, conspiratorially, into the garden of the neighbouring bungalow and had peeped though a convenient gap in the carelessly, closed curtains of the lounge. The occupants, a two years' married couple, had given him several, unintended opportunities to play voyeur to their nightly love making. Like Alan, they delighted in viewing erotically charged, explicit movies. But whereas Alans's wife deprecated the habit and refused to watch, simply because she wanted him to be aroused by her alone and not by some tawdry movie, these two took mutual pleasure in the sexual arousal they experienced through their salacious viewing.

    The television occupied the right hand corner of the window. From his vantage point, he had an uninterrupted view of the sofa and the amorous pair, who were blissfully unaware that they were providing entertainment for the observer outside. They watched and re-enacted the erotic actions in the movie, whilst he watched them accompanied by the titillating sounds from the video which were clearly audible to him. He watched their act of slow, reciprocal undressing and the ultimate, total revelation of their young, athletic bodies which added to Alan's appreciation of their performance

Alan envied the husband whose wife obviously adored his body which was youthful, muscular, with a substantial penis, although, somewhat inferior in length and girth to his own, he noted. She was fixated by its size and the life it seemed to develop as she played with it. She could not take her attention from it, so captivated was she of its power. His own, rapidly enlarging, penis began to chafe irritatingly against his trouser leg as he watched the drama unfold on the other side of his personal window-glass screen. She ignored the rest of her husband's body, concentrating all her attention on his rampant cobra-like organ which was standing upright and rigid, from his reclining body like the deadly snake getting ready to strike. She took its swollen cobra-like head and used her mobile tongue to lick and tickle it into an even greater enormity, then in a sudden movement she thrust it into her mouth as if bite off its attacking head. She was dissuaded from her too early energetic movements as her husband clearly wanted to extend this activity for some time. He arranged her body on the sofa so that she sat legs splayed giving him access to her female parts. As he knelt before her, Alan had a perfect view into her inviting female chasm with its surrounding curly, black shrubbery. He could almost feel and taste those freely flowing juices from her innermost parts. Her husband soon obliterated his view as he nuzzled his probing tongue into the folds and depths of her pink vagina. Her body responded as she moved her body to give easier and more pleasurable access to his snake-like, flicking tongue.

The final act, which Alan had been desperate for, finally arrived as the husband placed his wife in the best position for his penetration of her from behind. She presented to him a wide open target. He ensured his weapon was at its optimum size, rigid as a ramrod and in the correct position for discharge; he engaged with his target and thrust his weapon home, time after time, repeatedly until all of his ammunition had been spent. After eight minutes of furious motion punctuated by encouraging groans, developing into screams of increasing intensity, she let out a final exultant scream, so loud that Alan feared it would wake his sleeping wife next door. Alan, exhausted, like his neighbours and presumably those in the movie, now was aware of the sticky dribble of his own semen as it trickled down his leg. Reluctantly, Alan had pulled himself from his vantage point and sneaked stealthily away with his faithful, silent companion whose tail was now wagging furiously in anticipation of the promised walk.

Alan once again became aware of Sian lying on top of him apparently dozing. He was also conscious that his penis was as erect as it had ever been. Gently nudging Sian from her sleep, he encouraged her to take hold of the unaccustomed swelling. He felt like a fussy pupil intent on displaying to the teacher the correct answer to a sticky problem. She willingly applied herself.

'Alan, my sweet, I knew all would be well.'

'Yes, all thanks to your hard work, my dear. I must admit that all my problems either stem from my worry about that trouble with the wanker, Portland, our secret meeting in this room and of course, my wife.'

'We love each other. Divorce her and I'll marry you.' Her response was immediate.

Alan had no intention of committing himself permanently to another woman, especially Sian Waite, who he considered to be a temporary dalliance. She was about to lower her receptive, lubricated opening onto his proudly presented torpedo when the horror of her marriage proposal caused his noble manhood to shrivel like a deflated dirigible and the intention to re-enter her proffered vagina vanished like a rapidly sinking ship.

'Oh. FUCK!' she yelled out, her frustration with the situation unconcealed.

At this point, stay as she wanted to, Phoebe Spong needed to make her escape quickly and without a sound. She left as she had entered.

Alan Bairstow sighed, unsure whether Sian's outburst was an instruction or a recrimination. He started to weep and she attempted to soothe him with a soft voice and apologies. She was unused to this kind of behaviour from a man. She did not know how to proceed. His movements signalled her to move off him and he suggested that they dress quickly as time was now against them. He sat on the edge of his chair, his head in his hands, rocking backwards and forwards, with whimpering sounds emanating from his lips and his usually ruddy complexion drained to a pasty pallor as Sian dressed soundlessly.

Furtively glancing to the left and right and finding the corridor quiet, Phoebe marched triumphantly onwards to the Science wing where she found the empty laboratory of Sian Waite. She spotted Peter Smalley in the Science prep room and made it known to him that she was in search of Ms Waite.

'I haven't set eyes on her since break.'

That delicious titbit of illicit human coitus on school premises had fairly set Phoebe's own juices running. Back in her office she rang Alec, wishing to see him urgently that afternoon at four o'clock. He was concerned about the insistency of her request and immediately agreed thinking that she had a grave problem. Her sponge-like face assumed a broad smile; life was suddenly becoming good for her. She would retain the information on Waite and Bairstow for a rainy day. She'd got Alec dancing like a marionette and the school was hers.

Sian left Alan still nursing his short comings. Arriving at the exit of his office, seeing the reality of the apparently locked door, she nervously peered out. Classes were still in progress and no-one was about. Miraculously, they had escaped discovery. She let out a sigh of relief in the belief that their assignation had gone unnoticed. She decided not to burden Alan with this revelation. She considered that he had enough to worry about.

CHAPTER TWENTY-FOUR

Wednesday, 22 July, 1992.

Tom settled with surprising calm and composure into a life of enforced retirement. After twenty odd years in the teaching profession, he had imagined that staying at home would be traumatic to the *nth* degree. Soon, he was able to confirm the words of former colleagues, who after taking early retirement, had said that they found it difficult to understand how they had had time to go to work. Tom busied himself in study, home and garden during the day and in the evenings he and Maudie also were able to make more regular visits to their Bridge club.

Days had turned into weeks and not a word was heard from Slater. Tom was not to know that Slater was attending school in a very irregular fashion. Slater, remained resolute in his unpreparedness to subject himself to an inquisition by his doctor, and so was in the habit of taking only a couple of days' sick leave at a time, so that he did not have to supply a doctor's note to explain his absence. His attendance at school was not productive. Phoebe had taken command. He thought little about Tom's predicament. He could survive the day only by the constant consumption of caffeine provided by Jennifer Bird interspersed with furtive visits to his car boot to top up his whisky consumption.

There were only a couple of days left of the summer term. Tom had imagined that within two or three days of his suspension a telephone call would signal the end of the investigation and he would have been back in harness, the whole episode forgotten like a bad dream. On every occasion that he walked past the telephone, he checked to see whether he had missed a call and that there would be a recorded message for him but he had been disappointed every time. His loyal supporters had not forgotten him. There had been telephone calls from the members of the group who he used to sit with in the staff anteroom at break and lunch time. David Southwich tried to bolster up his spirits with his latest jokes: Keith Dawson kept him informed about the school's performance in the summer sports tournaments: Donny Ross had told him about the successful Year Ten outing to the Textile museum at Helmshore: Paul Sawyer had asked his advice about final details of the new timetable. Anne Jones, Lucinda Terry-Smith and Jill Field had all sent their support in letters and cards. Jennifer Bird and Irma de la Haye, however, kept in touch more than anyone else. Jennifer, briefed him on the to-ing and fro-ing of, and, the inevitable contretemps between Ted Slater and Phoebe Spong, whilst Irma maintained as much coverage of staff room opinion and gossip as possible. Considering he had not set foot in the building for over two weeks, he felt as if he knew more about the day-to-day affairs than he had ever done when on site. These colleagues knew well of the concerted effort to 'stitch him up' as one of them verbalised. There had been many comings and goings of Union Officials, County Officers and each of the complainants had been interviewed and had presented statements. Pupils, too, had been interviewed though sworn to silence. Tom remained in ignorance about the precise allegations against him.

Tom and Maudie racked their brains in order to review the events of the previous few weeks. What possible catalysts to his present predicament could there have been? Prominent in his memory remained Phoebe's occasional allegations that he was given to handling children, girls in particular. Then there had been his obligation to intervene in Alan Bairstow's conduct of Maths GCSE coursework. Tom had become aware that a handful of favoured pupils had been given their teacher's own work to copy whereas what was demanded was an original, researched Mathematical Investigation. He had repeatedly challenged Bairstow upon the practice. Coursework ought to have been the child's unaided work, he had contended. An approach to Slater on the matter had led to an investigation by the Maths Adviser who had found in Bairstow's favour, there being no rubric from the Examination Board which outlawed the practice which Tom had alleged. Despite his better judgement upon the matter, Tom had had to accept defeat. Perhaps Bairstow's evident chagrin at Tom's intervention had led him to combine with a group of jaundiced women in order to get even with him. And there had been that embarrassing episode in the staffroom, when he had asked Sian Waite to do a cover for Monica Dickinson who had gone home, at short notice, unwell with a migraine. It had been such a mundane, every day run of the mill request that he had thought nothing of it. On reflection, he realised that he had been set up. He had been so determined to be wide awake when dealing with any of this gang and yet he had walked right into the trap they had set for him. Never in a million years would Sian Waite have responded as she had, to a request from the Deputy Head unless she was part of the deliberate entrapment. She had been right on cue to get the maximum effect from that innocent request that he had made of her. All credit to her for her acting ability, Tom thought. And how convenient it had been that Trudie Long and Peter Smalley had been there to witness the entire affair. He tried to remember exactly how the scene had been enacted as she had had her back to him. He remembered touching her shoulder to get her attention. She flared up immediately. That should have warned him off. How could he have been so dozy as to touch her arm again in an attempt to calm her down? His action had merely acted as a fan to an already raging inferno. And then, stupidly, he'd tried again to reason with her as she was going through the door. He remembered touching the door handle. Oh yes, that would be construed as barring her exit. How cleverly and with cunning they had planned his demise.

Cogitate as he might, he could think of no incident involving pupils where allegation of improper conduct might have arisen. There had been, of course, the incidents concerning Lesly Atherton and Phoebe Spong and the sexual misconduct of Greg, James and Kevin with Gillian Sumner on the school playing field but such was his management of those affairs and such the nature of his relationship with the pupils concerned that he could not for the life of him imagine them to be the source of any complaint against him.

He had experienced difficult management relationships with such as Vivienne Lowther, Trudie Long and Sharon Crabtree but he could remember nothing of particular note. Such difficulties were par for the course in school management. They had obviously held grudges against him for his response to some of their habits of which he did not approve. But was that good enough reason to have him hung drawn and quartered? He remembered having words with Vivienne about the state of her register. She had not seemed to realise that the register was an official document and had to contain an accurate record of a pupil's attendance or absence and be marked accordingly with a stroke for attendance and a zero for absence. It had been impossible during a fire drill to have trust in the reliability of her register. He could remember nothing at all about Sharon Crabtree, a junior member of the English Department of which he was also a member. As for Trudie Long, he had little time for her. He had to acknowledge that. He had disapproved of her past live-in relationships with Keith Dawson and Donny Ross and then of her to shacking up with Peter Smalley. It was beyond the pale in his view. That would be her gripe.

With his wife, Tom dissected the various aspects of his personality, his opinions on the news and matters of the day which had caused so much offence to certain colleagues. He knew that a number of staff had been offended by his unashamedly reactionary life view. He had made no secret of his fear that western society was crumbling on account of family instability. His concern had been for the welfare of pupils but those colleagues who had experienced domestic breakdown had felt that Tom was blaming them personally. Repeatedly, as he had reviewed Southwich's Sex Education Policy with Phoebe whose special responsibility it was and who did little more than show interminable videos on 'The Birth of a Baby', he had been appalled by Schools' general impotence to affect adolescent sexuality. His heart ached at the inevitable confusion experienced by the teenager faced with the school's Social Education values which suggested that sexuality had its place only in the confines of stable, married relationships whilst all around them, cultural practice suggested otherwise. It had seemed like swimming against the tide. Any discussions he had tried to have with Phoebe were halted from the start. The state of her own private life caused her to be a substantial part of the problem.

Tom had ample time to review his attitudes towards the gender discrimination debate within which he assumed the malicious allegations to have arisen. He knew himself to be regarded by some as a misogynist. Such slanderous talk had hurt him bitterly. Passionately, he upheld the right of all women to invariable parity of esteem, in education, employment and domestic circumstances. Life with mother, sister, friends and his revered wife, Maudie, had conditioned him to this view. And yet he could not avoid his opinion that Feminism was a strident clarion call to the revolutionary upheaval of the state of society. The demand for women's rights on the grounds of the equality of the sexes had actually done more harm to the cause of female emancipation than to enhance it.

The Equal Opportunity legislation of the nineteen seventies, whilst ironing out anomalies of industrial remuneration, had actually reduced the number of significant managerial posts taken up by women despite the odd epoch-making exception. Posts formerly reserved virtually exclusively for women, had been seized by men once dual gender employment advertisement had been established in law. Appointments were made on the basis of the best qualified for the job and inevitably, but not always, the male applicants were better qualified. This major change in the law had not been an advantage to women after all. Women really wanted positive discrimination in their favour. Twenty years on, there were still no female Heads of major industries, precious few female judges and a ridiculous paucity of female Members of Parliament. Not even a female Premier had appointed more than a single short-lived female Cabinet Minister. The Law had enfranchised females in employment competition; something else was holding them back.

Tom was, indeed, horrified by the increasing frequency of marital infidelity and he had to admit that he did go on about it in the staffroom. Perhaps he should have kept his own counsel more often. Though he acknowledged every woman's right to extricate herself from an abusive relationship, he felt that if women perceived themselves to be the victims of men's assumed superiority then that was the cause of the deterioration of marital stability.

Tom and Maudie had discussed the effect of the contraceptive pill in their relationship. They had both agreed that for them, like millions of others, it had been a godsend for the purpose of family planning. It had placed women in the driving seat of their sexual relationships. Freedom from the fear of unwanted pregnancy, if used correctly, had given the woman what had formerly been the male prerogative – a carte blanche to follow the dictates of fickle sexual urges. They both recognised it as the single most significant social event of the millennium. The male sex had always been polygamous; it was part of their genetic make-up; it was something to do with spreading their sperm far and wide, but the female sex was naturally monogamous. The contraceptive pill had allowed them also to become polygamous. He did not condone promiscuity by either sex but there was so much of it in the movies, TV and even in *The Archers*, no wonder ordinary people considered that it was quite normal for them to behave as their idols in the media. People sharing his views needed to stand up and be counted but unfortunately they did not dare put their heads above the parapet for fear of recrimination.

The sexual emancipation of women doubled the deleterious consequences of promiscuity of both sexes not least of which was the pernicious spread of the Human Immunodeficiency Virus leading to the incurable condition known as AIDS. Once personal relationships had been freed from the domination of commonly agreed moral codes by the decline in the influence of organised religion, responsibility seemed to have been sacrificed to the demands of individual freedom. He wished that the Women's Liberation Movement would count the social cost of their flaunted emancipation. He wondered if any of them ever had.

Most painful to Tom was the cost borne by the children - the products of the broken home or the single parent. He saw the victims every day walking the corridors, sometimes shy and quietly dishevelled, frequently absent through sickness - real or imagined, having a reluctance to abide by school rules with regard especially to smoking and adherence to uniform, disobedient in class, often aggressively defiant, with usually poor academic achievement. He estimated that such children formed the greater number of those referred to him by subject teachers for discipline. He believed that they should be sacrosanct. Their welfare was the primary professional mandate. He knew of no child at the school during his tenure as deputy Head who had displayed serious signs of social disturbance whilst living in a contentedly balanced nuclear family. Contemporary social statistics shocked him. The spread of HIV, AIDS and other Sexually transmitted diseases, the preference for trial marriage and single parenthood together with the burgeoning incidence of abortion, and the development of the abortion pill aroused in him intense anxiety precisely because of their cost to individual happiness and thus social cohesion.

The modern male had become fearful of emasculation in the wake of the demand for female equality. Having suffered shameful suppression for centuries, women understandably had sought to redress the balance but the desire for equality had been relegated in favour of the desire for role reversal. In Tom's opinion, women would never achieve true parity with men because men had too much to lose. The male ego would not be subjugated by fanatic feminists. Once embattlement occurred, men would behave according to type. In these terms alone was misogyny understandable. Society's stability would be the inevitable casualty. The family, he conceived to be the building block of the fabric of Western culture. It followed that inviolable marriage was its cement. Marriage, increasingly, had been going out of fashion enabling both parties to walk away without the inconvenience of a costly divorce. Currently, the cement was crumbling under the pressure of adult promiscuity. Raised in an amoral milieu, the young emulated their parents' generation's moral indifference and entered relationships without faith that they could offer permanence. Thus, future family units were doomed. The family's salvation and with it Society's, lay in the development of the view of the family's sanctity. Youthful romance needed to be seen as a precursor to mature love, responsibility and permanence and not as it was becoming, an end in itself. Love should be selfless; it necessarily encapsulated service; in pursuit of their justifiable goals, feminists had relinquished and become ashamed of their role as helpmate; service had been understood as servitude. Fulfilling love called for mutual give and take. In present society, giving selflessly had become a sign of weakness. Traditional Western culture would only survive if the stable family as its constituent unit survived.

The alternatives were too awful to contemplate. As mentors of impressionable Youth, teachers must stand up and be counted amongst those willing to risk social unpopularity by preaching a gospel of old-fashioned, ethical, social values. Tom had no interest in the churches' view on all this. It was a simple utilitarian philosophy. Promiscuity was lethal. How could committed teachers not make every effort to improve the future quality of their charges' lives? What quality of life lay on offer after Youth got sucked into the descending vortex of premature pregnancy, abortion, early and therefore doomed marriage, or no marriage at all, repeated divorce, promiscuity and consequential deterioration of health?

The trouble was as Job discovered, no one liked a prophet of doom, especially if the message conflicted with one's chosen lifestyle or philosophy of education. Tom's chagrin was compounded by the realisation that since his personal and social ethic contravened the predominant attitudes of the day, he fell foul of yet another contemporary communal tyranny– Political Correctness. He was experiencing the fate of the dissenter down the ages – the witch hunt if not now lethal was at least calculated to injure and thus dissuade. The heretic of the Inquisition and the Reformation had been executed by blade or by fire. The modern free thinker against Political Correctness faced a more subtle sanction, but each faced the tyranny of conformity. It struck Tom as a powerful irony that the modern life view was essentially irreligious and that he, an atheist, advocated the opposite view. Further irony resided in the fact that the age had totally inverted what was considered Politically Correct. In Victorian England, even the table legs had to be covered for the sake of modesty. The attitudes of those days, towards legs, were a far cry from those of the modern day young woman whose wardrobe might contain a mini skirt or hot pants. Political Correctness had become the new Puritanism with all the faults of that philosophy. Tom assumed it to have been largely North American in inspiration and what occurred in the USA inevitably found its way in to UK usage sooner or later was his cynical but apt view. It was fundamentally praiseworthy in its essentials but manic in its extremes. At its heart, it preached the fine qualities of equality, freedom and tolerance but in its detail, common sense disappeared. Words like *wife* and *husband* were now frowned on, preference being given to the neutral *partner.* Girls were given traditional boys' toys and vice versa. Even in school, all the craft subjects had to be tasted by both boys and girls. Before long he envisaged that the words *girl* and *boy* would be out of favour and illegal if this new morality were to continue to its natural conclusion. Tom thought of some ridiculous examples of the potty nature of political correctness. The term chairman was now considered non-PC. Other variants he had heard used were chairwoman, chairperson and simply chair which was the most popular but seemed the most barmy to him He considered that his use of the words *potty* and *barmy* would also be considered non-PC by some. It would have been a good joke if it were not such a serious matter. Continuing along these lines, he could imagine that in the future, History books would be rewritten to censure the true facts - giving a distorted view to suit the politicians of the day. The agents of Political Correctness infiltrate the Government, offer a distorted view of the past which may be untrue, but such is their current ascendancy that they pervert Society's understanding of the past and insinuate their own view which determines future experience. Those in current control of political thinking had expunged the understanding of a bygone age. He remembered reading George Orwell's *1984* in which the Party slogan was 'who controls the past controls the future: who controls the present controls the past'. He wondered how far away was the dystopian future as portrayed in the movies and in literature such as *The Handmaid's Tale.* This was not the goal of the modern woman, but Tom could foresee this kind of future once men took the offensive and rebelled. They were the stronger sex after all, being the hunters and protectors whilst the women bore the children. At the end of the day, the inescapable fact was that men and women were biologically different. No amount of Feminism and Political Correctness could alter that fact. There had to be a fundamental reason for it and the sooner Society accepted it as a reality, the sooner relationships between the sexes would improve and progress could be made. Tom recognised that he was politically incorrect. No-one was going to make him conform if he did not agree. Only changes in the law would make him toe the party line. Even if he disagreed, he would not flout the law, but he would not remain silent. But failure to abide by the dictatorship of political correctness would lead to virtual pariah status, which is where he currently found himself.

Tom imagined that his shameless political incorrectness to be a likely catalyst to any complaint made against him. For the time being, he waited, somewhat tickled by the irony of his enforced role reversal with Maudie who took to returning home from the library with the greeting,

'And how's the plucky little house-husband then?'

And he would reply, remembering *The Worm that Turned,*

'You promised me a new dress to do my chores in. When can I have one?

Tom suffered no undue strain. He had been angry and unnerved by a professionally imposed inability to retaliate when suspended. He was particularly irked at the thought of sexual misconduct when he had believed that he had spent his adult life attempting to combat the effects of just that in others and being considered a preacher for his pains. He had been embarrassed as the news circulated on the jungle telegraph. But there was no depression. When innocence was as palpable as it was in his case, he anticipated the pleasure of responding to Slater's abject apologies yet again and witnessing the culprit's punishment. As the days of his suspension turned to weeks and still no call came, this anticipation lost some of its appeal. Clearly, there was going to be no retraction. But still his innocence buoyed him up – this and the accumulating evidence of massive support for him in the school's community. It was just a matter of time and since the Local Education Authority was prevaricating, he was prepared to sit back and enjoy the summer sunshine.

CHAPTER TWENTY-FIVE

Monday, 10 August, 1992.

Six weeks after his suspension, Tom received, what was for him, earth shattering news. A bombshell had been dropped by the District Education Office. The morning post consisted of a weighty envelope with a Manchester postmark. His face white and his breathing rapid, he contemplated what lay in store for him inside the envelope. He took a kitchen knife with which to slice open the package. No sooner had he opened the envelope and saw that the first document was a letter from the District Education Officer that his nerves were further jangled by the piercing ringing tone of the telephone.

'Oh, Good morning, Mr Portland, it's Peter Jolly from the Longborough Echo here. Could you please confirm that you are under suspension from your duties as Deputy Head of Southwich High School?'

Tom's nervousness subsided as his brain sprang into action in order to respond to the voice at the other end of the line. How had the Press got hold of this piece of intelligence? Could this be a further piece of malicious action? He had been suspended for six weeks without a murmur from the press. It was altogether too coincidental that on the morning on which he had received notice of the Hearing he should receive a Press enquiry about his circumstances.

'May I ask you, Peter, how you became aware of the suspension?'

'Sorry, Mr Portland, we never disclose our sources.'

Tom considered for a moment how he should respond to the question. He decided that there was no point in prevaricating. After all, the reporter was only doing his job and he sounded a decent sort of lad. Tom answered,

'OK. Yes. I can confirm that I have been suspended.'

'Can you confirm that a Disciplinary Hearing is to be held on Thursday 27th August to consider your case?'

'Yes. I can confirm that too.'

'Would you be prepared to make a statement about the cause of your suspension?'

'I am forbidden to enter any discussion on the matter. So, all I can tell you is that I have been suspended pending investigations. Those are complete. Any further information you require will be made available in the form of a Press release following the Hearing.'

'Thank you Mr Portland. We do understand that there is a great deal of disquiet in Longborough about your suspension. We understand that you have been Deputy Head for thirteen years and that you have the support of the parents, the pupils and the majority of the staff.'

'You will forgive me, Peter, if I make no further comment. Good day to you.'

Whilst horrified at the prospect of the publicity which would be given to his suspension and the embarrassment which would inevitably follow, at least the matter could be seen to have entered the public domain and the satisfaction which he might achieve from proving malicious accusation would be all the more lucrative in consequence, he thought.

Tom returned to his documents. Whilst he read through the contents of the envelope, the peaceful equanimity he had enjoyed vanished like the mist on a scorching summer morning. There were a number of documents either in the form of letters or statements seven of which were from members of staff, four from female pupils and two from officials.

The first document was a covering letter, dated Wednesday 5th August, 1992, written by Marcus Bristow, the District Education Officer in Longborough. He wrote,

Dear Mr Portland,

Following the investigations into allegations of sexual misconduct towards staff and pupils, a decision has been made that the issue should be considered at a Hearing by the School's Governing Body. To this end, the disciplinary committee of the Governing Body of Southwich High School will meet at County Hall on Thursday 27th August, 1992 at 9.00am. The meeting will consider the allegations.

You are recommended to be present and to be aided by a trade union representative or a solicitor. You will be given the opportunity to present a case to the committee. The Hearing will proceed in your absence should there be no explanation for your non-attendance.

A copy of all complaints against you by staff and pupils is enclosed. Should you wish to submit any documents of your own which will be used in evidence by you, they should be directed to me for onward circulation to the committee at least five days prior to the Hearing.

It is felt inappropriate that pupils should be asked to appear before the Hearing though the Headteacher may call any member of staff who has made a complaint.

The next document was a copy of a letter from Mandy Hewitson, the Northern Area Secretary of the Secondary Schoolteachers' Association to Ted Slater. It concerned a complaint from Sian Waite.

Dear Dr Slater,

I am writing in the capacity of Northern Area Secretary of the Secondary Schoolteachers' Association on behalf of our member Ms Sian Waite. We wish on her behalf, to record a complaint against your Deputy, Mr Thomas Portland.

Ms Waite complains that on the afternoon of Tuesday 2nd June during a discussion about cover between herself and Mr Portland, in the staffroom. Mr Portland put his arm across her shoulders, to which she took particular exception, and later prevented her exit despite her repeated request to be allowed to leave.

Ms Waite further complains that Mr Portland causes her frequent sexual harassment by threatening and intimidating behaviour, a habit of turning conversations to sexual matters and by deliberate sexual innuendo.

My Association believes that these allegations which will be corroborated by and added to by six other members of our Association call for disciplinary action by the Governors and that Mr Portland should be forbidden to:

1. Touch pupils or colleagues.

2. Interview female colleagues.

3. Make sexual innuendos.

4. Discuss any matter of a sexual nature with pupils or colleagues.

We understand that a copy of this letter will be presented to Mr Portland and that he will be forbidden from discussing its contents with any member of our Association who makes a complaint.

Document three was the specific complaint from Sian Waite.

The specific catalyst to my complaint was an incident which occurred on Tuesday 2nd June but it has to be said that I have felt sexually harassed by Mr Portland since joining the staff of Southwich High School in September 1989.

Times without number, he has engineered a sexual direction in our conversations, constantly touched myself and other female colleagues, touched children, particularly girls, made specific reference to myself and pupils of our gender, undermined our confidence and intimidated us.

'All lies', expostulated Tom out loud.

I wish to demonstrate that I (and others) have had our rights as individuals in the workplace undermined by Mr Portland. I wish it to be known that we are alarmed and dismayed that female pupils (who desperately need our protection and support) have been similarly sexually harassed.

On Tuesday 2nd June, Mr Portland approached me in the staffroom (empty of all but my colleagues, Trudie Long and Peter Smalley, who witnessed these events and who will give corroborative statement) asking me to cover a lesson in a non-teaching period. I expressed reluctance to cover the lesson in view of the lack of notice. I was, at the time busy on a curriculum development exercise. He violently accused me of idleness, put his hand on my arm and further alleged that it was my duty to respond to his request.

'More lies...when have I accused you of idleness? What rubbish!'

I felt threatened and intimidated, not by his assertion of my duty but by the way he thought that he could touch me about my person and treat me in a patronising manner.

He went on to say that I had on several occasions refused to do cover. That was untrue as colleagues will confirm. I then asked Mr Portland whether he would be so kind as to ask someone else. His response was to put his arm around my shoulders. At this, I became highly agitated. My heart thumped as though about to burst. Tears welled up in my eyes. I felt like a cornered rabbit. He then leant over me. Put his face right up close to mine, stared at me harshly and said, 'You women are all alike; you do not carry your weight in the school. You should be obliged to stay in your place by the kitchen sink and the marital bed.'

'Absolutely not true! I can't believe I'm reading this.'

With wildly racing emotions, I begged him to leave me alone. I was appalled by what he had said but I desperately needed to get out of his way rather than to take up his usual bait. He stepped back and barred my exit from the staffroom. I begged to be allowed to leave but he just leant against the door, appearing to enjoy my discomfiture. Finally, Trudie Long jumped to my defence. She said 'Leave her alone, you great bully. I suggest you cover the lesson yourself.'

'Absolutely not true!'

I took the opportunity of his looking towards Trudie and rushed from the room. Trudie followed me to the ladies' toilet where I sat for half an hour crying uncontrollably. At last, Trudie felt obliged to ask permission of the Head for me to be taken home.

I have not recovered from this shameless harassment. I believe that it is only just being recognised what effects sexual harassment has on we female employees. They include loss of personal confidence, humiliation, anxiety and extreme stress.

I further wish to say that in previous conversations, Mr Portland has put his hand on my arm, my shoulder, and on two occasions on my leg. These latter occurred when he had invited me to his room ostensibly to discuss the Science curriculum. I always felt cornered and unable to prevent unwarranted physical contact. On this occasion, he deliberately brought the conversation round to Sex Education when the topic for our meeting did not merit such a turn. It is his invariable habit to bring matters round to sexual concerns. Then we are regaled by rambling discourses about his sexual exploits as a young man. I am appalled by any man in the workplace making sexually motivated approaches to me and this was certainly how I interpreted Mr Portland's approaches. I felt he was taking advantage of my youthful, feminine vulnerability and I felt thoroughly uncomfortable. I feel that we, as women, have to make a stand against such unacceptable male behaviour.

'Complete distortion of the truth!'

Furthermore, I know of dozens of girls who have made complaint that Mr Portland has both placed his hands on their persons and talked perpetually about sex, occasioning them immense embarrassment and discomfort. One such girl is Elizabeth Richey of Year Eight who, I believe, will make a separate complaint. Many girls, who other complainants will cite, have complained of Mr Portland's tendency to use sexual innuendo.

I believe that Mr Portland's colleague, Mrs Spong, to whom I have made frequent complaint about Mr Portland's unwelcome attentions, will confirm that she has spoken to him about such matters and warned him of their intimidating effects upon young and vulnerable female employees such as myself.

Ms Sian Waite

Assistant Science Teacher

8th June, 1992

Tom read and re-read this first specific complaint, the veins in his temples, throbbing and distorted, his eyes almost popping out of his head in disbelief at the outrageous lies and defamatory comments made by this young, precocious whippersnapper who had obviously been set up just as he was by Phoebe Spong. What a monster she had made him out to be. If indeed his behaviour was as described, in great detail, by her, then he truly deserved his punishment. But she did protest too much in his opinion. He felt safe in the knowledge that what he had read was a pack of lies with the occasional grain of truth.

With a sigh, Tom picked up the next document. Lengthy, like the previous one, it was the specific complaint by Monica Dickinson. What on Earth had he done to Monica to make her so angry, that it took two pages to make her complaint?

I have a catalogue of complaints to submit against Mr Portland, but first of all, I ought to explain why I have felt it necessary to voice them at this particular time. For many years, we women have been subjected to unwarranted sexual harassment by the male Deputy but we have been reluctant to bring specific complaint out of fear for our careers, being fearful of being branded trouble makers. Recent shifts in social attitudes reflected inevitably in this as in all other workplaces, made manifest by the Secondary Schoolteachers' Association of Guidelines on Sexual Harassment, together with a collective determination by all female employees inside and outside education, has enabled us to feel confident enough to wage war on unwarranted sexual attentions by managers such as Mr Tom Portland.

From almost my first entry into Southwich High School, I have been made to feel distinctly uncomfortable by Mr Portland's apparent enjoyment of seamy conversational matter in the staffroom, held deliberately and for the specific purpose of embarrassment of female company. He, invariably, in private conversation, brings up the topic of sexual philandering by the adult in Society. He seems to take particular delight in insinuating that we who have suffered matrimonial discomfort have done so in consequence of sexual indulgence. Insinuations of this sort, I have found dreadfully hurtful and a personal slight. He seems to enjoy unnatural pleasure in cataloguing the social malaise of the age in terms of sexual morality.

From the time I attended for interview at the school in 1981, I have noticed that Mr Portland stares at me, though not at my face; it seems always to be my body and my breasts in particular which have attracted his attentions. I frequently find myself unable to sleep at night. I awake to find myself trembling uncontrollably at the prospect of his unnatural attentions.

'What absolute nonsense!

I hate to be touched by anyone. Mr Portland seems quite unable to hold a conversation without placing his hand on the arm, the shoulder or the back. On one occasion, during one of his usual lectures masquerading as a conversation about modern society, he actually fondled my buttocks, lingeringly whilst ostensibly removing a piece of Sellotape from my skirt. I believe that this will be corroborated by a further complainant.

'Fantastic fairy tale! If my hands were to linger on anyone's buttocks – they certainly would not be yours, Madam!'

As the member of staff responsible for Social Education, I have occasion to discuss the issue of gender discrimination with Year Eleven girls. It has been during lessons on this theme that there have been frequent complaints from them that Mr Portland 'is always talking sex in his English lessons'. They consider this a deliberate attempt to embarrass them. A number complain that he should be prevented from teaching them. I believe that at least two senior girls are prepared to make written complaint.

I do feel most strongly that Mr Portland, like all other male managers, must be prevented from harassing we vulnerable women and it is to this end that I present this complaint.

Mrs Monica Dickinson

Head of Personal and Social Education

8th June, 1992

The next document was a complaint from Sharon Crabtree, a junior member of the English Department who Tom hardly knew. He could barely remember speaking to the woman. Why had she got it in for him?

As the youngest female member of the Southwich staff, I must complain that I have been made to feel distinctly uncomfortable on several occasions by Mr Portland. I believe that the occasion of a specific complaint by another female colleague and the fact that the effects of sexual harassment on women in the workplace generally, are being recognised nationally, makes this an appropriate time to voice my complaint.

On a specific occasion shortly after my appointment to the staff in September 1990, I was invited by Mr Portland to his office. He asked to see me ostensibly about my probationary activities but I felt that he spoke with unnatural inquisitiveness about my personal life, seeming to take delight in enquiring about my relationship with my fiancé. I felt trapped in his office. At the point where I wished to end the meeting, he stood by the door and seemed to deliberately block my exit. I made no complaint at the time since I felt disinclined to appear to be a trouble maker. There were several touches about my person on that occasion which made me feel sickened.

'Yes, I vaguely remember the interview about probationary activities. As for the rest - Miss Crabtree, you have a good imagination. If you had the slightest anxiety, why did you not confide in Irma? She's the most approachable Head of Department on the staff. She would have soon sorted me out. Sorry, Sharon, this won't wash and it will not have done your career any good. Getting mixed up with Monica and Phoebe will have scuttled you for sure.'

Other colleagues and pupils have mentioned to me the unacceptable tactility of Mr Portland. I distinctly recall the tremendous embarrassment suffered by my colleague, Mrs Monica Dickinson, on the occasion that Mr Portland, under the pretext of removing a piece of Sellotape from her skirt, actually allowed his hand to linger unnaturally on her buttocks. At the time, we women were appalled by this act.

'Use of the words *linger* and *buttocks* in two documents – indicates collusion, methinks'.

Many senior girls have mentioned to me in the context of discussion about the gender issue that Mr Portland touches them and that that makes them feel threatened and patronised. We, as female teachers, really are the guardians of female pupil welfare and I have thought frequently that attention ought to be brought to Mr Portland's and other male colleagues' tendency to handle girls inappropriately.

'What is it I or we are supposed to have done? What do you mean by *touch* and *handle*? Why have you not reported any complaint to Irma or anyone else before? When is it supposed to have taken place? There's no answer because it's all a fabrication'.

I do recall a specific unease during an English Departmental meeting when Mr Portland was holding forth on how we should interpret the poem set by the Exam board, Thomas Hardy's 'The Convergence of the Twain'. It seemed that he was determined that we should all get involved in sexual discussion and mention of phallic symbols. I was myself, greatly embarrassed and felt sure that such an approach was far from suitable with Year Eleven mixed gender classes. I could see no necessity whatsoever for such insinuation where Hardy's poem was concerned. I mention this issue since it substantiates my view that Mr Portland always brings the topic of sex into any conversation. I have been appalled by his apparent titillation by issues concerning pupils' and adults' sexual conduct. I have become heartily sick and tired of his constant preaching about society and its short comings, especially as far as sexual morality is concerned. I fear for the welfare of the girls in his hands.

'You uneducated goose! The whole point of this poem is that it concerns the rape of the Titanic by the iceberg. If you can't appreciate that then you've no business being a teacher of English in a Secondary School. In any case, Irma, as Head of Department, would have been at the meeting. If she had been unhappy she would have spoken. Why didn't you raise any concern with her? Any discussion, as I recall, was totally relevant'.

I must add that one occasion I was dreadfully embarrassed by Mr Portland's use with a year Eleven English group of a photocopy of naked boys being pursued around a park lake by a policewoman wielding a cane. This was supposed to be an illustration for a lesson on Deviance, a subject upon which Mr Portland seems to be unnaturally keen. I felt at the time that this came into the category of the display of sexually offensive or pornographic material in the workplace about which the Secondary Schoolteachers' Association Draft procedures on Sexual Harassment speaks.

Miss Sharon Crabtree

Assistant English Teacher.   8th June, 1992

'More accusations without substance! A bone fide photograph, from 1926, used to stimulate discussion on moral hypocrisy. How is a group of naked little boys sexually offensive or pornographic? The offensive part is the policewoman chasing them with a big whipping stick! It shows, young Sharon, that even as late as 1926, Victorian hypocrisy concerning socially acceptable sexual behaviour remained current. There is nothing criminal in little boys' innocent but impudent nakedness. They are simply determined to shock. The policewoman's moral outrage and vicious intent with the weapon is morally more appalling than the boys' prankish naughtiness. The whole point of the exercise is to stimulate class discussion.'

Tom's razor sharp mind was dulled after perusing only four documents. He felt in need of an energy boost to get him through the next one which was the complaint by Phoebe Spong. He took a break and an injection of caffeine in the guise of a mug of strong, black, sweet coffee.

She wrote,

The composition of this complaint has been a most painful responsibility. I realise that it impugns the Senior Management solidarity which ideally ought to be maintained. However, when the welfare of the female staff and pupils of the school has been placed at risk, I feel that my greater moral duty is to the better good of the larger number.

'Huh! Moral duty – what do you know about moral duty? As for the greater number – you've always looked out for number one!'

I have warned Mr Portland on many occasions against a tendency to be inordinately tactile in his dealings with female pupils and colleagues. I have further counselled him to desist from a habit of preaching interminably to all and sundry about what he alleges is the disintegration of Western culture through adult promiscuity. His conversation in staff and pupil groups alike is frequently sexual in its nature. His intimidating manner with all female adults is overbearing and he has an obsequious, unnecessary counsel-orientated approach to pupil welfare. He is the school's Curriculum Deputy and ought not to interfere to the extent he does in Pastoral concerns. He seems particularly and unnaturally animated by sexual deviance. Despite my frequent warnings, he persists in interviewing female pupils alone.

'What a load of exaggerations without substance. I am also entitled to my views and as they say, 'If the cap fits....'

If I get involved in Pastoral concerns, it's because those pupils concerned come to me and not to you, Madam, for advice! I certainly don't seek the extra workload from your back.'

My most recent warning to Mr Portland occurred following an incident on Friday 15th May, concerning the Year Eleven pupil, Lesly Atherton. During my disciplining of the child, Mr Portland officiously and unnecessarily intervened, placing his hands around the girl's upper body and positively cuddled her...

'In fact, Madam, by my action, I stopped her from giving you a second black eye. As for cuddling her – what ridiculous nonsense you talk. I was acting as a strait jacket to prevent her from attacking you.'

...I was outraged. And I told him so, warning him that we adult women of Southwich High School were sick and tired of his constant pawing of the girls and ourselves. He took the girl alone to his office and supported her in her indiscipline. I felt that as a colleague, he gave me no support whatever.

'Frankly, Phoebe, you didn't deserve my support.'

There have been a good many complaints by female pupils about both Mr Portland's tactility and inappropriate talk. Four of them are included with my statement.

I have witnessed a considerable reluctance on behalf of female pupils, particularly of the Upper School, to be dealt with by him in disciplinary situations. They have alleged repeatedly that they feel uncomfortable with him – that he is always talking about sex and that he makes them feel like second class citizens when compared with the boys. Frankly, he allows the boys to get away with the most heinous of crimes, I believe out of gender-biased sympathy. For instance, he recently engineered a trouble-free passage to three senior boys who had committed an appalling sexual crime against a Year Eight pupil, Gillian Sumner. He took their rapacious attack on the girl in characteristically light hearted vein, in 'boys will be boys' fashion. No action was taken against the boys after he had extracted them from my disciplinary involvement.

'Phoebe , take note and learn...The boys needed correctional treatment .The parents of all parties were entirely satisfied by my minimising the humiliation for all….and….the Head agreed with me for once!

We bear an awesome responsibility to maintain the welfare of young girls in schools. Like we adult women, they are subject to constant gender discrimination. Far from supporting their interests, Mr Portland patronises and humiliates them.

'When have I done that? You don't give any evidence.'

I have had frequent cause to object to his attempts to interfere in my proper concerns with the School's Sex Education policy. Constantly, he attempts to lecture me as he does everyone else, upon the need to protect pupils from the ravages of adult sexuality. What he has failed to respond to is my repeated warning that his 'state of the world' speech gives very great offence to all women since they assume that he is directly accusing them of sexual promiscuity.

'You always seem to be showing the same video. We need to teach girls to avoid giving birth until they're mature - physically, mentally, and financially.'

I cannot claim like others whose statements accompany my own that he has inappropriately touched my person. His attentions seem to be towards the more junior and vulnerable. But such is his perpetual 'holier than thou' tone, his over-authoritarian, patronising and intimidating manner that I have received in confidence dozens of complaints from female colleagues and pupils in equal measure.

It is clear that women will no longer tolerate sexual harassment in the workplace. We must make a stand if we are truly to enjoy anxiety-free, equal employment opportunity. The Draft Proposals of The Secondary Schoolteachers' Association on Sexual Harassment make a laudable start in that direction. Mr Portland is undoubtedly guilty of a series of sexually harassing behaviours as defined by that document. His 'unwarranted sexual attentions' have occurred in physical and verbal form; they have been deliberate, persistent, unreciprocated and unwelcome; they have taken the form of comments of a sexual nature, intimidating behaviour, sexual innuendo, unacceptable touching and even the display of pornographic material. The statements which accompany my own give ample evidence of each.

Mrs Phoebe Spong

Deputy Head

15th June, 1992

'Well, wheel out the evidence then. I'll get some more coffee to keep me awake.'

The next document was from Tracey Smith in Form Eleven MD.

'One of Monica's', thought Tom.

Me, mandy and jane was sent to mister Portland for fiting and doing grafiti on the toilet walls. We was to be done for it. Mister Barestow sent us. We dident want to go cos we new he would go on about it. He went on about are having boyfrends and them fiting and how fiting solvs nuthing. Then he shoked us all by torking about his wife. He said it were grate wen we got marred we wood be able to do it evry day for the rest of us lifes just so long as we didnent fite. We was dead fritened and shoked and embrassed. He made us clean the lavs.

Signed   Tracey Smith

'Oh my God! Whoever is her English teacher? She must be bottom set – slow learners.

What's all this talk about my wife? Beats me... Some misunderstanding's taken place.'

The second statement was from Tracey's partner in crime, Mandy Johnstone, another member of the bottom set – the slow learners.

She wrote,

Tracey Smith Jane Tomlinson and me were sent by Mr Bearstow to the deputy head for fiting, we don't like to be sent to mr Portland becawse he shows you up. Hes allus going on about his happy famly life. But we were ded shoked wen he sed he has a smashing sex life becawse he dident hit is wife. It was very embrasasing. We couldent understand what having a good sex life as to do with wat we was accused off.

Mrs Spong ast us about it after becawse we wer so shoked, she ast us what he ad sed and we told her all about this sex tork. I told her that we had seen him tuch a girl and she was embrassed.

Signed Mandy Johnstone

Form 11MD

The final statement from the Year Eleven girls was from Jane Tomlinson from Form11TL. Trudie Long was her form tutor.

We had been fighting – me, Tracy and Mandy. Some girls had been doing graffiti on the toilet walls and we got blamed. Mr Bearstow set us to Mr Portland. He were dead mad and we was dead scared. When you get sent to him you allways get done right bad. Hes allways getting your parent's in. we would not of wanted them to now becawse we'd get done some more.

Then he said waht a good sex life his wife and he ad, then he said we'd ave a lot of sex if we dident fight. We couldent understand all this and we was dead frightened and we was very embrassed. Mrs Spong torked to us about it. She ast wether he had torked to us about sexual intercoarse. We told her what he had sed. She ast if we'd seen him touch enybody. I think Mandy sed she had but I hadent.

Please. I don't want my mum to now about this becawse she'll kill me. She thinks hes ded good, and I don't want enybody *else to now neither, other kids will get us if they now what weve sed about Mr Portland but its all true I sware.*

Jane Tomlinson Form 11TL

Tom considered these three statements and tried to remember the details of their offence. The three girls were all low achievers – two of whom he had identified as slow learners. Their English and spelling was appalling for sixteen year olds, but it apparently had not been corrected by whichever adult had asked them to write the statement. Jane was from a respectable family compared with the other two. She had obviously been brought down to their level of behaviour. He could understand why she did not want her parents to learn about this business. He suspected that something which he had said, while he was trying to reason with them, had been misinterpreted. One of his accusers, probably Phoebe, since she was mentioned by two of them, may have embroidered what they had said and had put her embellishments into their half empty heads. He regretted mentioning his happy home life with his wife and family because these girls had been encouraged, if they needed any encouragement, to equate his advices with talk of sex.

Feeling rather disconcerted that his endeavours to help and give advice to these adolescent girls had come back to bite him, he pressed on with his reading. The next statement had been written by a Year Eight pupil, Elizabeth Richey from Form 8VL.

Miss Wait asked me to write down what happened when Mrs Smally and Mrs Spong and her saw Mr Portland carry me to a car belonging to a tempry teacher what he'd got to take me home wen I'd hurt my leg in PE. I couldent walk so he carryed me. As he carryed me he touched my leg where it joins my bottom. He felt my leg where it hurt to. I dident say enythink to eny boby becawse I dident want to get into trouble.

Mrs Spong asked me if I new any boby else who he had touched. I said that Jane Pilkington said that he'd touched her leg when she went all num but now she wont say enythink becawse she says all the labs will get her becawse sh's allways making things up and she says all the labs like Mr Portland.

The End

By Elizabeth Richey.

Tom remembered both incidents. He had carried the injured Elizabeth to the car of supply teacher Mrs Brown, who had offered to run the girl home. He remembered Jane Pilkington and the numb leg. He did indeed touch it to determine whether or not it merited a visit to the hospital. In fact, she had merely been sitting on the leg in such a way as to cause it to 'go to sleep'. The numbness disappeared and she went back to class.

Tom considered the four statements from the girls. If they had not constituted a serious threat to his future, he might have considered turning the illiterate garbage produced by such pupils into a money-making venture. He had, indeed, read books consisting of schoolboy 'howlers' and other hilarious scribblings.

He picked up the next document. This had been devised by Trudie Long. Before he started to read, he cogitated about what she might have written.

'She's bound to mention my distaste for her having co-habited with Ross and Dawson before taking up with Smalley. And she'll complain about my complaints about those people who are letting down the young in our society by their inadequacy as rôle models. And she's bound to mention the incident with Sian Waite... and the touching of women and girls. Let's see.' He frowned and pushed his glasses on to the bridge of his nose with his fore finger.

I have been seriously concerned about the behaviour of the Deputy Headteacher, Mr Tom Portland, for some time. He invariably treats me with a high-handed and patronising manner. I have noticed how affably he relates to most of the men but with the women on the staff, he seems to adopt an authoritarian approach.

I am appalled by his tendency to share sexually explicit jokes in the staffroom. He seems to do so with deliberate intention of embarrassing the females on the staff.

'I'd like to know which joke you're talking about. Was it the one about the boat to the West Indies, I wonder? If so, I was only one of a mixed group and you were not there. How do you know about it? This is just hearsay you're repeating'

On several occasions, I have felt personally intimidated by him. I particularly object to the view of life which he constantly preaches, namely, that divorce is the source of all problems in young people and that promiscuity amongst adults is the primary cause.

'There you go!'

I sympathise greatly with Ms Sian Waite in her altercation with him yesterday.

'Ditto.'

I too have experienced his intimidating ferocity when I have questioned his requests or opinions. It is useless to argue with this man. He bears down upon you unmercifully, peers straight into your face and frequently enough seizes hold of you. I have been held by him several times. Each time I have shown, by backing off, how I've not liked it.'

'Balderdash!'

Most alarming has been his behaviour towards girls. Girls in my own form in Year Eleven have said that he should be forbidden from touching them and that he always brings sex into the English lessons.

'All talk and no substance. As I remember, these were naughty adolescent girls and likely to bear a grudge. It's an unfortunate characteristic which some people have.'

As well as Ms Waite, I witnessed last October an event which made our stomachs turn. The Year Eight pupil, Elizabeth Richey, was obviously very embarrassed when he felt the need to carry her from, the gymnasium. We distinctly saw him touch the top of her leg and her bottom as he carried her to a waiting car. I believe that the child has given an account of this incident. We women shared our concerns in the staffroom about the incident at the time when it happened.

'All recorded in the Accident file....and Ms Long... just explain to me how you'd carry a girl without touching her body?'

In view of all the anxiety being voiced both nationally and internationally about the amount of sexual harassment in the workplace, I would find that I was not doing my duty if I didn't add my voice to the list of complaints being gathered against Mr Portland.

Trudie Long

Assistant teacher of Modern Languages.

3rd June, 1992

'Pretty much as I expected, but a rather poor letter...'

Tom saw that the following statement was from Peter Smalley. He was in no doubt that Smalley's letter would back up Trudie Long's complaints absolutely, because they were partners. He had been surprised when the po-faced Smalley had moved in with Trudie Long since he was aware of her former relationships with at least two of his male colleagues who were still members of staff.

'Obsequious toad! The eyes and ears of the Head in the staffroom: Another member of that tyrannous sect.'

I have received several complaints from members of my department concerning sexual harassment by the Deputy Head, Tom Portland. Yesterday's appalling treatment of my colleague, Sian Waite was characteristic of the sort of treatment he metes out to women exclusively. I know of no male on the staff who has been treated with a similar authoritarian and demeaning manner.

As a committed Christian, I must complain about the way in which Mr Portland joins the openly anti-Christian group of staff, making ribald comments about, for example, the wearing of Ichthus badges by we who are saved. I always feel that the Deputy ought to set a worthy example. By public acknowledgement of an irreligious perspective, he is seen not only to side with the more disreputable element of the staffroom but to display a lack of support for the Head, who we all know as a most devout Christian. Solidarity within the Senior Management Team, I consider crucial to the success of the institution. With Mr Portland in post, this eventuality is unlikely. I know him to have criticised the Head on several occasions. His liking for sexually ribald joking amongst his male cronies in the staffroom also causes me much embarrassment, not least of all since it is invariably within the hearing of our female colleagues who I know to be greatly offended by it. My own partner certainly is and I think that hers is a typical feminine response. The ladies feel that their femininity is scorned by the kind of humour in which Mr Portland delights.

'You're making an incorrect assumption about my taste in jokes, Peter. If you were rather less proud and pretentious, you'd appreciate that David Southwich is a very funny man and a gifted teller of jokes. The women listen and laugh as well as the men... you're too pious by far.'

I do object most bitterly to Mr Portland's constant harping on about the troubles of the world in terms of sexual depravity. He arrogantly and publicly deprecates divorce, attributing all the evils of the modern society to this phenomenon about which he knows nothing. He is insensitive in the extreme to the pain which we divorcees experience in the light of our Lord's recommendations, in St John chapter 19 and St Paul's, in I Corinthians, chapter 5.I know many children of single parents who have shared their embarrassment with me after listening to his denunciation of divorce.

'You totally misread me, Peter. I don't object to divorce when there's no saving a marriage, but people get hitched by marrying too soon or by co-habiting. Divorce these days is too easy. People don't try hard enough to stay together and ultimately the children suffer. Look at your own children and your current partner as examples.'

I have been obliged on several occasions to avoid sending pupils to Mr Portland for chastisement after being begged by them not to carry out that threat. I understand that such is their fear of his sexually harassing them that they would face any sanction in preference to being handled by him. This has been much discussed by myself and the female Deputy. Of late, we as a group of senior staff have determined to avoid sending female pupils to him to save them from unnecessary discomfort.

'Who are these girls? Name them! I suspect their names are Tracey, Jane and Mandy'

I submit this complaint out of no personal acrimony. In emulation of our Dear Lord who was moved to turn the money changers out of the Temple, I submit it in a spirit of Christian duty.

Peter Smalley

Head of Science

3rd June, 1992

'Sanctimonious squit!

The final complaint had been written by Alan Bairstow, the Head of Mathematics. Tom could understand why Bairstow would bear a grudge, even though it was not justified. He started to read it.

As Head of the Mathematics Department, I have occasion to refer naughty children up the line of command. I have noticed for some time a strong reluctance by the girls to be dealt with by Mr Portland. It seems as if they are afraid of being touched by him and of their tickings off being turned into a sex talk.

Recently, a parent of a Year Eleven boy told me that she did not want to have her boy dealt with by Mr Portland since her other child, a Year Ten girl, had told her that Mr Portland always started talking about sex.

Whilst I was preparing for some research for my Master's Degree course, I interviewed some Year Eleven pupils who were in Mr Portland's English group. Several alleged that his lessons consisted of little more than accounts of his family life and sexual innuendo.

'I can't, for the life of me, understand what I have said, to these kids, that could be so readily misunderstood?'

In the staffroom, I am very uneasy in the presence of those men amongst whom Mr Portland enjoys a certain bluff popularity. Their conversation is always full of sexually explicit humour which seems to be picked just to upset the ladies. For this reason, I never go into their half of the room. What I have seen of the way he talks to the ladies, I have not liked. He touches them all the time and usually talks to them as if they were naughty children. His treatment, yesterday, of the young, sensitive and highly vulnerable Ms Sian Waite was a disgrace. When in the past I have felt a lady to have been badly treated by him, I have felt the need to challenge him but have not done so out of fear of physical assault.

Parity of esteem between the genders is something I feel strongly about. Women, I respect a lot; the female members of our own staff, I hold in the highest esteem. It therefore causes me tremendous grief that one of my gender should cause upset as great as that by Mr Portland towards our female colleagues. He seems to regard them as sex objects or beings of an inferior order. About a year ago, at a school Technology meeting, I remember that he caused distress to our Food Technologist, Mrs Vivienne Lowther, when he succeeded in causing lot of exaggerated mirth amongst a largely male audience by making out that 'Pud' teachers could not be expected to take part in teaching concepts which proper technology deserved. When I stepped in to support her, he started to lecture the meeting on the theory of supposed right-hand-side-of-the-brain deficiency. He ended by saying that women were not able to deal with the empirical concepts of technological thought. I tell that story since I think it fairly typical of the man.

Not unnaturally, the women of this staff do not think Mr Portland is able to manage the school in an atmosphere of equal opportunity. As a man, I am proud to align myself with that element of the Senior Staff who can. Knowing that at least some other men feel like I do, I can deny any suspicion that these allegations are exclusively from the women. The complaints are justified. I would like to see this school make an unashamed stand against the sexual harassment whose characteristics the Secondary Schoolteachers' Association Guidelines make very clear and against which criteria Mr Portland stands thoroughly condemned.

Alan Bairstow   Head of Mathematics 3rd June, 1992

The reading and assimilation of the morning's post had occupied most of Tom's day. He could hardly believe the evidence of his eyes. He had anticipated correctly that Phoebe's insinuations about his supposed tactility and his tendency to re-iterate his view of society would form the backbone of the allegations. It came as no surprise that the altercation which had developed in the staffroom with Sian Waite formed the catalytic event out of which the other complaints mushroomed. But the complaints about repeated sexual innuendo before colleagues and pupils alike, apparently substantiated by complaints from three senior girls, gutted him. The statement from the little girl whose ham-string had been injured left him dazed. However had these pupils been persuaded to produce statements so patently fabricated? He had been further shocked by the leakage, malicious or otherwise, of the date for the Disciplinary Hearing.

The plan of campaign was finalised that evening with the Union's legal representative, Derek Jones. Irma de la Haye would be asked to appear in person in order to give evidence of Tom's personality and conduct in school. She would also give account of the conversation which she had overheard between Monica Dickinson and others which proved that a conspiracy was being hatched. Tom would solicit from a number of male and female professional colleagues' statements as to his precise nature in school. Jennifer Bird would give an account of his intervention into the Lesly Atherton case, his behaviour towards herself and her colleagues and her belief that Phoebe Spong had displayed a chronic history of complaint against Tom. Accurate accounts would be given by Tom concerning his disciplining of the Year Eleven girls and the carrying of the injured child. Should Ted Slater choose to bring to the hearing the complainants as witnesses, their written evidence would be subjected to critical cross-questioning. Their manifest collusion over the allegations would be laid bare.

Tom anticipated the Hearing with a considerable degree of composure, content that its outcomes would be complete exoneration, leaving the way clear for legal recompense consequent upon malicious accusation.

CHAPTER TWENTY-SIX

Thursday, 27 August, 1992.

A sudden ear-piercing, blaring assault on his tympanic membranes spurred Tom into a violent awakening. Not being accustomed to opening his eyes at such an early hour, he cast his eyes to the small innocuous device which had emitted that ear-drum fracturing signal. It was six o'clock. After having his pattern of sleep for the previous eight weeks brought abruptly to an end, his bleary eyes and fuzzy head required a few minutes to adjust themselves to the impending events of the day which would become one of the most significant of his professional life.

A calm, clear morning followed a night of tossing and turning. Tom was grateful for the weather, at least. The topsy-turvy pattern of storm and sunshine, which had dominated the spring and summer, had been quite unnerving. Torrential rain and thunder would not have helped his spirit on this pivotal day of the Hearing of the complaints made against him by his colleagues at Southwich High School.

Maudie, already wide-awake, brain alert and thinking about what lay before them during the forthcoming hours, almost leapt from their bed. She also had pondered which paths their lives, after the decisions largely out of their control, would take them. This day was almost as important to her as it was to Tom;

the conclusion to the events of this day would mark the beginning of the rest of their lives.

'I'll make some tea whilst you come round', she offered, showing not an iota of the nervous tension which she had successfully internalised, ever watchful of her husband's mental state.

'O.K, but I'll get my shower. I need to get my brain working then I'll come down', was his matter-of-fact reply, also apparently unmoved by the fear of the momentous consequences which could determine his fate.

There would be three for breakfast. Freddie was staying overnight with Dan from next door. Tom did not want him at the hearing. Jack was adamant that he should attend to support his father. After all, he was going to be studying Law for his degree at Warwick University. His three top grades at 'A' level had guaranteed his place. All arrangements for his accommodation had been organised before Tom and Maudie had given him the shattering news about his father's problems at school and the subsequent Hearing before the Governing Body. Jack had requested that he be allowed to see all the evidence contained in the bundle which Tom had received earlier that month and Tom had agreed. His son was going to be studying Law. 'Let him have some real-life material to study', had been his immediate response.

Surprisingly, selection of an appropriate suit for the day troubled Tom. He had not had much experience of such anxieties but he needed to be smartly attired. After much deliberation, he chose a Navy blazer, light blue shirt, grey trousers and a startling red tie. As he stood before the mirror adjusting his tie, he was strangely reminded of his childhood days of Whitsuntide Sunday School processions when all the children wore their new clothes. There would be no popping into neighbours' on this occasion in order to show off the new clothes, hoping for the invariable gift of money which rewarded such visits. Why the strange thought entered his mind on this day of all days, he could not imagine. For sure, this was the first time in eight weeks that he had felt the need to dress formally. But thoughts of childhood pride in new clothes in a context of religious observance, he had imagined so far back in his past as to have been forgotten. Had he not been always greatly embarrassed by the event anyway, fearful of being seen in the Sunday school procession by non-church–going school friends who subsequently would rib him unmercifully?

He dismissed the curious memory and looked out of the window again. Maudie re-entered their bedroom and kissed him reassuringly on the cheek. As he watched the idyllic pastoral scene, he noticed a hawk of some kind, hovering with menace. All the usual flurry of hedge sparrows which normally fluttered around the feeder station like furry moths around a light bulb had disappeared. The hawk had some creature in its sight. In the blinking of an eye, the bird had dropped like a stone then it soared and Tom saw it flying off at speed with a wriggling grass snake caught in its talons.

'Your tea's getting cold. What do you fancy to eat?'

For the previous eight weeks, Tom had slept late, enjoyed a leisurely shower and breakfasted like a king, but his appetite had disappeared. He knew that he had to have something in his stomach otherwise the whole assembly would have to listen to the rumblings which would inevitably issue forth from that organ. He ate a pauper's breakfast of dry toast and cold water. Jack tucked into a full breakfast of fruit compote, nutty granola, scrambled egg, toast and home-made Seville orange marmalade. He was not suffering the dread of the forthcoming event at County Hall which had taken away his father's appetite. Tom did not think unkindly of his son's apparent lack of empathy; he took the optimistic view that the intended lawyer had an intuitive realisation that his father would be exonerated by the end of the morning.

Maudie disappeared into the garage and instructed her car,

'Now, Bessie, please don't let us down, Get us all there and back intact with Tom back to his former self.'

She took the wheel with Jack in the passenger seat. Tom sat in the back where he could concentrate on his rehearsal of the questioning of his accusers. He reminded himself of the sang-froid and brevity he had promised Derek Jones, his Union legal representative, he would demonstrate. He reminded himself also that it was crucial that the women did not become upset. The last thing he wanted was to appear bullying of his opponents. Anticipating this day of the Hearing, he had imagined that he would have to battle against the usual symptoms of nervousness. On the contrary, he felt alert, anxious to see the proceedings in progress, but essentially calm.

At half past eight, the traffic was relatively light. In another fortnight - school holidays over - the scene would be very different. Parking at County Hall was always a problem; the double yellow lines, edging the rather bare streets, prohibited Maudie stopping for any length of time. She dropped Tom off at the main entrance whilst she and Jack drove off to the public car park a few streets away. There, they encountered, Jennifer and Harold Bird and the other allies of Tom. Together they strode as a single unit towards the forbidding edifice of County Hall. This monstrosity of a building dated from 1882. It presented a flat, ugly, front facade of red brick, admittedly somewhat relieved by window sills and mullions of Portland stone, once white, now sullied by decades of soot and grime from smoking chimneys and traffic exhaust fumes. It was topped by a black slate roof. The main entrance consisted of double doors of oak, flanked by grubby pilasters topped by a crumbling pediment. The starkness of the austere frontage was not mellowed by any form of natural planting. Instead, a single row of black, painted, pointed iron railings separated the fabric from the pavement. The prospect was not an inviting one.

How different was the interior! Tom entered the ornate, octagonal foyer of the Longborough Council chamber, reminiscent of the Central Lobby at the Palace of Westminster. It was constructed from the same white stone, but unsullied and gleaming, with arched doorways, bearing elaborate carvings, which led to the various meeting rooms. The intricately cream and black tiled floor had a central black tiled circle which bore around its circumference, the inscription

'JUSTICE IS TRUTH IN ACTION'.

He was struck by the mosaic which decorated the façade of the chamber itself. He had seen it dozens of times before when, as the school's representative deputising for Slater, he had attended District Heads' meetings. Now, for the first time, he understood its design. Scales of Justice stood out plainly, superimposed upon an intricate web, though in such subtle mixture of glistening, kaleidoscopic tiles that the total picture could only be appreciated from a distant, angled perspective. The solitary figure of his Union Legal representative, Derek Jones, was sitting on one of the green leather-upholstered benches, waiting for him. Across the foyer almost huddled in a corner, he was aware of the gathering of his accusing colleagues. Gone was their usual staffroom demeanour of exaggerated gaiety and confidential tête-à-tête chat. Each sat as though awaiting judgement against them in a mediaeval witch trial. Faces were drained; postures were stiff and erect; there was no effort to seem part of a group. The women appeared unmoved by Tom's appearance, seeming to stare straight through him. He noticed that Peter Smalley and Trudie Long were surprisingly not with the main group but sitting together at some distance away. Their faces, pale, with furrowed brows, showing signs of anxiety. Alan Bairstow and Sian Waite, although sitting together appeared not to be communicating to any degree. Tom was surprised as whenever he had seen them in the staffroom, their heads, always, had been close together.

He walked over to greet Derek Jones, just as Ted Slater emerged from the council chamber. Their eyes met, locked together like a couple of gunfighters in an old John Wayne movie.

Neither was willing to make the first move. Slater, acutely embarrassed, averted his eyes. Tom noted that his usual florid complexion was now blotchy like a reddened version of army camouflage. Beads of perspiration decorated his forehead and upper lip, like condensation on a silver chalice. At the bottom of the deep pits which were his eye sockets, lay his once-glittering, snake-like eyes - now dulled with fatigue and worry. His once much envied, wavy, silver mane had lost its colour, texture and had thinned so much that he wore it longer in an attempt to hide the paucity of hair. His Ichthus badge, illuminated by a sunbeam entering via a stained glass window, shone out from his lapel, reminding Tom of the tyranny in which the Ichthus wearing members of this company held him.

The impasse was breached by the feigned cheery intervention of that forked-tongued, medusa, named Jacquie Erne, the current Chair of Governors. He averted his eyes. She held out her hand to him; he ignored it. Totally disregarding his reluctance to greet her, she enquired,

'Good morning, Tom. I do hope you are well. How are Maud and the boys?'

Tom frowned, annoyed by this woman's failure to name his wife correctly but at the same time he felt as though disembodied, unable to fathom from such quarters the enigma of bonhomie at such a juncture. Nevertheless he responded after a moment's supreme effort of will with a polite though restrained acknowledgement. She continued,

'Perhaps, Mr Portland, Mr Jones and Dr Slater, you would come into the council chamber and take your places? The committee have been here for some time. We are anxious to proceed.'

Ted Slater gazed around, almost absent-mindedly to see who else was waiting in the foyer. He nodded to the eight complainants who then made their way into the council chamber.

Tom looked round to where Maudie and Jack were hovering, waiting for him to beckon them. They moved forward to join Tom who was waiting with Derek Jones, along with Paul Sawyer, Vernon Longstaffe, Keith Dawson, Donny Ross, David Southwich, Jill Field, Anne Jones, Lucinda Terry-Smith and Harold Bird,. Tom's witnesses, Jennifer Bird and Irma de la Haye, who were expecting to have to wait in the foyer until called, were also ushered in. The whole group moved forward as one supportive unit. As they passed through the ornate arched doorway, Tom looked up to see a bas-relief carving in the Portland stone of St George slaying the Dragon. For a moment in his imagination, the carving took on another form - that of St Michael vanquishing Satan. It had the immediate effect of raising of his spirits a couple of notches.

The council chamber was a vast ecclesiastical stateroom with massive, green leather, upholstered, oak pews disposed in semi-circular form, with a central aisle leading to an imposing table, of oak, mirror-like from decades of enthusiastic polishing. On the right, in the front pew sat Tom with Derek Jones – rather like the bridegroom waiting with his best man. Tom's entourage of supporters took seats behind. Maudie and Jack sat directly behind Tom. To the left of the central aisle the eight complainants arranged themselves on the first two rows. Ted Slater took a seat at the table at the front at which were already seated the Governors' Disciplinary Committee of three- the Brigade of Ichthus - Jacqui Erne in the Chair, flanked by the local Anglican vicar - Reverend Routledge and a parent governor, Simon Jessop - one of Slater's supporters for the position of Pastor at their United Reformed Church. To right and left of them sat the County's Legal representative, a senior County officer and the District Education Officer, Marcus Bristow. Tom could not help but smile to himself as he was put in mind of a typically sparse congregation at his boyhood church shortly before its demolition.

Jacqui Erne asked if all would join in a moment's prayer – 'that they might seek guidance and wisdom in order to arrive at a just resolution to the current problem'. To his surprise, Tom found himself saying 'Amen' with a degree of sincerity unknown to him since his flirtation with religion in his adolescence. As he scrutinised the officials before him, rays of sunlight were streaming through the large rectangular stained glass windows behind him illuminating their persons with an eerie green light. And then he counted the Ichthus badges. Each of the seven people facing him wore one. They were like a school of sharks waiting for their lunch. Tom sat straight – backed, upright, his body taut, his head high and his eyes fixed on the face of his old adversary – the spitting cobra-like Ted Slater. He wondered what venom was about to be ejected in his direction. In an uncharacteristically shaky voice, Jacqui Erne, from the Chair requested,

'Dr Slater, would you please present your case against the defendant, Mr Portland.' Tom noticed the reddening rise from her exposed throat until the whole of her face was flushed. He could sense her discomfort. He was aware of her white knuckles on her tightly clenched fists which she tried to disguise by shuffling on her seat and leaning forward as if in eager anticipation of Ted Slater's impending oration.

Ted Slater rose awkwardly to his feet. He held in his trembling hand a single piece of paper. A voluminous folder of papers lay unopened on the table before him. Tom watched him intently. The Head looked older than his years. He swayed; his shoulders were hunched; his body was stiff – still cobra-like, but now lacking its determined intention. He looked a complete travesty of the former sportsman that he had been.

The vast council chamber, whose floor was covered with gleaming, polished woodwork but whose massive volume was filled with air, was silent. Tom could hear his beating heart as could his supporters hear their own. The silence seemed to be interminable. So intense was it that he felt suffocated. He had been holding his breath in anticipation of Ted Slater's accusation. Tom became aware of the echoing sounds of a clearing of the throat –the squeaky, fidgeting on the leather upholstered pews – the shuffling of papers. Outside, in the street, the dulled sounds of traffic and the occasional call, *Sheffield United* of the wood pigeon could be heard. Ted Slater seemed to take an age to propel himself into his prepared script. There was, in his reading, the clarity of verbal expression which Tom had witnessed only on the occasion of his suspension.

'I'm afraid, Madam Chairman and gentlemen, that I must announce to the Hearing that we are no longer able to substantiate the allegations against Mr Portland.'

As he proceeded, Tom felt an increasing crescendo of wildly racing emotions. His composure exploded. Imperceptibly at first, his pulses quickened, his temples throbbed and he began to fidget in his seat. He controlled the urge to leap from his seat to admonish those before him who had been about to pronounce his fate. He battled with himself to concentrate on the words being delivered by the Head. A flitter of disturbance passed between the personnel at the table. Derek Jones touched Tom's arm and looked at him in amazement. His face white, changing to a rosy hue, a broad smile appearing on his lips and in his eyes, he said,

'You're OK...and we haven't had to utter a single word in your defence.' He stopped talking as Slater continued,

'Early last evening, two of the complainants whose written testimonies are before you, begged to visit me at my home, Mr Peter Smalley and Ms Trudie Long. They were distraught. They had a story to recount which leaves me no option but to intercede with you on behalf, not as you expected, of the eight members of the Secondary Schoolteachers' Association, , but on behalf of my Deputy Mr Tom Portland. I am afraid that when I have shared new evidence with you, it is I, myself, who will be obliged to appear before the Disciplinary Committee. I am prepared to offer my resignation from the Headship of Southwich High school. I have allowed myself to be persuaded, perhaps out of personal acrimony, jealousy and malice, that Tom Portland had been guilty of sexual harassment and worse where children were concerned. I now find him to have been the victim of the most perfidious conspiracy imaginable. May the Lord forgive me?'

Ted Slater's voice had been cracking progressively during this presentation. At this point, his knees gave way. He sank to the seat and buried his face in his handkerchief, sobbing piteously.

'Take five, Ted. We can wait until you've composed yourself. This is a momentous development. Take your time', Jacqui Erne intervened, her face and voice softening in her concern for her old ally.

Ted Slater rose again to his feet after a moment or two.

'Thank you and apologies. I'm at my wit's end, as you can see. If you wish it – Mr Smalley and Ms Long will themselves tell you what they conveyed to me last evening. They will say that during the last few weeks they have been wrestling with their consciences over their own complicity in what they now acknowledge has been a deliberate conspiracy against Tom Portland.

'On Tuesday evening, already racked with guilt like the Pastor in Nathaniel Hawthorne's *The Scarlet Letter,* Peter Smalley attended a prayer meeting, during which, he will confirm, he experienced a visitation from the Holy Spirit which racked his body and flung him to the floor where he was left for some moments in spasm. Helped by his neighbours, he rose and spoke in tongues. The message was interpreted by the pastor. The message was clear. A tremendous injustice was about to be perpetrated. It was his bounden duty to witness to the truth whatever the cost to himself.

'Having shared the intelligence with me last evening, that the whole group of complainants, led I'm afraid by my other Deputy, had conspired to write complaints about Mr Portland's supposed sexual misconduct, Mr Smalley suggested that together we visit the homes of the four pupils whose statements you have before you. They too, admitted giving evidence out of chagrin at having been disciplined by Mr Portland. They had been encouraged by Mrs Spong and Mrs Dickinson to lie.

'I have to tell you that when, last evening, each of the three senior girls in turn were challenged in front of their parents on the matter, each acknowledged that Tom, in chastising them for fighting and graffiti daubing had said nothing about sex but that he had said quite properly that if girls fought, they would attract the interest of boys who fought and then would form relationships with boys who in later marriage would be more likely to assault them. In the case of Mr Portland and his wife, they confirmed him as having said, a perfect friendship existed precisely because no violence had ever occurred. They confirmed that Mrs Spong had encouraged them to write as they had, saying that she would protect their interests.

'I assured the girls that no official sanction would be taken against them. I trust that you will accept this new evidence from myself and Mr Smalley and not require, as we agreed formerly, pupils to appear before you.

'The fourth child was a year eight pupil. She confirmed that Mr Portland had quite properly carried her to the car of the supply teacher who had offered to provide some transport since her mother had no vehicle. She assured us that it had been Mrs

Spong who had told her that Mr Portland had touched her upper thigh and since she had been carried in a PE skirt she assumed that must have been true.

'For my own part, I have to admit that despite five weeks of exhaustive investigation, I have found no pupil prepared to give written statement of allegation against Mr Portland and this despite the claims in the statements of four adult witnesses that such statements would appear. It became clear that the overriding majority of pupils thought Mr Portland beyond reproach.

'Additionally, I must admit that apart from the statements you have before you, no single word of criticism from other colleagues was uttered. A good many statements were made in his favour.

'I acknowledge that I should have had the complaints treated as a Grievance rather than as a Disciplinary matter. I acted over-hastily in my response to the letter from Ms Mandy Hewitson of the Secondary Schoolteachers' Association, a copy of which lies before you. I permitted myself to believe that we had a case of gross moral turpitude in view of the strength of feeling exhibited by Ms Hewitson's accompanying letter. Mr French, as County Legal Officer, you will confirm that once allegations of sexual misconduct were received, it was the county's view that suspension should occur. That decision, I regret wholeheartedly. Mr Portland has suffered public humiliation and damaging Press coverage at goodness knows what personal cost.

'I wish the Governors and County officials to record my very sincere regrets for what has occurred. As I acknowledged earlier, I bear a substantial portion of the guilt and I will face my Maker accordingly. Now, perhaps I may be permitted to call Mr Smalley and Ms Long?'

'Just a moment Dr Slater,' Jacquie Erne interrupted, casting him a sideways glance, glaring at him down her nose at the tip of which were perched her gold-rimmed spectacles. 'I should like to suggest a short recess whilst my fellow Governors discuss how we wish to proceed. My own feeling is that we have heard enough.'

This was followed by nods of vigorous assent from her neighbours. A dry-throated, Mr French, hoarsely acknowledged that should the Governors' Disciplinary Committee choose to suspend the hearing in view of Dr Slater's desire to withdraw the allegations, there was no further obligation to hear witnesses. Jacquie Erne was itching to bare her teeth and snarl. Looking in his direction, but not at him, seeming to be staring at some unknown object in the middle distance behind his left ear, she smiled.

'Mr Portland', Jacqui Erne addressed Tom in the most professional of voices, 'The Committee finds you exonerated of all allegations. You have been the victim of a most heinous conspiracy. We offer you our most sincere apologies. Every effort will be made by the Governors of Southwich High School to ensure that you receive just compensation. We do hope that negotiations involving Governors, The Local Authority and your Union might result in an out-of-court settlement which is to your satisfaction. We should be honoured to have you back in your post as Deputy Head as soon as possible. Sanctions against the leader of the conspiracy will be considered jointly by the Governors and the Local Education Authority. Have you, Mr Portland, or indeed Mr Jones, anything you would like to say to the committee before we declare the Hearing closed?'

'From Mr Portland's Union's point of view, we should like to thank the Head, Dr Slater for his ethical refusal to continue with his previously prepared presentation, in view of the last minute findings. We should like to compliment him on his frank acknowledgement of his own partial culpability in the matter. We see no reason for the Governors to accept his offer of resignation not least of all because since we understand him to be awaiting the Local Education Authority's response to his application for Early Retirement. We are grateful to the Chair for the offer to ensure that our member is adequately compensated for his defamation and we as a Union would make every effort to ensure that such matters might be settled out-of-court, including sanctions against the malicious accusers. We take the assumption that the financial compensation which the Local Authority will offer Tom Portland will be at least that which the courts would award.'

Tom heard the words spoken by Jacqui Erne,

'The Committee find you exonerated of all allegations...back in your post...Sanctions against...anything you would like to say...'

His face, drained of all colour, his knuckles white on his clenched fists and his body, hitherto tensed like a coiled spring, now relaxed with such immediacy that he relaxed so abruptly on his seat that both Maudie and Derek Jones believed that he had fainted. Tom started to think; the cogs in his brain turning slowly then gathering momentum in an effort to unlock the compartments containing memories from long ago. He knew that he would remember, sooner or later, the quotations from the Bible which he had been made to learn by heart all those years ago. They had been safely tucked away in the recesses of his brain never to be resurrected until this moment. He knew from experience, that those memories would not return merely by concentration – they would suddenly reappear for no apparent reason when he least expected them. He raised his head and looked behind at the assembled personnel, some of whom were looking in his direction with some concern. He smiled briefly at his supporters, Irma in particular, and at his wife and son. He heard only the final words of Derek Jones,

'...financial compensation...at least that which the courts would award.'

Tom stood. All sounds, in that vast council chamber, ceased in an instant. Everyone waited. All breathing paused; only the hysterical thump-thump of heart beats in unison could be detected. Anxiety and eagerness were in the ascendant in the expectation of Tom's response. The quotation from Deuteronomy suddenly surfaced from his memory bank as if by divine intervention. He spoke quietly, with deliberate menace in his voice - using skills from his days in amateur dramatics to their utmost.

'To me belongeth vengeance, and recompense; their foot shall slide in due time; for the day of their calamity is at hand, and the things that shall come upon them make haste.'

He sat down, exhausted.

Gurgling noises came from the direction of Ted Slater. He groaned; his face was contorted in terror; frothy saliva trickled from his gaping mouth; he slumped in his seat; he clutched at this chest.

'My God! He's having a heart attack', shouted Peter Smalley.' Someone, get an ambulance for Christ's sake.'

Ted Slater in his semi-consciousness was being pitched into a long, dark narrow corridor. The pain in his gut and in his chest had eased. He was surrounded by pale figures, their mouths in frantic motion, emitting unintelligible soundless voices. He could see light drifting in, hazily, many hundreds of metres away. He had an urgent need to make his way towards the brilliance. As he moved relentlessly towards his goal, threatening serpents squirmed in his path and the walls of his cloistered walkway were damp and hung with a myriad of interwoven, interminable webs in which were trapped the bodies of flying insects whilst the patient, voracious spiders sharpened their massive mandibles.

The meeting was never formally closed. Ted Slater regained consciousness on his way to Longborough Hospital. He prayed. He implored his God for forgiveness and for protection from the demons which were all around him. The silence of the council chamber changed abruptly to loud applause and shouts of approval as Tom uttered the final words of his short response. He was oblivious to them as his brain was fixated on the words spoken by Ted Slater,

'...I am prepared to offer my resignation from the Headship of Southwich High School...I now find him to have been the victim of the most perfidious conspiracy imaginable...'

And the words uttered by John French,

'...exonerated of all allegations...financial compensation...'

Derek Jones, congratulated Tom on the outcome of the Hearing, and made his exit. Tom's attention was fixated on the prematurely old, frail body of the Headteacher, Ted Slater and the major stumbling block to his own promotion to Headteacher. Tom did not wish him the sort of punishment he was enduring in the presence of all those gathered there. It was a blessing that he was only partially conscious. The first-aiders attended to him until the paramedics arrived and whisked him away in the ambulance with its blue light shining and its siren baying *weewooweewooweewoo*.- shattering the relative peace of the warm August morning. Tom and his entourage walked briskly and cheerfully to their waiting cars. The morning was yet young. Jennifer invited them all back to 'Robin's Nest' in Crossechester for elevenses. Later, the two Birds and the three Portlands walked to 'The Three Fishes' in Crossechester where a table for five had been reserved in the name of 'Bird', in anticipation of a favourable conclusion to the morning's events.

CHAPTER TWENTY-SEVEN

Autumn Term,

Tuesday, 1 September, 1992

Maudie sat up in bed and wrote in her journal.

'What a start to the new school year!...Tom newly released from eight weeks on 'death row' where he awaited his fate...saved at the eleventh hour by the testimony of Peter Smalley, a man whom Tom detests for his Uriah Heap association with Icky. The satanic Icky now hospitalised with a suspected heart attack. You couldn't make it up! Now, Tom has to dive right back into the deep end, and try to work alongside those bloodthirsty sharks which were out to devour him. He'll need the patience of a saint to survive.

On the previous Friday morning at six thirty, Tom, already showered, dressed and ready for breakfast, had said to the assembled family,

'Today is the beginning of the rest of our lives',

What a hectic day it was; the telephone never stopped ringing. Barely had they finished eating when the first call came from County Hall. After consultation with Violet Bluett the re-instated Chair of Governors, the District Education Officer formally asked Tom to take over the running of the school in the capacity of

Acting Headteacher in the absence of Dr Ted Slater who, after a suspected heart attack, had been forced to take extended sick leave. Tom, bursting with newly discovered energy reserves could not wait to get back into harness. He said his *goodbyes*, kissed his wife, wished his sons a good day and was off to his car, in whose boot he had already placed his ancient carver chair and his Renoir print.

The car park, grey and forlorn, was bare as he drove through the school gates. He was not surprised; he was very early; he needed to lead by example. The border was aflame with the colours of late summer – the sunshine-yellow Rudbeckias and devilish-red Crocosmias were flowering in abundance. How appropriate it was that the variety *Lucifer* had been planted in the border adjacent to the Head's window. Their brilliance added an extra boost to his self-confidence which was still slightly below par. Tom noticed the groundsman, Harry Wilson, emerge from his shed; he made a detour in order to congratulate him on the orderliness of the lawns and the spectacular, colourful borders; he wondered if Slater had ever spoken to the man; he doubted it.

Entering the building after an eight weeks absence, he was aware that the foyer appeared tired. Dull, drab, walls devoid of any art did nothing to enhance the initial impact on a visitor to the school. Tom decided to ask Jennifer to check the funds in order to provide for the purchase of some pictures to brighten up the area; then he would approach Lucinda Terry-Smith, the Art teacher, to make the necessary decisions about which to buy. As Acting Headteacher, he would occupy Ted Slater's office. He opened the door and immediately memories of his last visit to this room flooded back. The décor remained unchanged. Tom rang the internal telephone number to the caretakers den; he asked for some cardboard boxes. Tom removed all paraphernalia which was associated with Ted Slater. He placed them, for their safety, in boxes to be stowed away. The bookshelves were cleared of his eclectic collection of books and photographs; his cabinets of exotic curios, including the vile shrunken head were emptied; his valuable ink stand was carefully encased in bubble-wrap and packed away; the wooden cross and his tub of sharpened pencils –cum-toothpicks were hastily discarded into the box; the only evidences of Ted Slater's existence, which Tom retained, were the hip flask, to remind him of the danger of resorting to alcohol in a crisis and the print of Epstein's sculpture, *St Michael's Victory over the Devil*. He collected his own two possessions from his car boot and installed them in the Head's office. He took from his brief case the mounted photograph of his wife and sons and placed it on the desk.

    Monday was the last day of the summer holiday, but for Tom, there was much to be done at school. He was the major administrator in school. He foresaw, quite accurately, that the accumulated paperwork from the previous eight weeks of his enforced absence would be in an unholy mess. He did not blame anyone. He just needed time to get matters back into some kind of working order. Jennifer Bird had worked far more diligently than she need have done to ensure that all examination results had been received by Year Eleven pupils. Paul Sawyer had tweaked and refined Tom's timetable magnificently. Jennifer was in her office, ready with a mug of hot, sweet coffee waiting for him as he entered. She rushed to him, spilling the contents of the mug, decorated with an owl design, especially for him. She gave him a mighty hug and replenished the spilled drink. Throughout the morning, the more diligent staff came and went; he was aware of their comings and goings from the window from where he had an all-encompassing view of the car park. Many sought him out to voice their support; some merely waved; others gave him the V for Victory or the thumbs-up sign. Not at any time did he see Phoebe Spong - his fellow Deputy or any members of her ghastly cohort; he was not surprised.

Tom prepared his opening remarks for the staff meeting which would be held at nine o'clock on the following day. Although it would be the first day of the autumn term, it had been designated a holiday for pupils. The staff continued to refer to the day as a 'Baker Day' even though that particular Secretary of State for Education after whom the day was named had been replaced three times over. It was a day for preparation for the new academic year, and members of staff were expected to put in a full day's attendance.

Friday, 18 September, 1992.

Maudie wrote in her journal,

Today, Tom learned from the District Education Office that Icky's not likely to be back at work yet. Tom will be unfazed by that news. Icky's been off the premises on and off for the last thirteen years. Nothing's new about that. The DEO was rather cagey about the whole business. I'll ask Jennifer. She might know more.

Friday evening's meal from the Chinese chippie arrived as usual, collected by Tom on his way past. As they settled down to eat, Jack asked,

'Has anything been done yet about the staff who tried to get you fired? Weren't they supposed to be taking sanctions or something? What about the out-of-court settlement they talked about?'

'All in good time,' Tom replied.' The wheels turn very slowly at County Hall. You'll learn that as you get older. But to answer your questions...no...yes...nothing's been mentioned yet.'

'How long are you going to wait before you say something to make them get a move on?'

'I'm sure everything will fall into place in its own time. I'm perfectly content with the way things are going at school. I don't intend to rock the boat.'

'But you won't let this bunch get away with it, will you?'

'Don't you worry about me, Jack; it'll all come out in the wash. I'll be OK.'

'Anyway how's the job going at the chair factory?'

'I hate it. They give me all the worst jobs. Every Tuesday I spend all afternoon sanding ... breathing in dust and more dust. They have me cleaning sawdust out of the extractor on a Friday afternoon. It's such a filthy job, and I'm breathing in dust again. Every Friday afternoon, I do this same job while everybody else is in the pub. I spend all my time surrounded by dust.'

'Don't they give you a mask to wear?'

'The men don't bother to wear them. They're such a pain to use…but I do wear mine but it's not good enough.'

'Well, it's not for long, thank goodness. At least it gives you a bit of pocket money and you're finding out what some people have to do week-in, week-out to earn their living. Just be glad that you're off to Warwick before long and on the road to a clean, dust-free, well-paid job.'

In fact, Tom was not totally content. They were now eighteen days into the new term and he had heard nothing about Ted Slater's health. Tom appeared to be trapped in some kind of limbo. The first few weeks had gone as smoothly as he could have expected. The Head's absence made little difference to the running of the school. Tom was able to carry both jobs quite comfortably but he did ask Peter Smalley to take on the task of provision of cover for absent colleagues. Although a participant in the plan to overthrow Tom, Peter's turning of queen's evidence, gave both he and Tom an opportunity to redress the balance and appreciate each other's talents. The other plotters gave him a wide berth and he did not seek them unnecessarily. In their turn, they were summoned to County Hall to be admonished for their conspiracy to oust the Deputy Head, for attempting to blemish his good name and character and they were encouraged to seek employment elsewhere.

This was Jack's last weekend at home before attending the Freshers' course prior to embarking on his university career at Warwick. Although the term did not actually start until October, he had decided to make contact with some family friends - solicitors in Coventry - who had owned a stunning fifteenth century house in Warwick town, on the beautiful Mill Street, which in his opinion was straight out of the illustrations in a book of fairy tales.

Maudie had no time to contact Jennifer Bird in order to discover more about Ted Slater's condition.

Friday, 2 October, 1992.

Maudie wrote in her journal,

At last, some news! The DEO made an unexpected appearance at school today with the latest news about Icky. He hadn't had a heart attack after all. It was just a very bad attack of indigestion brought on by nerves. Tom was told that Ayna was glad that Icky had been taken to hospital, because she had been telling him for months to see a doctor about his stomach and belly aches. Huh! He had belly aches? He usually gave Tom the belly ache! Icky hadn't been prepared to ask a diagnosis from his GP. – seems he doesn't like doctors. Now Ayna was in a position to get a diagnosis of his problem. They did lots of tests on the various parts of his gut and found no reasons for the griping pains he complained of - leading Ayna to believe he had been simply attention seeking all along. Ayna described some of the other odd symptoms which he had displayed over the previous few months – not just the normal run of the mill type. He had been acting strangely as if he had a screw loose (my words not hers).For instance, at church, where he was hoping to become pastor, provided he got early retirement from Southwich, he started hugging and kissing all the women in the congregation and talking to them in a lewd manner, commenting on their legs, bosoms and bottoms. I would love to have been there and seen Icky doing the sort of things that Tom was falsely accused of and more so. What a turn up! They decided to have a look at his brain and discovered that he has a brain malfunction. Some cysts have grown in the spider's web part (whatever that is.) of his brain. On the basis of Ayna's observations, they have diagnosed him as suffering from Hypomania.

It won't kill him.

Friday, 30 October, 1992.

Maudie wrote in her journal,

Jack arrived home today for a long weekend – he goes back on Monday. He wanted to know all the latest on his dad's situation; we had some good news for him.

The DEO and Violet Bluett called Tom to a meeting at County Hall yesterday. They told him that Ted Slater's application for early retirement had gone through successfully - particularly speedily, on account of his hypomania. Because of staffing levels at Southwich High School and a fall in pupil numbers, the decision had been taken to offer the post of Headship to Tom commencing 1st November if he chose to accept the post.

So tonight we're celebrating! Champagne will be served with our Chinese takeaway!

The not-so-good news is that no mention of financial compensation was made. The authority is strapped for cash. They suggested that the prize of the Headship might be compensation enough especially if the county helped to off-load the plotters sooner rather than later. Tom was overjoyed to get the job he has wanted all along and agreed to their suggestion without hesitation. He said that he could not stomach the long drawn out battle which his Union would pursue to get him his rightful compensation. So they got off lightly - the penny-pinching pen-pushers!

So...it's no expensive holiday or a new car for us.

I'll have to put all my research into Cornwall on the shelf for the time being. (sigh).

Wednesday, 25 November, 1992.

Maudie wrote in her journal,

Great news for Tom! County have found a potential position for Phoebe Spong. It's an advisory post...a promotion for her...but will get her away from Southwich High. The staff, on the whole are cock-a hoop! It does mean an increase in her salary; that leaves a bad taste in the mouth, but you can't have everything.

Monday, 18 January, 1993.

Maudie wrote in her journal,

Two weeks into the new term and Tom came home with some bad news...rumours about reorganisation of education in the borough. Nothing concrete as yet but someone has leaked the info so there must be some truth in the rumours. Jack came home for a long weekend to coincide with the spring half term break. He was livid that the financial compensation promised to his father at the Hearing had not materialised.

'Are you going to sue for defamation of character? As it stands, they've got away...lock, stock and barrel.'

'Look son,' Tom said, 'I've got the Headship I wanted. Icky's left the scene and out of my hair. The plotters have been shown up, for what they are, in front of county officialdom. They've been hauled over the coals to boot. They're pariahs in their own school and will have to find other jobs. Why would I want more vengeance? Anyway it would be too costly to go to court. I'm not interested in pursuing the matter further.'

Friday, 19 February, 1993.

Maudie's entry in her journal read,

Well, isn't that just great! All that angst we went through last year...then elation about the Headship...now more angst! The news broke today about the rumoured re-organisation. Tom got the details in his post this morning. It's bad news for him. They are only turning Southwich High into a school for 10 to 14 year olds...a middle school. Tom won't want that. He wants the full range, 11 to 16 year olds.

So it's back to the drawing board. I'll get all my stuff out on Cornwall again...at least one bright spot in all the murk.

EPILOGUE

Sometime later.

After the absolute failure to rob Tom of his respectability, not to mention depriving him of his professional status and his ability to earn a living as a teacher, the Governing body made the decision, that because his and the school's hitherto good name had been brought into disrepute as a result of the evil intentions of a few misguided personnel, they should be made to attend a meeting of the disciplinary committee in an attempt to start to try to put the matter right. They were urged to make a new start by applying for posts elsewhere and they were assured of full support from the County.

Ms Jacqui Erne, as soon as the verdict on Tom's culpability was announced, immediately resigned her position, not only from the Chair, but from the Board.

Mrs Violet Bluett, the former Chair was delighted to be re-instated.

Trudie Long, Sharon Crabtree and Vivienne Lowther were all successful eventually in securing posts elsewhere. Trudie Long split up from Peter Smalley.

Uncle Bertie, the Director of Education ensured that his niece, Sian Waite, the precocious, talented, but misguided young teacher, found a new post in the administrative section of County

Hall. She and Alan Bairstow broke off their relationship. This decision was wholeheartedly agreed by both parties. Sian Waite soon became besotted by Marcus Bristow, the District Education Officer. Bristow, a married man with three pre-school aged children, had been in the habit of sending her love letters and flowers for some time. As they now worked in close proximity, their affair proceeded with gusto.

Monica Dickinson secured a post in the newly formed Department for the Co-ordination of Equal Opportunities at County Hall.

Alan Bairstow, resigned from his post of Head of mathematics and left the town. He and his wife, Charmaine, relocated to the south, back to their roots, where he hoped he could rekindle his marriage.

The Deputy Head, Mrs Phoebe Spong was unsuccessful in her applications for Headships. Likewise, sideways moves to other Deputy Headship posts were blocked. She was given a post at County Hall. She received an increase in salary. All the pupils at Southwich High School were pleased to see her departure, likewise the teaching staff, but a sour taste was left in their mouths with the knowledge that she was being rewarded with a better paid job. Later, she was advised to apply for the post of Adviser for Personal and Social Education in the adjacent county where she would carry responsibility for its delivery in schools, by organising courses for teaching staff. She would have no further contact with pupils, only with their teachers. Consequently, she lost the hated nickname of 'Sponge face', given to her by the pupils, but it was soon replaced by another one - this time coined by the teachers over whom, theoretically, she had authority. 'Rosa Klebb' dictated policy, but autonomous Headteachers, could ignore her policies frequently and did so. Only the ambitious, sycophantic, greasy-pole-climbing, individuals took her seriously. So, ultimately, she was side-lined and her sphere of influence reduced significantly.

The Headteacher, Dr Edward (Ted) Slater, accepted with alacrity the offer of early retirement on the grounds of ill health. Miraculously, his health began to improve as soon as he had left behind the stresses of Headship. He resumed his quest for ordination into the church of which he was a member along with the Director of Education and other influential members of the council. These individuals closely bound by their Ichthus connection came to the conclusion that although Ted had been, hitherto, a faithful member of their fraternity, he had become, through his diagnosed condition of Arachnoid cysts and hypomania, which had led to inappropriate behaviour and ipso facto caused distress to the matrons at the church, together with the recent bad publicity about his unsatisfactory dealings with his Deputy, a liability – a chink in their armour. He needed to be sacrificed for the greater good of the other members – for the maintenance of their very existence – for their careers - otherwise he might bring them all down.

He was counselled that, because of his record of ill health when under stress, the role of pastor to a large flock was probably not in his best interests. It was suggested that he take on some voluntary work in the soup kitchen at the church's hostel for the homeless in the centre of town. This was not the message that the defunct Head wished to hear. His vanity was still at its peak, despite his mirror image showing a frail, aging man with thinning white hair, and their suggested activity of serving soup to the homeless was not on his agenda. Thwarted by those with superior positions above his own, he attempted, unsuccessfully, to renew cordial relationships with his wife but she had found other interests to pursue with her female friends and they did not include husbands, partners or boyfriends.

    He tried to insinuate himself into the lives of Jennifer and Harold Bird, but he was now the biter bit and Jennifer took delight in informing him that her loyalties lay with her devoted husband, Harold, and their explorer son, Robert. His bouts of hypomania intensified. He would not go to bed; he existed on little sleep. He perpetually harangued the elders at the church with his protestations of his suitability for the role of pastor. He began to suffer from severe headaches. Nausea returned but accompanied, now, by vomiting, his hearing and vision became distorted and his muscles weakened. He entered a downward spiral of depression exacerbated by a dependence on a regular intake of whisky. Ayna was at the end of her tether with him. Her instincts told her to leave him to his fate. In her opinion, she had led a dog's life because of his narcissistic nature and his unsympathetic treatment of her needs as a woman and his wife. Repeatedly, in the past, she had advised him to seek medical help but it had been totally rejected. *'Let him stew in his own juice'*, she had thought, but ultimately, after his diagnosis, she came to the conclusion that he was like an old dog and did not deserve to be kicked.

Ayna, remembering her marriage vows, realised that her future role would be as his nursemaid. Any other hopes and dreams for a brighter future she might have had would remain in suspension rather like the fatigued fish caught on the hook at the end of the line.

Jennifer Bird continued in her post until the date for re-organisation, at which time she decided to retire to enjoy a quiet life indulging in favourite pastimes with Harold. Gardening remained their favourite hobby. In September 1993, Harold's autumn crocuses flowered for the first time. He had planted new corms for a couple years without success. He called his wife, excitedly, to show them to her; she expressed delight in his pleasure. She had not the heart to tell him that every time he had planted them, she had dug up the Colchicum corms and ground them to a pulp after which she had administered a dose to Ted Slater in his morning and post-lunch coffee - just enough to upset his bowels, give him some physical pain and cause some hair loss - but not enough to kill him. Ted just needed to be punished for his mistreatment of her in the distant past, of Tom more recently and ultimately his attempts to thwart any plans Tom might have for the future. All had gone well; Tom's future was secure, Ted had got his comeuppance and so the cultivation of Harold's Colchicums could proceed without any more interference.

Tom had been appointed to the Headship of Southwich High School, with minimal formality, on the departure of Ted Slater. He was at that point older than Ted Slater had been when he was first appointed to the Headship. The old goat had misled Tom all those years about his age. Tom was determined that his tenure of Headship, however long it might be, would not in any way enable the tyrannical or character assassination traits within the staffroom that had been the norm previously.

Within six months, the news had broken that education in the county was to be re-organised and Southwich High School was to be designated a middle school catering for pupils from the ages of ten to fourteen years. Tom, from that moment, decided that Maudie's dream of returning to Cornwall would, by hook or by crook, take place. Feverish activity ensued henceforth in the Portland household. The national newspapers and the *Times Educational Supplement* were devoured and digested in the search for suitable teaching and librarian posts. The estate agents in Penzance were bombarded for details of properties for sale. Their own house was marketed.

Tom Portland and his wife Maudie, eventually, found a new life in West Cornwall with their younger son, Freddie. Jack had left home for university in Warwick, returning like his mother had before him, to Cornwall for the holidays.

Tom had received outstanding references and soon was attending interviews on a regular basis. He simply had to make sure that from the posts offered to him, he chose the optimal one. A new secondary school was to be inaugurated on the outskirts of Penzance. The newly appointed Headteacher would be in a position to select staff and to a large extent dictate policy on the curriculum. On opening, the school population would consist solely of Year Seven pupils. There would be no amalgamation of existing schools. The position offered enormous potential to the right applicant. The school governors were searching for a person with strong personal values, a diligent work ethic and a pillar of the community. They had been well informed about Tom's trials in his recent history but were impressed, absolutely, with the reference supplied by his superiors at County Hall. They were also cognisant of the fact that he had a Cornish wife. Tom applied and was successful; he remains in post.

Peter Smalley was appointed Headteacher of the new Southwich Middle School where he placed a strong emphasis on Religious Education. He dispensed with Trudie Long, realising that sooner or later she would tire of him, just as she had tired of Keith Dawson and Donny Ross before him.

The provision of early retirement for Ted Slater and the promotions of Phoebe Spong and Peter Smalley, all of whom wore the badge of Ichthus for all to witness, proved to the cynical Tom that the Tyranny of Ichthus remained in the ascendant at County Hall, where it continued to bind together the hierarchy and benefit its members.

Tom was prepared to forgive Peter Smalley as it was Smalley's evidence that enabled Tom's exoneration. It did occur to him that the Tyranny of Ichthus had ensured the removal of the atheist from its midst, albeit to a higher position, but it was ever thus.

END

Made in the USA
Middletown, DE
27 August 2019